Old Flames

A Novel
By
Dewi Griffiths

If You Can't Shake Off Your Ghosts:
You're Dead Too

Garland Stone Productions Ltd
Wales, UK

Old Flames
First Published in 2018 as an eBook, in 2022 as Paperback
By Garland Stone Productions Ltd, Wales, UK
© 2018 Dewi Griffiths

The rights of Dewi Griffiths to be identified as the author of this work has been asserted by him in accordance with Section 77 of the Copyright, Design and Patents Act 1988. Copyright Registration is in effect in the UK, US and other territories including at the Library of Congress, Washington DC.

All Rights Reserved.
No part of this book/e-book may be reprinted, or reproduced or utilized in any form, or by any electronic, mechanical or other means, now known or hereafter invented, including photocopying and recording, or in any information storage or retrieval system, without permission in writing from the publishers.

Any similarity between characters in this book and any person, living or dead, is purely coincidental.

Acknowledgements:
The quotation from R.S Thomas' *Welsh Landscape* is used by kind permission and taken from Selected Poems 1946-1968 (Bloodaxe Books, 1986) www.bloodaxebooks.com

English Language Biblical Quotations taken from the Holy Bible - King James Version.
Welsh Language Biblical Quotations taken from Y Beibl – William Morris translation 1588

Cover Artwork by Chris Crow © Garland Stone Productions Ltd

Map of Cwm Celyn. Sophia Wulf © Garland Stone Productions Ltd.
www.sophiawulf.de

Author Photograph: Ray Kilby
Cover Layout & Design: Gareth Hughes

Identifiers:
ISBN (eBook)	978-1-9999263-2-8
ISBN (Paperback)	978-1-9999263-3-5

Garland Stone Productions Ltd.
www.garlandstonepublications.com
www.garlandstone.com
www.facebook.com/garlandstoneproductions
dewi@garlandstone.com

About the Author

Dewi Griffiths is a native Welsh speaker from the coast of Pembrokeshire in West Wales, Great Britain.

Pembrokeshire is the setting for many of the stories from the Ancient Celtic Myths written down a thousand years ago in the Mabinogion. This scenery, remoteness, mythology and the supernatural were strong early influences on Dewi.

Combined with a love of storytelling, photography and film making, Dewi entered a career in feature film and high-end television drama, working worldwide.

Dewi worked on four continents for such production companies as BBC, S4C, ITV, Sky, Merchant Ivory, and Full Moon.

Dewi was head hunted by senior staff at the AFI and USC Film School to head up Producing at The Red Sea Institute of Cinematic Arts in Jordan, teaching award winning film makers from across the MENA region.

Dewi runs Garland Stone Productions Ltd, which builds on his connections and experience, to produce horror films, TV and literature: contemporary stories grounded in folklore.

Today Dewi is Senior Lecturer in Film Producing at The Film & TV School Wales at the University of South Wales.

www.dewigriffiths.com

About Old Flames

The inspiration for Old Flames came from my work on the S4C television drama series, "Dihirod Dyfed", directed by Oscar nominee, Paul Turner.

One of my early tasks was hunting for locations to suit this period drama series, based on real historical murder cases.

I found a disused farmhouse near Carmarthen which was a perfect filming location, except that it turned out to be haunted by the ghost of an old lady who had lived there every day of her life.

This was my first experience of an angry ghost. She definitely did not want a film crew in her house. During filming there were atmospheres, cold spots, bizarre unexplained incidents and sightings of the old woman. But most alarming were the injuries to the cast and crew including myself in the week we were at the property.

On a later series of the same show, I spent some time in Talley, where large tracts of land are now forestry plantations. One of the local farmers told me of the numerous farms which used to exist under what is now the blanket of trees. I found a few of these abandoned homes forgotten and derelict in the trees; a community and landscape which vanished beneath the plantations forever.

According to UK government figures for 2018, 15% of the surface of Wales is forested in this way.

Dewi Griffiths, August 2018

Dedication:
To my Dad, Aneurin.
And my uncles Ieuan, Leo, Tom, Rhidian and Elgan.
And before them my Grandpa Robert, great-uncles Wynford and Ebenezer.
Together with the fathers of friends like Roy Lewis, Brian Richards,
Jim Washbourne and Tony Williams
You shaped how I think.
What I know.
It makes me who I am.
To those now gone I miss you.
I wish I'd learned so much more in the time we had.
I know I still have so much more to learn.
Thank you. Diolch.

Thanks:
With Thanks to Chris Crow for his work on the cover.
And to Sophia Wulf for the map of Cwm Celyn.

Old Flames began as a feature film script.
I would like to thank particularly Keith Northrop of Goodman Derrick, London, who spent many hours discussing the project with me and honing my producing skills in developing this and other projects.
Also, Ros Hubbard of Hubbard Casting, London, who likewise was a strong advocate of the project for which I am extremely grateful.
And my fellow faculty members at the Red Sea Institute of Cinematic Arts in Aqaba, Jordan, Sharon Doyle and Mo Twine who helped me channel a cold haunted cottage in mid Wales whilst sitting on the shores of the Red Sea.

Also Available from Garland Stone:

Black Valley	By John Washbourne and Dewi Griffiths
Blood Eagle	By John Washbourne and Dewi Griffiths
Away Game	By John Washbourne and Dewi Griffiths
Witch Sight	By Dewi Griffiths and John Washbourne
Folk Devil	By Dewi Griffiths

Coming in 2022 – 2023
Witch Sight 2	By Dewi Griffiths and John Washbourne
Old Flames 2	By Dewi Griffiths

For details on purchasing all Garland Stone titles see
www.garlandstonepublications.com

Contents:

	Map of Cwm Celyn	Page	v.
Chapter 1:	From the Bright City to the Old Country	Page.	1
Chapter 2:	The Old Country Has Changed	Page	7
Chapter 3:	Meeting Future Ghosts	Page	14
Chapter 4:	A Merciful Release	Page	19
Chapter 5:	Toili – A Ghost Funeral	Page	26
Chapter 6:	From Grief, A New Beginning	Page	30
Chapter 7:	Doors Opening	Page	36
Chapter 8:	Visitation	Page	41
Chapter 9:	Doors Closing	Page	46
Chapter 10:	Into the Outland	Page	52
Chapter 11:	A Not So Empty House	Page	57
Chapter 12:	Oppression	Page	63
Chapter 13:	History Haunts Us	Page	67
Chapter 14:	Hangover	Page	72
Chapter 15:	You Are Never Alone	Page	77
Chapter 16:	Ghosts at Sunset	Page	81
Chapter 17:	Missed Calls	Page	86
Chapter 18:	Shrines and Shadows	Page	91
Chapter 19:	Back to the Grindstone	Page	99
Chapter 20:	Detours	Page 105	
Chapter 21:	Visitors at Dusk	Page 112	
Chapter 22:	Lights in the Night	Page 121	
Chapter 23:	The Blinding Light of Day	Page 125	
Chapter 24:	Afterglow	Page 133	
Chapter 25:	Cleaning House	Page 141	
Chapter 26:	English Girls	Page 148	
Chapter 27:	The Dark Grove	Page 152	
Chapter 28:	Remorse	Page 159	
Chapter 29:	Trying to Burn the Past	Page 162	
Chapter 30:	A Little Prayer	Page 169	
Chapter 31:	Regression / Possession	Page 177	
Chapter 32:	Beneath	Page 183	
Chapter 33:	Within The Woods	Page 190	
Chapter 34:	Coming Home	Page 196	
Chapter 34:	Passing	Page 202	
Chapter 36:	Burial	Page 207	
Chapter 37:	Wake	Page 215	

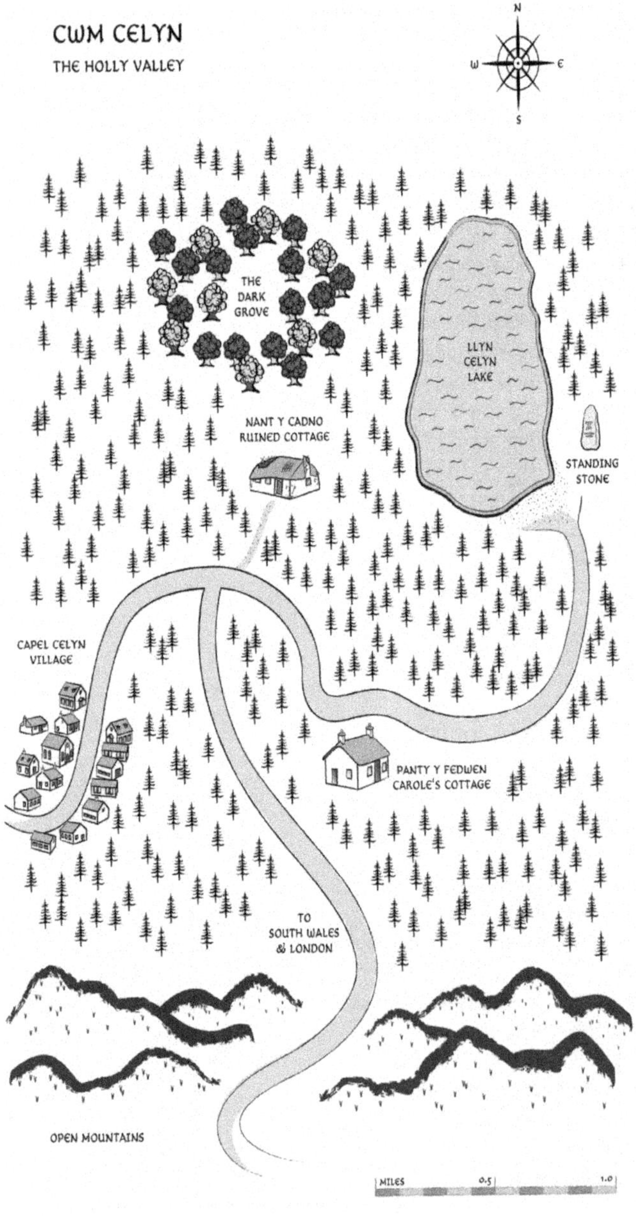
CWM CELYN
THE HOLLY VALLEY
N
W
E
S
THE DARK GROVE
LLYN CELYN LAKE
NANT Y CADNO RUINED COTTAGE
STANDING STONE
CAPEL CELYN VILLAGE
PANTY Y FEDWEN CAROLE'S COTTAGE
TO SOUTH WALES & LONDON
OPEN MOUNTAINS
MILES
0.5
1.0

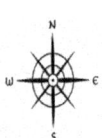

Chapter 1: From the Bright City to The Old Country

"There is no present in Wales
And no future;
There is only the past"
(RS Thomas - "Welsh Landscape")

1904. A new century. Queen Victoria two years in her tomb. The Edwardian British Empire dominating the world.

Great Britain continuing the hardships of the previous century into the new one with its all-pervasive industry. Too self-absorbed to foresee the horrors to come in ten brief years. Looking outwards to the world, rather than inward on itself.

Within Britain's borders, a wild land to the west. Never quite conquered. Never quite defeated. Its mountains and valleys making it difficult to master, which is why it had more castles than any other country in the world. Castles are control. To a level. Wild Wales.

Wales. Its very name means 'stranger.' A difficult place. A new religious revival bringing back God to what some called a Godless Land, whilst others call it God's Own Country ringing to the sound of the Language of Heaven.

Edward VII's British Government in London still seeking to make Wales a part of England, which Kings had been struggling to do since Edward I's army killed the last of the Welsh Princes in 1282. Now using universal education where military might had not succeeded. Using the lure of knowledge and advancement to kill the native tongues of the isles in the classrooms of Wales as in Scotland and Ireland: shaming the young of their heritage, their language and their history, making them wear the label 'Welsh Not' and beating the last speaker of their own language at the end of each school day.

But now Wales is rich. Or rather its landowners like the

Earl of Bute are rich. Men from the Welsh countryside and indeed men from all over Britain pulled to two Black Gold Rushes. In North Wales slate is blasted from the face of the earth. In South Wales the Black Gold Rush is for Coal to be dug from deep underground. Making the machinery of the Empire move - the ships, the trains and keeping the home fires burning wherever in the world the map was red. Millions of tons of Wales being shipped to power the Empire. A country burning bright at night leaving black smoke and ashes in the morning. A country blown away on the wind. Diminished to tiny black particles floating in the cloudy skies.

In Cardiff, not yet deemed by London worthy of city status, much of its area is railway sidings rammed with cars full of coal heading like a row of migrants for the port. Docks full of ships full of coal ready to sail on the tide, empty for mere moments before the cranes start to fill their bellies with their black cargo. Coal moves by rail and by ship day and night. Night and day like a black river of rock. The very bedrock of Wales sold and sailing away.

The heart of Cardiff's dockland. Tiger Bay. Wealth and notoriety cheek by jowl. The centre piece is Mount Stuart Square, named in honour of the richest man in the world, the owner of much of the land of South Wales. Coal Exporters' Offices forming a ring around The Exchange Building. Grand Victorian architecture in the heart of these dark boondocks. Ship owners and ship hands rubbing shoulders in the warm summer air. Gossip on the forecourt of the Exchange Building between clerks and ship owners. A cargo of coal has just changed hands for a million pounds. A sum unheard of anywhere on God's Earth.

Something on the street below catches the ear of one of the ship owners, Henry Radcliffe. Tap. Tap. Tap. Rhythmic, but sharp and striking. The impact of a stick on the paving slabs below. A drunken hymn sung in deep baritone rumbles within the cacophony. Mr. Radcliffe moves to the edge of the forecourt. Below, unsteady but persistent, a large figure dressed in Methodist black making his way drunkenly around Mount Stuart Square. Passing the smart shipping company offices, pushing through the clerks, sailors, the local Somalis and Yemenis who crewed the ships. Parting the conversations of prostitutes and drunken sailors, charting a course for the Ship and Pilot on the corner of the Square.

"Ifan!" Radcliffe's call unheard or unheeded over the chatter on this hot summer night in Tiger Bay. Ifan disappears pushing his way into the Ship and Pilot.

Radcliffe checks his pocket watch. "Nine o'clock tide tonight?"

"Aye sir" replies one of the clerks. Radcliffe inhales on his cigar. "Damn you, Ifan." He turns to the clerk. "Find James and Robert. Hurry!"

Inside the Ship and Pilot, the fading sun is dimmed further by the heavy leaded windows, coated with tobacco residue. Pipe and cheap cigarette smoke fill the air. Small lamps dot the interior like little lighthouses in the fog.

Beneath one sits Ifan, his black clothes blending him into the darkness. At thirty five, a middle aged man in a seaman's world. Working himself to an early death at sea, now drinking himself to an even earlier death on land. Ifan drinks directly from a whiskey bottle. He is large but compact and powerful. Scarred hands where ropes have burnt him, and a face which remembers for him the many fights on drunken nights like this. A nose broken back into his face and then broken sideways. Blue eyes burning beneath thick black eyebrows and the black hair which falls masking his face. He is reading, lips moving as he studies the text of a little black book in his hand.

The sawdust strewn floor muffles some of the footsteps. The whiskey keeps out the raucous laughter and talking. Ifan is immersed in his own world. Reading. His mind in a hot land he sailed past once as a boy, his captain keeping a respectable distance from Ottoman soil. Heathen bastards in Jesus's country. It hurts him to think of that now. Now. After his conversion. After he heard the preacher Evan Roberts and how he had been told he was one of the one hundred thousand who would be saved. Now he read so much wisdom in the Book he laughed at as a child in the mountains of Cwm Celyn. The book now clutched tight in his hands. Lighting his way in this world. Reading Exodus. The journey of a people to find their way back home. Home... Bang!

A drunken sailor nudges Ifan's chair. Ifan instinctively on his feet, staring wild eyed from beneath the black fringe. Teeth bared. Stick and bottle ready for what's coming next.

The sailor recognises Ifan, sobering immediately, "Sorry Ifan... sorry sir."

Ifan sips from the whiskey bottle. The sailor backs off from standing where the whiskey bottle could open up his face. Ifan's coat knocks the Bible to the floor, sending a piece of paper off across the floor at the sailor's feet. The sailor gingerly passes it back to Ifan. He quickly melts back into the fuzzy crowd around Ifan.

Ifan resumes his seat. He looks at the piece of paper returned to him by the sailor. A photograph of himself with his wife, Mari. A formal, joyless wedding pose outside the chapel in Capel Celyn. Ifan mutters to himself in Welsh. "You witch Mari". Mari. Ten years younger than he. He married her when her father died. Took pity. An honest mistake. Some mistakes you regret for a lifetime.

Ifan recites a prayer. "Lord, let me see the best in my wife..." Ifan can't go on. He closes his eyes and slips the picture back into the Bible. He takes another sip of whiskey and starts to read Exodus further. Chapter 22. Ifan walking the Holy Land as he reads on. Verse 18. "Thou shalt not suffer a witch to live." Read aloud. Clarity. Guidance at the time of need. Ifan stops and slams the good book shut. Ifan's lips moving as he mumbles. His entire frame shaking. "Mari..."

Shadows fall across him - two sailors. Ifan's eyes snap open. "Robert. James. You are disturbing me in prayer."

"Sorry sir, we sail within the hour." The man's voice is breaking. Fear gripping him.

Ifan stares into his eyes. "Then be gone."

"Mr. Radcliffe. He said we should bring you with us to the ship sir. To ensure your attendance. Now sir."

"Ensuring my attendance? Tell Mr. Radcliffe I shall not attend this voyage. I have other matters which need my urgent attention. He can go to hell. I'm going home."

"Sir, Mr. Radcliffe was very clear." Both men step forward.

Ifan jumps to his feet, wielding his heavy walking stick like a club. He pushes the tip under Robert's jaw, pushing him backwards. The two sailors back off. The pub falls silent.

Ifan pushes the Bible into his jacket pocket followed by the bottle of whiskey. "I have my own journey I need to make. 'Thou shalt not suffer a witch to live'. Those are the words of the Lord. Spoken to me of my wife right this moment. Out of my way, I have the Lord's work to do."

The sailors step aside as Ifan strides purposefully out of the pub into the Sodom and Gomorrah that is Tiger Bay after dark.

A train. A journey into the dark valleys, obscured by steam and coal smoke. A town at the head of the valley. The sky aglow with iron foundries lighting up the town and the bare mountainsides above. Merthyr. Martyr. The place a princess was killed by Pagans. They are still out there. Pagans like Mari and her kind. Beyond that acrid air.

Another railway. Sleeping on a bench until the first train. More whiskey.

Brecon. A coaching inn. Mountains. Farmers. Some Welsh spoken on the street. Heading west on a coach. Sleep.

Sunlight. Bright. Hurting Ifan's eyes. Clean air in his lungs making Ifan cough. The sun burning through the leaves of the trees. Bird song heard through the rumble of the wheels and the clopping of the two horses. Opening the Bible. Exodus 22. Verse 18. 'Thou shalt not suffer a witch to live." Ifan's brow furrowing.

A coach stop. The bare high mountains beyond. Ifan on foot. His book, his bottle and his staff easing his way into the centre of the country. High Country. Sheep Tracks. No one to be seen anywhere. Two days of walking. Two pubs to sleep in. He is too old to sleep out at night, even in summer.

Ifan walking up another steep mountain road. Knowing every rock in this landscape. Sheep his only company.

The crest of the hill. Below open farmland. Cwm Celyn. 'The Valley of the Holly.' Home. Every inch of it etched in his memories wherever in the world he went. The holly grows in the dark grove of trees where he first met Mari. So many shades of colour after the greys and blacks of Cardiff and Merthyr. A handful of scattered farms. The lake, shining in the summer sunlight. Across a ways, the little village of Capel Celyn. Holly Chapel. Ifan needs to visit there. Before....

A rushing sound behind him. Roaring closer. The Devil coming to divert him from his task?

Ifan spins around on the road. A black shape rushing at him faster than a train. Lower. Faster. Upon him in a second. Ifan drops the bottle. It smashes on the roadway.

A black Saab estate car swerves to avoid the broken glass as it slows to a halt at the brow of the hill.

Chapter 2: The Old Country Has Changed

The view through the car windscreen stretches out for miles. Miles upon miles of uniform pine trees. A grey-green carpet across the contours of the valley and carrying on to the lowlands in the distance.

Carole, mid twenties, a pretty blonde haired and brown eyed woman studies the landscape in front of her as she sits at the wheel.

"So, what can you see in those bloody trees?" A soft West Wales accent. Carole's father sits wrapped up in the front passenger seat despite the car heater humming away.

Carole smiles and points. "There's the lake." A flatter London accent.

"Llyn Celyn. Good." Her father smiles.

"Capel Celyn." Carole points out the village, only just visible through the trees and in the grey mid-winter light.

"Can you spot the grove? Tough with no leaves on the trees."

Carole squints. An area of grey black in the green black. "There."

"Good." Carole's father, Dai smiles. David at work. Davey to his wife and family. Dai when back here at home. "I was a boy when that Commission started planting these trees. There used to be little farmhouses everywhere, but the forest has swallowed them. No one remembers them. All gone."

"That's enough Davey! You're getting upset. Carole. Get us to the village for goodness sake. It's getting dark." Carole's mother in the rear seat. Impatient for the long journey to end.

"Of course it's getting bloody dark. It's the solstice. The shortest day." Dai coughs due to raising his voice.

Carole puts the car into gear, and it pulls away descending the steep slope down into the forestry.

Within the forest the direct winter sunlight is gone. Gloom. Half-light. A different world. The road suddenly cracked, and frost shattered.

Carole switches on the headlights. The pool of light illuminates the road but does not penetrate into the forest all around.

The grey pine forestry plantation's form is obvious now. Regimented. Starting a few feet from the edge of the road. No light for anything to thrive. No room for anything else. Just enough room to walk between the trees. Like rows upon rows of soldiers as far as the eyes can see. The trees taller than buildings on a big city street. Thirty feet tall, more. Keeping out what light there is on this the darkest of days. The forest already in near darkness even before sunset.

The Saabs taillights disappear as the car is swallowed by the gloom created by the forestry.

Carole brings the car to a halt at a road junction. One signpost.

To the left is CAPEL CELYN — 1 MILE. Carole turns right.

Mother's frustration boils over. "Where are you going? It's the wrong way Carole! It's getting dark!"

"It's ok, we've got time. Right Dad?"

Dai is lost in his thoughts. Not miles away. Years away. Back when this very spot was open country. Sheep. School friends. The people of Capel Celyn.

"Carole!" Her mother tensing in the rear seat.

Carole turns to her mother in the back seat. "It's not far Mum. And it's Christmas."

Dai grabs the wheel. "Look out!!!"

Carole slams on the brakes. Everything slows down. Seeing and steering around a shape in the middle of the road.

The car skids to a halt. Carole looking out of the

driver's side window at the old man who stands beside the car in the middle of the road.

Thin. Hardly filling his grey overcoat, carrying an empty shopping bag. He stares into space and seems to come back to his senses. He turns angrily to Carole. Bulging eyes. Maybe drunk. He locks eyes with Carole for a moment then continues on his way, limping down the middle of the road in the gloom, lit red by the car's brake lights.

Carole thrown. Shocked. Shaking. She climbs out of the car. "Are you ok? Sir?"

The man doesn't respond as he limps away further into the gloom of the forest. Ghost like.

The hiss of the wind in the trees masks every sound except the thump of the car engine.

Tap tap tap. Carole's mother tapping on the car window. "Carole. Get back in the car. Get us to the village before it gets dark for goodness sake."

Her father coughing again as the cold air hits him. "Phillips! I'm surprised he's still alive."

"You know him, Dad?"

"Aye, he lives in the cottage just up the road here. Leave him alone, mad old bastard."

"That's no way to talk Davey. He might hear you."

"He's as deaf as a bloody post he is."

Carole stands for a moment catching her thoughts. Realising how close she came to hitting the old man. Getting shakily back into the car. Carole drives off down the road. In the rear-view mirrors Phillips continues to walk until the gloaming swallows him.

Carole accelerates away down the forestry road into the encroaching gloom.

The car drives past an old traditional single storey Welsh cottage on the roadside, surrounded by the tall forestry trees. The cottage is character personified - beautiful but is very unkempt, fighting off dereliction. Once white, now more grey with damp and moss. Carole doesn't notice it as she concentrates on the road ahead in the gloaming.

The road dips and dips again for the next half mile. Around one more bend and the Saab descends to the end of the road at the shore of a beautiful lake surrounded by the forestry trees. A magical sight after the darkness of the forest. Carole kills the engine. Awed, she reaches for her phone.

All is silent as Carole and Dai get out of the car. Not even the hiss of the wind in the trees here. The sun is already low - winter purples and blacks colour the water. Hardly a ripple on the surface. "Dad. Smile." Carole takes a photo of her father against the sunset; the phone camera flashes. Carole looks at the picture on the phone's screen. Darkness looming behind her father. The colours not as true as real life. And he looks pale. Old. Tired. Unwell.

Dai wanders off down towards the lake shore lost in thought.

Carole opens the car's rear door. "Come on Mum, it's a lovely sunset."

"It's too cold Carole. Get your father back in the car, you know he's not well."

"Mum. Please. Come on." Her mother closes the door. Carole bites her tongue. Her mother doesn't do any emotion except annoyance. Right now, that's the last thing she needs. The old man has asked to spend Christmas in Capel Celyn. With her too. She had plans. But something told her to change them. They haven't been here in Cwm Celyn as a family for maybe five years. Why now? Midwinter? Christmas? The weather won't be great. "He's not well" is her mother's phrase to explain the trip. Carole doesn't want to think about it any deeper than that.

Dai has walked around to the standing stone on the shore of the lake. He leans on it, a little unsteady. Carole sees his unsteadiness, and hurries to join him. Suddenly overcome with a feeling of not wanting to be far from him.

"Thanks for bringing me here, Carole. It's good of you taking time off work. I know you'd rather be with Peter in London."

"I know this is home for you Dad. That little flat you bought with Mum... she's happy there, but are you?"

Dai turns and looks at the low sun. Carole is struggling as much as Dai. Thinking of what to say next when there's too much to say.

"We'll have a quiet family Christmas, like we used to have. Just you, me and Mum."

Dai is drifting away. "There are so many memories here... so many ghosts..."

"What's the matter Dad? Don't you feel well?"

"Listen, I've made sure you'll be ok when I'm gone. When the money comes through promise me, you'll find yourself down here as often as you can, get away from that damn city. This is where you're from Carole. Our blood runs deep in this country, you can't forget that. Promise me, will you?" Dai grabs Carole's arm. Earnest.

Carole worried. "Dad. Ok, I promise. But listen…"

Carole's phone rings. Carole checks the caller - Peter.

"You going to answer that? Might be important."

"It's only Peter."

"So, it's important." Dai makes his way back towards the car.

"Dad, no…" Carole exasperated. Why won't her parents talk to her? She answers the phone. "Hello, Pete?"

A west London square surrounding black iron railed gardens. Georgian white pillared townhouses. On the outside back to their former glory. As everything in London, going through a new lease of life behind the facade. Within this one, it's high end flats. A single one-bedroom flat on each floor. Bedroom, bathroom, kitchen, lounge. Theirs is on the second floor.

Thirty years ago, it would have been bedsits in this once dodgy neighbourhood. Today it's worth a good million more than even Peter and Carole could borrow together to pay for it, even with their two good City jobs. Renting it takes over half of their monthly wages.

Bright spotlights. White walls. Fitted units in each room. A few books on the shelves but little else. Decorated for Christmas by a fibre optic Christmas tree. A gas fire burns in the grate. Large screen TV with sound bar. A handful of Christmas cards. A shaggy little dog. Photographs from foreign holidays on a digital photo frame. A Facebook lifestyle.

Peter, Carole's boyfriend. Four or five years older than her, pushing thirty. Dark haired, handsome, sitting on the leather sofa, tie-less in a designer suit. Relaxed for a change. The tone of his voice brings Sammy the dog up on the sofa beside him, nestling on Peter's lap.

"Hi babe, have you made it to wild & woolly Wales yet?"

Sammy's ears prick up to Carole's voice on the phone. "Yes, just watching the sun go down. It's lovely. Everything ok?"

"Yeah, your dog's being very affectionate for a change. I'll be lucky to make it out the door with my virtue intact!"

Carole's coy laugh still gets to him. Such a sexy girl. Pretty. Great body. And nice. Not usually his type, but with Carole there is no drama, just plenty of light entertainment. What a difference from the previous couple of bunny boilers.

"I'm off out now to the Christmas bash. I wish you were

here.· But family is important. Mine doesn't work, so I should bloody well know. So you enjoy babe, OK?" A pause. Swallowing. He has to ask. "How is the old man?"

Carole looks across at Dai, standing at the water's edge, watching the sun sink over the horizon. "Not himself. I brought him down to the lake where he used to take me fishing, I thought that would cheer him up a bit. Something's up. And Mum, well, is Mum."

"I'm sorry babe. You have fun though eh? They'll appreciate it, I'm sure."

Carole forces a smile. "Behave yourself tonight."

"Moi? Don't I always?"

"You never did with me."

"You never asked me to."

"Miss you hon. Give Sammy a hug for me."

"Yeah. Talk tomorrow, eh?"

Carole pockets the phone. Dai has wandered over to the car and climbs inside. Family sunset moment over.

Chapter 3. Meeting Future Ghosts

The sun is setting on the shortest day. It's on the horizon hidden by the trees. A cold sun. No warmth. Mid-winter. Bleak. A shroud of darkness is falling as the sun disappears.

Carole drives the Saab through the dark pine forest, watching for that strange old man walking down the middle of the road. No sign of him now. He must have got to where he was going in one piece.

Four days to Christmas. Carole feels no sense of festive spirit. No snow forecast for Christmas, thank God. She wouldn't want to be stuck out here. It doesn't feel like Christmas even if she is surrounded by literally millions of Christmas trees.

The village of Capel Celyn starts where the trees end. Suddenly you're in it. Off to her right, a small cul-de-sac of council homes, when new, a uniform white, now that they have been bought by their tenants are a mix of random colours, making them unique in their own way.

The main part of the village is one long narrow strip of houses, not continuous. A short terrace. A modern bungalow. A row of older detached houses. Many of these houses are dark, unoccupied, holiday homes probably. Others have Christmas lights battling the gloaming. A smattering of parked cars, Japanese pick-up trucks, family cars cum rally cars and local trader vans with names like Evans, Williams, Davies. In seconds the car has reached the centre of the village. A pub closed and for sale. The chapel, *Y Capel* giving the village its name.

Opposite the chapel, the little house Dai has rented for Christmas. Dai points it out to Carole. "End of the road. Just here on the left Carole." Carole gives him a smile and parks the car.

"Thank God. I thought we'd never make it." Mother in the back.

Carole undoes her seat belt and heads out. "I'll pop over to the shop and get the keys."

Opposite the little house, next door to the chapel vestry, a pool of light. The Village Shop and Post Office. Independent, not one of the franchises that dominate back in the city. A beacon of light in the gloom of the village.

Carole enters the shop with the doorbell tinkling. An Aladdin's cave. Freezers of food. Fridges of milk and cheese adding sound and light to the quiet cacophony. A newspaper rack stacked with magazines. A Post Office counter. Rows of shelves of tinned food, bread, essentials.

And Mrs Jones at the counter. Mrs Jones squinting to see who the stranger wrapped in the big coat is. Recognising the voice straight away.

"Hello there Mrs Jones. How are you?"

"Carole bach. Good to see you. You made it before dark. Good, good. Did you have a good trip love?"

"Great thanks, but I think the sooner we get Dad indoors the better."

Concern on Mrs. Jones' face. She reaches for keys on a hook on the wall behind her and makes her way around the counter to join Carole, giving her a peck on the cheek.

Carole becomes aware of a movement behind her. A figure moving from between the shelves which have hidden him from view. The man in the road. Mr. Phillips. Grey under the fluorescent lighting. He carries a half full shopping basket and wanders in front of Carole to the counter.

Carole is still embarrassed from the near miss in the road earlier. "I'm sorry, I never saw you."

This close, the old man smells. Poor old feller must not be looking after himself too well. A wife wouldn't put up with that.

Phillips hasn't heard Carole. Or maybe he doesn't listen. "Two of those", pointing at the whiskey bottles behind the counter. Welsh. Carole learned so little Welsh from her father. She gets the number but not the full meaning.

Mrs Jones speaking loudly. "I'll be with you now, Mr. Phillips. This is Dai Morris' daughter."

Phillips takes out his wallet to pay.

Mrs. Jones is in need of some help. "Geraint!?!" Smiling apologetically at Carole, "It'll do your dad good to spend Christmas back here where he was brought up. Tell him to pop in when he's feeling up to it. We can catch up on old times."

Mr. Phillips coughs. Impatient.

Geraint, Mrs Jones' teenage son appears from the rear of the shop. Mop of unruly blonde hair, tall, lanky, not filled out yet. Still dressed in his school uniform. He stops in his tracks when he sees Phillips.

Phillips gives him a long hard look. Cold. Menacing maybe.

"Geraint, take Carole and her family over to Idwal's cottage will you, and open it up. Get the heating on. Show them where everything is." She holds out the key fob.

Geraint takes the fob whilst keeping a safe distance from Phillips.

He then looks at Carole. Looking stunning with the fur of her parka around her face. Recollection from a few summers ago. The older blonde babe who came to the village for a week. She is even more beautiful now. Geraint clams up.

Deep brown eyes framed by dirty blonde hair. Lips move. A soft voice. "Thanks Mrs Jones. Hello Geraint."

Geraint almost crippled by shyness. "Hi. This way."

Geraint moves quickly passed Carole and towards the door. Carole smiles at Mrs Jones, and Mr. Phillips. He glares back. Recognition at last.

Carole follows Geraint out of the shop.

Geraint leads Carole across the road to the little house near where the car is parked. "Geraint, I'm Carole, thanks for helping."

"I remember you. You used to come down here a few years ago with your dad and mam."

"That's right, you've got a good memory. I haven't been here for maybe five years. You always hid when I came into the shop. I'm not that scary huh?" Carole laughs, Geraint lightens up. She remembers him.

Carole's Father and Mother get out of the car and start to pull suitcases from the rear. Geraint doesn't wait to be asked, he takes the largest case from Carole's Father.

"Geraint? You've grown. You're the image of your dad. Pity he's not here to see you. He'd be proud. How's your mother?"

"She's alright thank you Mr. Morris. You should go and see her. Catch up."
Geraint carries the case to the house, fiddling with the key in the lock. Carole takes her mother's case and her own and joins Geraint at the front door to the cottage.

Dai hangs back, closing the car's hatchback, then leaning on the car, catching his breath. He is in a cold sweat and wipes his brow. A door slam across the road. Dai looks across. His and Phillips' eyes meet. Mutual recognition, but no friendliness. Mr. Phillips limps off back up the road. Dai watches him go passed the Chapel and on up the street.

Dai crosses the road to the chapel fence. Bethlehem Chapel. Rebuilt in 1904 during the Welsh Religious Revival. Where Dai used to go to chapel as a boy. Now looking dark and unwelcoming in the half light. Shadows by the chapel door. Indistinct. Probably due to the cataracts Dai's been told need to be treated. But is there any point now?

Shadows becoming shapes as Dai looks harder. Three figures near the chapel door. Something on sticks. Tall. Almost as tall as the man in the top hat who is using it. A box. Concertina section. A little cloth to the rear. One of those old cameras. Who uses cameras like that anymore?

Outside the Chapel on the steps stand two grey figures. Becoming clearer as the light decays. Ifan and Mari, dressed for their wedding. Formal. Joyless. No smiles. The Photographer taking the picture.

Mari is unnerved. Her voice drifting to Dai on the breeze. The primal fear of a Welsh mountain girl faced with something new at the dawn of a new century. "Will this thing steal my soul, Ifan?"

The photographer raises the flash bar and presses the trigger. A flash of light - the headlights of a car speeding through the village.

The phantoms are gone.

Geraint appears from out of the cottage and sees Dai leaning against the chapel railings. Geraint walks over to the old man. "What do you see there Mr. Morris?"

Dai replies in Welsh. "A wedding."

Geraint looks towards the Chapel. "No weddings here as long as I remember. Maybe you were remembering one, Mr. Morris. Good night." Geraint walks off to the shop, shutting the door.

Dai stands staring into the gloom. Maybe something is staring back.

Chapter 4: A Merciful Release

Phillips limps back to his cottage through the darkness of the forestry. No streetlights out here and no moon or stars in the cloudy mid-December sky. This is the road he's walked almost every day for the six decades since he moved into that cottage with his new wife. No children because she didn't last very long. In that time, it is the forest that has grown up around him, not children. A forest that has grown to hide Capel Celyn from sight. Phillips doesn't miss it.

He reaches the spot where he usually stands when he has to get away from the cottage. Driven out of there. Sometimes he has to stand here for hours until things subside back there. Those times that he needs to be alone out here, where no one will bother him. He is not lonely. Living here has taught him that you're not alone even if there's no one else there.

Tonight, something has been following since he left Capel Celyn. There is something in the woods. It can't be an animal. There are no large animals in the woods.

Phillips stops. A sound coming from somewhere in the trees. No, not an animal. Strange. Unnatural. Something he has not heard before in his nine decades. The sound starting as a moan, building into a howl. What the hell is that?

Phillips' mind goes back to one of his early memories. Sitting on his grandmother's knee. Her explaining the sounds of the night to him. Fear mounting now as it did in his grandmother's arms. This is the sound no one wants to hear. The death portent. The sound you hear before you die. *Y Cyhyraeth*.

Dai sitting in the chair by the fireplace. Carole watching him from the opposite armchair. The holiday cottage is nice, cosy, but not Christmassy. Not a family home anymore. Just like the flat her mum and dad bought, to replace of the house where she grew up. That flat is not the family home. So why spend Christmas back there? Why not here? The Morris family home. Capel Celyn.

Downsizing. The term Peter uses to describe her Mum and Dad selling the place she called home. Making more money available for their retirement. Very sensible. But now Dad is ill. He may not have long to enjoy his retirement within that new flat's unfamiliar walls. And Dad seems to need the familiar more and more as he gets older.

Carole watches him sitting by the fire. Cold despite being almost close enough to burn himself in those flames. The burning logs from the forestry heating the house. Probably the only thing her father thinks the trees are good for. Firewood.

Dai is silent. Lost deep in thought. Communicating nothing. Carole watching her mother work on getting him to respond by nagging him. Remembering unsent Christmas cards. Worrying whether the Christmas dinner booked at the hotel in Lampeter would be any good. Would it be worth what they had paid for it? Would there be any of her favourite biscuits in the shop? Carole tunes out, closes her eyes and lets the last-minute rush at work, organising mum and dad for the trip, and the long car journey wash over her. She's asleep in moments.

Outside darkness and silence permeate Capel Celyn.

The City of London. Lit up like a Christmas tree. Peter at the bar with his work colleagues. Hardly mates. Tonight, the place is theirs. Private function. Christmas bash. Chessboard floor. Oak bar and furniture. Glass. Class. No tasteless trendy colour schemes here.

Every surface reflecting the eighty people who work together every day but seldom speak. Reflecting superficiality. No depth. No one really mingling. Staying in work groups even on this one night out a year. Loud music. Shouted conversations. Mostly about work.

Peter with no Carole means Peter on his own. When did that happen? Peter's world is already blurring. Champagne on tap. A few French brandies. A Christmas kiss from Frances the Office Manager. Not bad for a woman in her forties. Not bad at all. He's never seen so much of her as tonight. She should dress like that at work. That afro, the exotic dark skin and those curves. Damn.

No Carole. He is missing her a lot already. He was not expecting that. Wanting her, not really wanting anyone else here; not even Frances quite yet. He'll miss Carole even more later. Back at the flat. And at Christmas alone in the flat. No point going to see his family. A waste of time. Christmas is going to be as miserable as...

OK. Time to focus. Time to be as sober as fucking possible. TP, his boss. Incoming like a guided missile. Working his way along the bar. Talking to everyone with a pre-rehearsed off the cuff speech, as slick as his sales presentations no doubt. Late fifties. He's forgotten how to let his hair down, not that it's an appropriate description for a balding guy. Chatting to Frances. His turn coming.... NOW!

"Peter. Where's Carole this evening?"

"In Wales with her parents."

"Oh, damn yes. Her father. Not well I'm told. Your family? Well?"

"What are you doing for Christmas TP?"

"A quiet Christmas. Off to France on Boxing Day. Snow seems a little sparse this season but.."

Behind TP. Coming into the bar. That long black hair. Hazel eyes. It can't be. That body. Unmistakable. Patricia! Who's that wanker with her? She's scanning the place. Making eye contact. God it is her!

"Peter? Do you think you'll have it done in time?"

"The Altmeier Industries thing? Yes, no worries."

"Good. Merry Christmas. See you in the New Year."

"Merry Christmas TP".

TP is gone. Moving on to the next poor bastard in for the festive interrogation.

Patricia. Damn. Where is she? Talking to Frances and some bar manager at the door. So, she's not welcome? Shit. That's not good. Patricia leading the wanker out of the bar. A glance and a wink his way. She is still game! Damn! Good girl. Peter raises his glass, but she's gone.

Frances returning to the bar. A warning look to Peter. Peter mumbles drunkenly under his breath. "It's OK Frances. I was only looking." Frances turns to start a conversation with someone else.

Patricia. Outside the window on the pavement. Hailing a cab with the wanker. His girl before Carole came to the company. Working late with her took on a whole new meaning until that CCTV was put in. God she was good. Mad as a bag of snakes though. Incredible in bed. The two go hand in hand. Now she's gone. History once more. Fuck.

The Saab winds its way cautiously along the forestry track. Headlights on in mid-morning. Carole not wanting to run over the grey man and ruin her Christmas. Keeping straight at the road junction heading deep into the woods towards the lake.

Dai smiles. Carole's heart soars. Mum half asleep in the back seat. This could be good after all.

The Saab rumbles towards the traditional single storey Welsh cottage all alone out here in the woods. Carole slows the car. The cottage looks neglected. The closer she looks the more she sees the signs of an old person on their own in a place they can't maintain.

"So, this is where that man we almost ran over last night lives?"

"Phillips? Aye. He's lived there since I was a kid."

"Is he a widower?"

"Aye. Stories are it was his own doing".

"What do you mean?"

"Just stories. His wife drowned. People talk." Dai stares at the cottage. Seeing something. "Stop the car."

Carole pulls over. "What's the matter Dad?"

Dai stares through his eyes' clouded lenses. Taking things in.

"Dad. Do you want to go in to see him?"

"Hell no!" Dai watches the way the light is not quite right at the cottage doorway. Bastard cataracts! The shadow moves. Still indistinct. Then clear: the ghostly figure of Ifan at the front door, drinking from a whiskey bottle. Ifan brings down the bottle and returns Dai's gaze. Burning eyes from beneath the thick black eyebrows. Mean. Angry. Drunk. Vindictive. Dark.

A chill shoots through Dai. He visibly shivers. "Let's get out of here." Carole starts the engine.

There's a movement at the cottage window. A figure in the darkness within.

Carole puts the car in gear and drives away.

Phillips is at the cottage window watching the car leave. Something dark blocks the light. Phillips lets out a sigh of angry frustration. Ifan's face getting clearer outside the window.

Phillips growls at Ifan in Welsh. "So, Devil. Got your eye on someone new? Good!" Phillips turns from the window and heads for his old armchair.

The inside of the cottage is as unkempt as its owner. Phillips limps across the rubbish strewn floor towards a steaming cup of tea on the chair arm. Behind him the front door swings open as the dark shadow enters the room. Papers on the floor are driven by the wind.

Phillips spins around and sees the dark shape moving in the room towards him. Phillips' voice cracks as he shouts at Ifan. "Stop tormenting me, bastard!"

Phillips' cup of tea crashes to the floor, shattering. The shape, Ifan forming before him now. Phillips' fear is becoming alarm. Phillips coughs and retches at the smell. With mounting panic, he limps for the front door, but it slams shut. Phillips struggles with the door, but it won't budge. He is cornered. Phillips limps along the wall and into the bedroom, shutting the door behind him.

Phillips backs off into the bedroom, watching the door rattle. Then silence. Not a sound in the cottage. That will pass for peace for now. The devil will go away and leave him alone for a time. Then all this will start again. That's life here. Cycles of fear. It's over for now.

BANG!!! The door rocks on its hinges and swings open.

It's not over! Phillips backs further into the room. Three paces back something hits the top of his head. Phillips looks up. The noose. "Again?!? No!!!" Phillips sees himself reflected in the full-length mirror on the door of the old wardrobe. Ifan is beside him. The shape and the stench unmistakable. Watching him. Waiting impatiently.

Phillips closes his eyes. He lets out a sigh of resignation. "Bastard creature! Why do you make me do this? I am not your toy!" The smell is overpowering. The sense of something malignant beside him which he has lived with for decades. This repeated ritual which seems to put the ghost to rest for a period. Meaning he gets peace.

Phillips pulls up the bedside chair and climbs onto it. A grim routine. "So here we go again! Maybe this time I will die. Then I will be free of you, you Devil! You can go and torment someone else!" Phillips puts his head through the noose, and steps off the chair.

Phillips swings from the rope, coughing and spluttering briefly as Ifan watches him. The stench becoming overpowering. The noose tightens. Surprise and fear on Phillips' face. Phillips claws at the knot in panic. He can't loosen it. His efforts only tighten it further.

Phillips opens his eyes. He is face to face with Ifan. The stench alone makes it hard to breathe. The knot is tight. Alarmingly tight. Phillips tries to get his feet back onto the chair, but it falls over. Phillips swings free.

Seconds pass by, measured in slowing heartbeats. Seconds turn to minutes. Images and feelings passing through his mind like dreams. But he has had so few dreams.

Phillips' face registers surprise as he expires. Gasping. His tongue coming out. Body swinging limp on the rope. The struggle has ended. Phillips is dead.

His cheap electronic wristwatch beeps to mark the hour.

Chapter 5: Toili – A Ghost Funeral

The surface of the lake rippled lightly by the wind. One element kissing another in this remote spot like two forbidden lovers. The wind hisses through the trees sounding like a detuned radio. Static. White noise. Not random noise, but the whole audible spectrum created by the wind passing through these trees. Just as the light is white light, all the colours of the rainbow filtered through the low white clouds of midwinter. White light and white noise meet in Cwm Celyn.

People see and hear ghosts in static. Obsessed widows and widowers study Electronic Voice Phenomena in universities in distant cities in other parts of the world. Here in Cwm Celyn, a community now buried beneath the trees whisper and appear in the wind and half-light. Cwm Celyn is a place of ghosts.

The lake, Llyn Celyn, silent and grey under the leaden sky. The Saab drives out of the forest towards its shore. The low growl of the engine and rumble of tyres on the hardcore road drowned in the all-encompassing hiss. The car stops.

Carole helps Dai out of the car, while her mother gets out wrapping herself up against the cold. Carole leads Dai down to the standing stone at the water's edge.

"It's so quiet, Dad. No birds. Nothing."

"Dead. I know. When I was a kid, you'd see herons. Hawks. All sorts up here. They don't take to the pine trees. You only find birds up at the grove there." Dai points to a dark patch of trees, standing out on a small hill above the pines. These trees are leafless and black in the midwinter gloom, but more natural in this place than the evergreens.

"I used to love fishing here with you when I was a girl."

"You always wanted a boy, didn't you Davey?" Mother joins them, making herself heard.

"My fishing days are over, Carole."

"Don't be silly Dad. We'll come up here again come summer.

You've still got your fly-fishing rod..."

Dai is not there. Lost in memories. In another time, when this lake was so different. No forestry. Open farmland. Birds, animals, insects, fish, friends, girls.

Carole's mother draws her away. "He mopes like this wherever you take him. I don't know what to do with him."

"All we can do Mum, is cheer him up as much as we can. The rest is up to him." Carole gives her mother a peck on the cheek. The first in years.

They both watch Dai lean on the standing stone staring out at the lake. They don't see the tears in his eyes, knowing he'll never see the lake he remembers from his childhood again. Dai lost in his nineteen fifties Technicolor memories.

Dai's eyes widen. The colour drains. The sky darkens. The lake black. The sky black. The trees black. The wind hissing like an angry snake. Dai is alone. Then there are people. Phillips limping leading a funeral procession. A simple pine coffin. Coffin bearers. Few mourners. Mrs. Jones and Geraint, totally unaware of Dai as if in a trance. Other mourners have features Dai recognises. The adult children of his past friends and neighbours. The procession passing silently. Silence. Not even the wind now. Just the darkness. Growing more intense. Blotting out the last vestiges of the world.

A *Toili*. A phantom funeral, led by the person who has just died. Phillips.

Dai has never seen one but knows what it is. He knows very well. His blood turns to ice. Dai drawn to follow the procession, but he can't move. He is gasping for breath. Left behind. This is a funeral he won't be attending. The final figure in the procession, dressed in funeral black stops and turns to look at him. Ifan glowers at Dai.

Dai drops to the ground. The cold wet ground. Soon to be his eternal home.

Carole and her mother hear Dai hit the ground.

"Dad!"

"Carole, call an ambulance!"

Dai rolls onto his back. "I'm ok, I just had a funny turn is all. A couple of minutes and I'll be fine."

Carole kneeling beside him in shock. "We'll get you to the doctor in no time Dad."

"No need. I had a shock, that's all. Coming home like this. It's my mind playing tricks on me." Dai stares at where the toili had been. The world brightening, the hiss of the pines getting louder.

The Saab drives back through the forestry towards Capel Celyn. Dai closes his eyes as the car passes Phillips' cottage. Dank. Cold. Ominous now. He'll mention that someone should pop in to see Phillips. But he's probably dead already, the miserable old bastard.

Carole drives swiftly into Capel Celyn and pulls up outside the holiday cottage. Carole's mother rushes out and opens up the cottage, switching on lights.

Carole leads Dai from the car towards the cottage door. Time to ask the question that's been bothering her about how her father is acting. "What happened at the lake Dad?"

"I saw a Toili."

"A what?"

"A Toili. A phantom funeral. They're seen hereabouts when the person at the head of the funeral has just died."

"Come on Dad, you're seeing ghosts now?"

"I've always seen ghosts, girl. You know that. Now they're seeing me. That's the problem. I can't have long."

"Oh Dad don't be silly..."

Dai is not looking at his daughter. Rather up the road. Beyond what Carole can see. Capel Celyn, but a different time. Hearing a tap, tap, tap. Seeing Ifan walking up the road leading a bloodhound. Ifan, funeral black in dress and mood, head down, angry, determined. Ifan staring maliciously at Dai as he passes.

Dai drops into Carole's arms.

"Dad! Help someone! Dad?"

Dai dropping to the pavement. Carole screaming. Her mother coming out of the cottage. Mrs Jones running from the shop.

Shouts echoing up the street as Ifan walks out of Capel Celyn.

Chapter 6: From Grief, A New Beginning

Leaden skies. The retirement flat. Unfamiliar. Unwelcoming. Nowhere for Carole to sleep on Christmas Eve.

Peter's Porsche finds a parking space in the West London town house square. Peter with his arm around Carole protectively, wheeling her Cwm Celyn Christmas suitcase back to the flat.

Through the communal door. Up the stairs. Into the flat. Sammy the dog bounding to greet them. Carole on her knees playing with Sammy. Peter has already taken down what Christmas decorations there were. That probably helps. Christmastime will now forever have new connotations.

A photo of Dad on a shelf. That's enough. Carole bursting into tears. Carole asleep on the sofa, Sammy lying by her protectively. Peter watching Carole sleep. Helpless in the face of this.

Dai's funeral. A Crematorium at the centre of a massive cemetery across town in the East End. Conveyor belt grief. The minister mispronouncing Dai's name. Few able to sing the Welsh language hymn. Mum wanting to keep the ashes, not scatter them in Cwm Celyn as Dad wanted. Not letting go.

Carole's New Year's Eve on the sofa asleep. Followed by a day when the city is as quiet as she is. Then normality returns. Traffic. Noise. Frustration. Tension. Anger.

Back to work. Thank God.

The stinging cold and pervasive wet hitting the back of her nose. The tube station. Sickly yellow light. Thousands moving in and out of small spaces as one. Claustrophobia and an unprotected drop onto those tracks. The hum of high voltage electricity. The whine of the approaching red tube train. The rush of air. The taste of dirt in that air. A guy eyeing her up, moving closer. Carole trying to move further down the packed carriage. No chance of that. Peter stepping around her protectively. Changing to the overground and running down slippery steps. Carole checking behind her; the guy has gone.

Daylight rushing into the large windowed carriage. Blinding for a moment. Docklands gleaming up ahead. Tall glass buildings shining in the winter sun, reminding everyone that there were boom times. Not so long ago. Before Brexit. Before the Financial Crisis.

At the centre of this shining city is a massive fifty storey finger up to the outside world. The New London? No, this is the Old London. Once its docks traded goods to and from the Empire and the World. Now it buys and sells the values of companies, properties, even things yet to exist with the Commonwealth, the EU and the World. Billions changing hands up there behind that shiny glass through digits on computer screens. That's how money & wealth moves now. Not by ship anymore, but still in and out of the Docklands.

London is its own country. With its own electronic currency. London doesn't need the rest of Britain now it has been rescued by it. That's history. Forgotten history. Here at least.

Carole and Peter enter the office reception together. Frances the office manager rushes forward and hugs Carole.

"Good to have you back Carole. I'm so sorry about your father. You could still have a couple of days of compassionate leave if you need it."

"Thanks Frances. I'd rather get back into work. Take my mind off things."

"Keep it in mind. OK? Pete, TP wants to see you. Something's up. Altmeier Industries probably."

Across the office TP is in his glass fronted private office, beckoning to Peter. Peter gives Carole a peck on the cheek and heads off to meet TP.

Quiet efficiency all around. People catching up with whatever the hell happened in the ten-day Christmas break. The tap of keyboards sending emails world-wide in nanoseconds and for the urgent matters whispered frantic phone calls.

Frances at the centre of the rising storm. She looks at Carole with concern.

Carole smiles weakly. "Back to the grind then."

"Yes. First day of the New Year. You haven't missed much. Honestly. I've left a brief breakdown of what's going on, on your email. Team meeting at ten in Room Two. See you there Carole."

The rest of the day is a blur.

The entire week is a blur. Friday evening comes around without warning. And nothing huge achieved. It's that time of year. Minor victories. No real deals. Not enough to make conversation about with Pete on the way home. Nothing important enough to have to take home to work on at the weekend. To fill up her time. So, there will be too much time to think. Carole looks for Peter. He is in another meeting with TP. She tries to catch his eye. Fails. Sends him a text and heads out.

A snappy cold early January evening. London lit joylessly against the sky. Just the hint of daylight in that sky. The days are getting longer. It's dank now after earlier rain. The tube train is full of coughs and colds. Carole pulls up her scarf over her mouth. She can't bear to feel any worse.

By the time she is out of the tube, it's dark. Queues of traffic trying to escape the city. Walking through the square, passed Peter's Porsche, parked on a permit bay outside the flat. So, he won't be going anywhere this weekend unless it's essential. Parking here is a preoccupation, not just a chore.

Carole walks through the colonnade and opens the door to the building. Checking the mail. A solicitor's letter. To her. Carole's heart sinks. She doesn't need this. It's been a hard week. She opens the door to the flat. Sammy bounding over, overjoyed to see her. A bundle of energy at the end of a sapping day. Too much energy. Carole grabs Sammy's leash and heads back out with him and the letter.

Out into the square. Into the communal garden, her key opening the black cast iron gate. Sammy off the leash. Bounding around like a crazy thing. She hasn't taken him out. Shit, not all week! She's not thinking straight. Poor dog. Cooped up in a few dozen square feet with a maudlin girl. Carole flops down on the wet bench in the garden watching Sammy bound around, suddenly feeling much older than she is.

She looks at the solicitor's letter. This will focus her. She tears it open. Holding the letter close in the dim street lighting. A typical solicitors letter. No punctuation within labyrinthine sentences. Reading more like a contract than a letter telling her that her father has bequeathed her £175,000 on completion of probate on condition that she spends it on a property in Cwm Celyn. "Oh my God!"

Dad so earnest on the day he died. Holding her arm at the lake. "I've made sure you'll be ok when I'm gone. When the money comes through promise me, you'll find yourself down here as often as you can... This is where you're from Carole. Our blood runs deep in this country, you can't forget that. Promise me, will you?" She remembers every last word.

A solicitor's letter. Dad's way of making sure he gets his own way about this. Being careful. But there's no need. "Dad. OK, I promise."

Peter walking back to the flat. He hasn't seen her in the half light. Carole puts the letter back in the envelope. Into her coat pocket. Watching Sammy as her mind races. Making a To Do List in her phone. Call the solicitor. Look up estate agents. Call Mrs Jones. Check council tax bands. Look up broadband reach.

Until the phone rings. Peter. "Where are you babe?"

Monday lunchtime. Carole walks out of the office, through the shadows and out into the late winter sunshine of Canada Square. One Canada Square towers fifty storeys above her. The buzz of the Docklands Light Railway adding to the hum of a thousand conversations in the air. Numerous languages beneath this inversion of the Tower of Babel, where everyone now speaks the same language. Money.

Carole finds a corner of wall to perch herself. Checking her To Do list on her phone. 'Phone Mrs. Jones'. Carole searches her contacts. 'Mrs Jones, Capel Celyn Shop.' Carole calls the number.

Capel Celyn Shop. Lights on. No one home. The phone starts ringing. Mrs Jones unlocks the front door, rushing to the counter to answer the phone. Geraint brings in a delivery left outside. Both are dressed in funeral black just as Dai saw them in Phillips' Toili. He foresaw today down to the detail of Geraint's father's thin black 1980s tie around his son's neck. A tie two decades older than he is. A tie older than Canary Wharf.

Mrs Jones picks up the phone. "Prynhawn da. Capel Celyn Shop."

Carole is thrown by the Welsh. Damn what's the correct reply? "Hi Mrs Jones, it's Carole. Carole Morris. I'm calling to thank you for all that you did when Dad died."

"Carole bach, it was the least I could do, with you by yourselves here. It must have been terrible for you. I'll miss seeing Dai around. He'd been a good friend since we were children. I hope I'll see you coming back here as often as you can."

"You will. Dad made me promise something the day he died, that I'd keep coming down there to Capel Celyn. I intend to keep that promise. I'll be looking for a place there for myself and Mum to come down to, when we can."

There. Wasn't so hard, was it? She may well know of somewhere going. Shopkeepers know everything. Silence for a moment from the other side of the line. Silence can't be good. She's blown it.

"You're looking to buy a place down here?" Thoughtful. Not angry.

"I know it's not a good thing to do, with local people not being able to afford places of their own, but if you know of somewhere that may be going on the market, I'll be grateful if you could let me know."

"It's just… well I'm just back from Mr. Phillips' funeral. The poor dab died around Christmas in his cottage. I think he was in the shop when you arrived..."

Carole stands up in shock. Dad mentioned a Toil. She thought it was nonsense. The grey man. In that cottage where they stopped. Oh God. "The cottage near the lake? Alone out in the forestry?"

"Yes. That's the one. He had no family locally. The cottage will need to be sold. His poor wife's brother was telling me that was what they were going to do with the old place. I can put you in touch with him if you like. He'll probably want to put it on the market straight away."

"That's so very good of you. Thank you so much!"

"That's OK Carole bach, I'd rather see someone we know get the place, rather than some stranger."

"So, I'm not a stranger?"

"No, you're Dai Morris' daughter. That makes you one of us."

Chapter 7: Doors Opening

A Facebook message. 'Hi Carole. Lunch tomorrow? Pret? 12:30? Jenny x'

Reply. 'Cool, see you there :) x' Add it as a diary item. Done. Carole's first meet up with any friends in the ten weeks since the funeral. Where did her friends go?

Carole opens her 'To Do List' on her phone. Plenty of ticks in those little boxes. A box ticked but bothering her. 'Contact owners Pantyfedwen'. Done almost two months ago. Mrs. Jones predicted they would be super keen to sell the cottage near the lake. Obviously not. A pity. There's nothing much else in the area in her price range, and nothing with the character. Carole makes a new To Do item: 'Chase Owners Pantyfedwen'

Lying on her London sofa thinking about a dilapidated cottage in mid Wales. An escape from million-pound bijou luxury to densely forested isolation a mile from the nearest village. Absolutely. Bliss. *Pantyfedwen* apparently means 'Birch Valley'. Pretty. A name from an earlier time before those pine trees were planted. It could be a pretty cottage again with a bit of TLC.

Sammy climbing on the sofa to join her. She searches Capel Celyn on her browser to see if there are any estate agents listed. It's time to move on with this.

Top result. The online version of the local paper. In Welsh, and far beyond her abilities to comprehend.

OK, next. A national online paper for the whole of Wales. Run hours away in Cardiff, so there won't be anything, surely? Oh! Mr. Phillips found dead in the cottage. He had been dead for a week before anyone found him. The tale tied into a '*Lonely this Christmas*' campaign. Fair enough. What a miserable end, even for such a miserable man. No one reading this report would want to make an offer for the place, would they? What if the wife's brother had already accepted an offer? And when would Dad's money hit her account? A few weeks. Months maybe? One thing she has learned from her projects at work; nothing happens within in the timescale you want. This whole project is out of her control. All she can do is hope it all comes together.

The next item on the browser. Same newspaper. 'Fire Sparks Reigniting of Holiday Home Arson Campaign'. Sounds like it's written by their football reporter. Making puns seeming inappropriate here. What's this about? A suspicious fire at a remote cottage some ten miles from Capel Celyn. Way up in the mountains. No one hurt. No one living there. A holiday let. OK. So what? 'This fire will strike fear into all of those owning holiday homes in Wales, bearing a striking similarity to the Meibion Glyndwr holiday home arson campaign in the 1980s and 1990s. Over two hundred properties were damaged...' What the hell?

Searching on her browser quickly. 'Did you mean Meibion Glyndwr?' Yes, obviously! Sammy up and off the sofa. Peter is home. Carole shuts off the phone.

Queuing for an ethical coffee and an off-the-shelf-made-on-the-premises sandwich. Having a chat with Jenny in the over-crowded seating area. The first time Carole has been out with a friend in such a long time. And months since she last saw Jenny. So here she is squashed up against the best boss she ever had. It's nice to catch up, but there's something brewing here. Carole knows Jenny too well. There's never a free lunch even if you paid for it yourself. Jenny never gossips unless there's a plan.

"I was worried about you. I hadn't seen you since your father died. No sign of you out and about for a couple of months. Thought I should track you down."

"I've just been going to work and going home. And Peter's

been working all the hours."

"You need your friends to give you a bit of perspective. Are you OK Carole?"

"I just feel on my own. Pete is being worked into the ground. I'm not even stretched. I'm home at a decent time. He's home late. There's things I'm planning he doesn't even know about. We never talk."

"Minor stuff though, right?"

Carole bites into her sandwich. It means she can't answer that one. She hasn't even asked herself that question. What is she doing? Considering a major life decision and she hasn't even mentioned it to Pete. "Where would I be on my own?" Oh crap. Where the hell did that come from?

"Carole? Are you really that unhappy?".

Another question Carole hasn't asked herself. Why not?

"Want a change of scene?" Jenny leaning forward, conspiratorial. "There's a job coming up on my team at DIG. Starts in August. I know it's a little way off. A much better package than you have right now. I should know, right? Why not send me your CV. I'll get it to the right people. I can put you in the frame before they even think about head hunting."

Carole swallows her sandwich. "I'll get it over to you tonight."

Jenny smiles, necking her coffee. "Do that. And meet me at O'Neal's on Friday evening straight after work. I'll introduce you to a couple of people you should know from DIG."

Carole arrives back at her desk, mind racing, distracted now. Is she happy here? Facing an afternoon of hassle and not the day of getting stuff done she had planned at the start of this morning. Never seeing the man she lives with, here in work or at home.

She hacks in the password for her computer. Her phone buzzes on the desk. Email. 'Interest in potentially purchasing

Pantyfedwen Cottage, Cwm Celyn.' Carole opens the email and stares at the screen. Everything is happening at once!

Carole on her laptop. Why did she ever bother buying this piece of crap? An operating system seemingly designed to piss her off. As glitchy as hell. Items flying around or opening on their own. She's making the final adjustments to her CV. She hasn't updated it in the two years since she moved in with Pete. She hasn't needed to. It's taken hours but it's done now. Save As a pdf and email to Jenny. Hurry up! Jeez. Bloody computer. Done. Why is everything so bloody complicated on this thing?

Where is Pete? It's passed nine thirty now.

OK. Next. LinkedIn. Edit. Oh man. That photo has to go. This all needs some work too.

Sammy on his feet. Pete is back. "Hi Pete. You're late. Been out?"

"As if. Fucking conference call with Altmeir's LA office. It went on for hours and they wanted to break for lunch. Fucking Americans think the world revolves around them."

"What time are you going in tomorrow?"

"The usual. I need to write this shit up."

"I'll heat up something from the freezer for you."

"Don't bother."

"It's not a bother. If you're hungry I'll make you something." Carole gets to her feet and goes to the kitchen area. "What shall we do for the weekend Pete?"

"You go out with your friends or something. I'll have to go into work."

"Seriously?"

"Seriously."

"Can I borrow the car?"

"Why?"

"Well, you won't be using it, and I promise I'll look

after it."

"Where are you going to go?"

Carole thinking fast. "I thought I'd go to see my mother." Carole opens the freezer and looks through the ready meals.

"Yeah. I'm best off being in work then."

"Do you want Thai Chicken or Butter Chicken?"

"Neither. I'm off to bed." Peter heads off into the bathroom, slamming the door.

Carole puts the ready meals back in the freezer, any chance of a conversation over. Back to the sofa to update her LinkedIn profile.

Friday evening. Jenny and two men from DIG at a table in O'Neal's. No one there from work tonight, thank God. Chit chat doesn't last longer than two minutes. Probing questions. One of the men, putting his phone on the table mid-question, the screen showing Carole's LinkedIn page. Time well spent the other night!

This is serious. Mineral water because it's an early start tomorrow turns into mineral water because this is a job interview. Laughter. Nodding. Going well. Jenny leading the conversation as she is so good at doing. And these people are actually fun. Talking shop yes, but really clever, insightful. Not a single bit of bitching. When Carole hits the March night air, she feels a little drunk on it.

Back to the flat. Peter is already asleep.

Chapter 8: Visitation

The far-too-early-for-Saturday alarm wakes Carole with a start. Pre-dawn light creeping around the blinds. Peter rolls back to sleep. Carole leads Sammy to the car. The Porsche shining in the dawn light. It's 6am. The streets are practically deserted. London sleeping in on a Saturday morning. Sammy falls asleep right away in the passenger footwell.

The car roars as it rises out of west London on the motorway. When her Dad used to take her out of London as a kid there would be a Lucozade sign with the date and temperature to draw her attention. Now there are one hundred foot high TV screens advertising Korean cars and video game characters for today's children to remember. Then the buildings seem to stop. Flatlands. Jets stacked up shining in the morning sky ahead as if ready to land on the motorway.

After forty miles the Porsche purring at twenty to thirty miles per hour over the speed limit. Carole trying to shorten the five-hour trip to Capel Celyn. Carole selecting another album to play on the phone, picked up and amplified by the Porsche's sound system. Carole and the Porsche in perfect harmony. Sammy asleep.

Over the two-mile bridge into Wales, the land of her father. Dual carriageways give way to endless roundabouts and then the open hills. Narrower roads needing the Porsche's power to get around lorries, tractors and Land Rovers. Carole looking for a service station selling Super Unleaded Fuel. Finding one with a cafe opposite. A bacon roll for her, sausages and a bowl of water for Sammy.

An hour later she is on the single track mountain road coming to the drop into Cwm Celyn. Carole brings the car to a halt as she did when driving her Dad and Mum just before Christmas. Only three months ago. Carole looks at the valley's landmarks within the forestry through tear filled eyes. Counting off the lake, the grove and the village as she always did with her Dad, until eventually the tears dry.

Buzz. A text on her phone. 'That went really well last night. You were brilliant. Job as good as yours. Keep under your hat. Xpect formal interview soon. Jenny x.'

Everything happening at once. Coming together.

The Porsche banging around, out of its element on the bumpy forest road. Carole bringing the car to a halt on the verge in front of the cottage. The throbbing engine stops and there is silence. Except for the hiss of the breeze through the trees and Sammy whining.

Carole gets out of the car. Mrs Jones opens her door and Sammy darts out. She struggles to get out of the passenger side having been sitting practically at ground level.

Carole looking around. "It's so peaceful here."

"A fortnight ago there was snow. March comes in like a lion and leaves like a lamb. Spring is coming. Everything looks better in the spring. These trees cut out the wind. It's very sheltered up here."

Mrs. Jones looks at the house. Two windows like two dark eyes watching her. Like Phillips watching her with those dark and haunted eyes when he came to the shop to buy whiskey. And how those eyes were different, clear and glassy when she found him here just after Christmas. She shivers at the memory.

Is it really the right thing to do to get Dai's girl interested in this place? With this history? It's just everyone is leaving Cwm Celyn. Empty houses are fewer customers. Fewer friends. A smaller community. It can't become just another holiday home for some rich English stranger. Carole is practically family. Yes, it's the right thing for Cwm Celyn. Mrs. Jones fumbles for the keys.

Carole takes a photo of the traditional Welsh cottage.

White-washed in need of redoing. Welsh slate roof in good shape. Traditional wooden sash windows with signs of rot, they'd probably need replacing. A chimney in good shape. Carole bounds up to the cottage enthusiastically, Sammy dancing around her legs. Mrs Jones follows with growing trepidation.

Carole looks excitedly through the window through the part closed rotting curtains as Mrs Jones fumbles with the keys.

Mrs Jones struggling to turn the old key. The door unlocks with a squeak and opens with complaining hinges. "The place needs a lot of work, Carole bach."

Carole steps inside into the gloom, dark and cold. It's really cold. Mrs Jones switches on the light. The energy-saving low wattage bulb hardly adds any illumination. Sammy is still on the doorstep unsure of whether to go inside.

By now Mrs. Jones failing to hide her distaste. "It's such a shame the place is such a mess Carole. The family came up after the funeral and took away anything they wanted to keep. The rest of this rubbish comes with the house."

Carole is looking beyond the old newspapers, magazines, general tat and decades of dust and dirt. The house seems to have stood still for sixty years or more. "But it's lovely Mrs. Jones. Look at this fireplace, the beams, it's really gorgeous." Carole takes more pictures on her mobile phone. The beamed ceiling. The fire place. The ochre walls. Sturdy stuff behind the dirt and dust.

Mrs Jones coughs with the dust, or is it fungus in the air? Or is something else smelling? Something dead? She swears she can still smell Mr. Phillips.

Carole heads off to the left. Through the door into the kitchen. Mrs Jones stays in the living room, by the front door. Uneasy. Still coughing.

"Wow, a Belfast sink..." Snap. A post-war kitchen covered in grime. Snap. "I don't know if you know, Mrs. Jones. Is this cottage listed?" Opening the other door. A toilet with pull chain. A different stink. Pretty bad too. No picture this time.

"I don't know Carole. It was built around the turn of the last century by a ship's captain. It's not that old as houses go around here."

Carole is coughing now. There is a bad smell in here. The whole place needs airing. Another door. A bath and basin and filthy mirror. The 1950s white bath is black with filth. Snap.

"The water comes from the well, there's no mains out here. There's a Septic tank. No gas or phone either. Just the electric. It's very basic Carole bach. Too much work I'd say." That doubt remains. Mrs Jones is getting... nervous? Another coughing fit. The dog has come inside. The first spots of rain. Mrs. Jones closes the front door.

Mrs Jones walks to the bedroom but stops. She has to prove to herself that this is just an empty room now. The sad old man has gone. The dog runs in passed her, exploring wildly. Mrs Jones feels increasingly uncomfortable in here. Where she found him. Hanging there like a side of pork in the cold air. Cold staring eyes. Accusing. Why had she not popped up before Christmas? Why? Because her hands were full with Carole and her mother after Davey died outside her shop. Mrs Jones has had enough. She turns swiftly bumping into Carole.

"Sorry." Carole takes in the bedroom. Low beams. The bed and bedroom furniture. "I can do a lot with this place, there's so much potential. There's nothing a bit of tender loving care and some fresh paint won't fix. I love it Mrs. Jones. I'll phone the family today and organise a survey."

Mrs Jones regretting this now. "Surely this is too much work for you?" She can't stand being in here, even with Carole.

The sudden sound of rain hammering down on the roof. A heavy shower. Masking the sound of the front door opening.

Squealing as a shadow comes inside. Sammy whines and crawls under the bed.

    Carole not listening to anything. "Dad would be so pleased if he could see me in this place." The shadow moves behind her. Carole takes a picture of the bedroom. She and Mrs. Jones are reflected in the full-length mirror. Beside her Mrs Jones looks very uneasy.

    Mrs Jones wanders off to close the front door.

    Carole looks at her watch. "Would you mind waiting while I measure up the rooms? I won't be long I promise."

    "I'll give you a hand. We need to be quick. The sooner I get back to the shop the better."

Chapter 9: Doors Closing

Carole at the bathroom mirror drying her hair after a shower. Combing through her dirty blonde hair. Mascara and eyeliner making her deep brown eyes seem black. Not thickening her eyebrows, that's tacky, for younger girls only. Red lipstick. Wonderbra making her cleavage more prominent but not too much. Dark stockings.

It's a job interview. Business but she saw how those men from DIG looked at her. It's a #MeToo world now. She can look good in person, as good as she looks on paper. She's aiming for business smart. The same style as Jenny. That girl has it to a tee. 'Yes, I'm attractive and I have a brain. Hire me and I make you look good. Because I'm REALLY good'.

Has she overdone it? She can't show Jenny up. No more mascara maybe.

"You never wear mascara." Pete, just awake, standing naked outside the bathroom door watching. Appreciating. Wanting. "Suits you."

Carole smiles. The first compliment he has given her in a few weeks.

"I thought you had the morning off? Where are you going looking like that?"

Carole steps out passed Pete who slaps her playfully on the bum. Carole goes into the bedroom. She pulls her best business suit out of the wardrobe and a business blouse. "I've got a job interview."

Peter's face falls. "You kept that quiet."

"It just came up. We don't get time to talk these days, Pete."

'We don't get time to talk?' Where the fuck has that come from? And why would she want to leave the firm? And not even mention it? "OK so tell me now."

"It's an interview with DIG."

Oh Jesus. A bomb goes off in Peter's gut. "Woah! Think for a minute. They're our main competition Carole! Think of the problems if my girl is working for a rival company?"

Carole puts on her blouse.

"Have you talked this through with TP? Ask him for a rise?"

"I want to talk to you first. If they offer me the job, do you think I should take it?"

"If TP won't offer you a raise, you should go for it. But it's complicated."

"Complicated?"

"Conflict of interest and all that."

"So, we'll be signing NDAs. What's new?" Finishing buttoning up the blouse.

"Would you get more than you're getting now?"

Carole nods aware of him watching her from the bedroom doorway. "Quite a bit more. And TP will behave. He needs you to do all the heavy lifting." Skirt on.

"Maybe. I don't know... Is that enough 'more' that we can get ourselves a mortgage? A place of our own at last?"

"Can we though Pete? Really? All of our money has gone by the end of the month right now. Have you got any money for a deposit?"

"I'll end the contract on the Porsche. That's almost a grand a month. Do you think you'll get any money after your father?"

"That money is spoken for Pete." Suit jacket on.

"What do you mean? There is money? Carole?" Carole puts her dress watch on. "London is one of the most expensive cities in the world! We need every penny if we're going to put a deposit down. I mean, your dad left it to you. For us! What else are you going to do with it?"

Keys. Handbag. "Let's talk tonight. I really have to go.

Get home as soon as you can, OK? Are you going to wish me luck?" Carole brushes past him, expecting a kiss.

Peter stands naked with his whole world falling away.

The door slams. Carole is gone.

Carole can feel eyes on her all afternoon. Who knows about the interview apart from Pete? Who has he been talking to? Would he screw things up to keep her here? He pulled some strokes to get rid of his ex-girlfriend Patricia when he and Carole started to see each other.

Men here can be devious. And as open as a book. Carole at the printer and two lads suddenly rushing to print stuff too. Ah... The battle dress has had an unintended effect. Walking back to her desk. The boys looking.

Peter glowering from across the office. Things are going to be rough tonight.

"How can you just forget what we've been doing for the last couple of years?"

"Don't be so melodramatic. I haven't. Dad has written a covenant. I have to spend the money in Cwm Celyn."

"Some back of beyond area you visited when you were a kid! Fuck Carole. Let's get a lawyer to look at it, see if there's any way..."

Carole leaps to defend her Dad. "What? No! It's his money and now its spoken for. I've already made an offer on a cottage there."

Peter's face pales further. What the hell is going on? "Really? So have you even seen this place?"

"That's where I went the other weekend."

Peter stares at Carole in disbelief. "You told me you were visiting your mother! You lied? Fuck Carole!!! Why didn't you tell me about this?"

"I am telling you about it. It's not a lot of money. The

place will make money as a holiday home. It will pay for itself easily."

"Is that your plan? And what about our plans? Here! In the real world!"

"It'll all work out, you'll see."

"You could lose me my job by working for DIG. It's called sleeping with the enemy!"

"You know TP has policies coming out of his ears about that sort of stuff. That's why we work in the same office but on different teams. Jenny left well over a year ago so she can now approach former work colleagues like me. Their job has me working with clients who have been with DIG for years. No conflicts. I checked."

"You've been planning this for ages, haven't you?"

"No! It's just things are coming together. Doors are opening Pete."

"No! Doors are closing!" Peter grabs his coat and storms out of the flat.

Hours later. Carole lying half asleep in bed, still upset, holding Sammy. Sammy woofing, the front door opening quietly. Someone in the doorway. "Pete?" The door closes. Someone flops heavily on the sofa.

For the next month everything flows. Faster than she even imagined. Offer accepted. Survey fine. Contracts exchanged. A bit of money left over to fix up the place. And DIG came through. Start date the first of August.

A whirlwind shaking up her life. But all Carole notices is Pete. Or to be more exact, the lack of Pete. Gone first thing. Home late. Sleeping on the sofa. Not speaking. Not speaking because of overwork has turned into not speaking on purpose.

Carole acquiring stuff for the cottage. A mattress filling

the entrance hall. Boxes of cleaning materials. Crockery. Bed clothes. A suitcase. Boxes of belongings from the flat. Her belongings. Peter doesn't do belongings, apart from clothes and tech.

So he feels all of this crap is just left there to antagonise him, to be tripped over as he tries to get in and out of the place as quietly as possible. So, Carole is not speaking now. Avoiding him at work and not speaking when he's at home.

"I'll miss you terribly you know." A warm hug.

"I'll miss you too Frances. But we'll see each other around, out at lunch or something."

A card. A bottle of Prosecco. An iTunes gift card. No TP or Peter, locked in a conveniently timed meeting. Carole knows that it's the end of the road here, and it's a one-way street. So onwards to elsewhere.

"Got any plans before you start up at DIG? A holiday or something?"

"I'm fixing up my cottage in Wales."

"You bought a cottage? In Wales? Bloody hell! I had no idea."

"It needs a bit of work, so I'm going to spend a few weeks down there sorting it out."

"So, what brought this on? I would have thought Peter and you would be buying a place of your own here in London."

"You know house prices."

"Yes, but there's no time like now Carole. The only thing that never comes down is house prices."

Carole uncomfortable in the face of Frances logic. "I bought it with the money my Dad left to me". Distraction always works with Frances. "Want to see some pictures?"

"Yeah! Too right I do."

Carole opens up the pictures on her phone. Shots taken on

her trip to the cottage with Mrs Jones.

"Wow... That's really old. It could be really lovely, eh?"

"I think so. It needs a little renovation, but you know me. I'm not scared of hard work." Carole keeps swiping through the pictures.

"What does Pete think of it?"

"He hasn't seen it. He's driving me down there on the weekend. He'll see it then."

"But he's back in work on Monday. You're not going to stay down there on your own or something are you? Don't get me wrong, it's lovely and all that, but it's a lot of work Carole." Carole still swiping through the photos to the shot Carole took in the bedroom. "Who's that?"

Carole looks at the still from the bedroom. "That's Mrs Jones. She's my Dad's friend who helped me get the place..."

Frances points. "No, not her. The man... there, behind you."

Carole and Mrs Jones are reflected in the wardrobe mirror. Behind Carole is a grey shadow. Something she hadn't seen before. What the hell is that? Dirt on the lens? But it's not on any other picture. "I've had these pictures for a couple of months and never noticed that. Weird. Trick of the light I suppose..."

Chapter 10: Into the Outland

Saturday morning. Carole stacking cardboard boxes outside the front door of the flat in the communal stairwell. It's much too early for anyone else to be about for them to be an inconvenience. The front door to the building slams. Peter comes up the stairs, carrying something inside his jacket. "Hi babe. I've got the hire van parked up out front. Better get moving."

Carole picks up the first box. Peter rolls a bottle of champagne onto the top of the box.

"I brought something for the new house. To say sorry... it's your money, your Dad wanted you to get a place down there. That's ok with me. I bet it's lovely."

Carole gives Peter an awkward kiss. Time was she could find his lips instinctively. It's been a while. "Thanks Pete."

The thaw is temporary. The chance to talk on the trip is wasted. Too much tension lately. Now they are in a small space together for a few hours it's very difficult to talk.

Peter still hurt by the fact Carole has kept such major life-changing events from him. Because he was overworked, apparently. How does that make sense?

Outside on the motorway the traffic is free flowing, but the hire van has a speed regulator. The ultimate pain in the arse on a long trip.

Peter could do with a coffee. Passing a motorway service station about an hour out of town, but they've not gone far enough to need to stop. The next he'd driven past without noticing it was there. Then nothing until after crossing the bridge over the sea into Wales but he missed that one too.

Off the motorway, onto dual carriageways and suddenly mountain roads. Reservoirs. Towns with at least twenty miles between them. Good thing he'd brought the sat nav. It sits on the van's dashboard showing oncoming nothingness as he keeps driving along a pink road into the unending greenery on the little screen.

The signposts are different, with Welsh on top. He never gets as far as the English version of names or directions, as his brain tries to make sense of the names he read first time. Peter is lost. Carole knows the way but isn't exactly forthcoming with the information. The sat nav does most of the talking.

Peter pissed off with the time this is taking and the country traffic. The odd tractor and omni-present lorries keeping them in a convoy at under forty miles per hour for dozens of miles. The skid marks on the road telling the story of other vehicles being stuck behind the same trucks who dared to try to pass. Peter praying that the lorries are turning off soon. But they never do. All this and the diminishing choice of radio stations as they travel deeper in country.

Lunch in the same cafe where she had stopped on the way to see the cottage those couple of months before. But it's mid-afternoon. Pete grisly after a six-hour drive, with at least another hour to go. He wanted, no needed his lunch three hours ago.

Well, he should have said so then, instead of clamming up all trip. Carole had calculated the trip in Porsche time, not hire van time.

The only one happy right now is Sammy with his sausages.

The hire van climbs up the mountaintop road. The sat nav saying "Unnamed Road", while on the screen it all still looks the same; pink line going through green. Dance music plays on the radio, the only thing keeping him sane.

No traffic up here. Carole is able to see for miles. Sheep

and lambs like white clouds on a green sky of pasture. Luckily Sammy is asleep after his feed.

Peter seeing only the single-track strip of grey tarmac and some broken glass before the road drops away into a world of trees. The sat nav speaks: 'You have reached your destination'. This couldn't be it surely?

"We're here. This is the valley." Carole's eyes light up as she sees Cwm Celyn spread out ahead.

She's fucking serious. This is it? You are having a laugh! "There's nothing but trees. I was expecting more of these open mountains. Sheep and shit."

The van dips into the forestry plantation. The music fades to static on the radio. Peter turns on the van lights. Where the hell did the daylight go? Peter retunes the radio while Carole holds onto Sammy, who is disturbed by the suddenly rough road.

Another radio station tunes in clearly. The jingle music fades, and the announcer speaks in Welsh. Peter listens in amazement. "Blimey! We still in Britain or what?" The announcement over, a folk singer launches into a heartfelt ballad. "Oh, come on lads, can't you play anything remotely funky, even on a Saturday?"

Peter re-tunes the radio, finding a news report in English, with a heavily Welsh accented announcer. "… and a spokesman for the organisation said that the renewed arson campaign against second homes in Wales would continue until measures were put in place to halt the purchase of holiday homes in rural areas…" Peter is confused. Whatever the hell that headline news was, it had never reached London. Where has she taken him? This is another country alright. He switches off the radio. There is a T-junction up ahead in the gloom.

"Not far now, Pete. Turn right at the junction."

Carole taking him down a road with no road sign. No, wrong. 'No Through Road'. Fucking hell, it's getting worse!

The van turns right towards the cottage and the lake.

The van continues its bumpy way down the forestry road. Would you believe it? A fucking cyclist. On a road to nowhere in the middle of nowhere. With no fucking cycle lane, no lights, nor one of those pratty helmets. And nowhere to pass. Peter changes gear loudly.

The cyclist hears the roar of the van coming up behind and pulls over to let it pass. The lad, maybe eighteen has a fishing rod and rucksack on his back and a mop top haircut. Geraint from the shop. A couple of inches taller than six months ago, and maybe ten pounds heavier. He's changed enough for Carole not to recognise him as they drive past. But Geraint recognises her.

The rush of the wind through the pine trees blots out every other sound for that moment. The van seems to arrive at the cottage in silence.

"This is it Pete. Stop here." Pantyfedwen. The small, single story traditional Welsh cottage is sitting waiting for her like a rescue puppy beside the road.

Peter brings the van to a halt. His eyes wide in surprise meeting those two dark window-eyes staring back. Aren't the eyes the windows of the soul? These are dark and as miserable as fuck. Peter sits aghast at the wheel, peering into the gloom at that... Shed. Unbelievable Carole. Never in his worst nightmare did he expect this. Unbelievable. The end of the road? Fuck yeah! Pete punches the Add To Address Book button on the sat nav. No way is he going to find his way back here without electronic help. Jesus wept.

Carole looks at the cottage with unbridled excitement. "Well Pete, what do you think? Isn't it fantastic?"

"It's... it's a bit out in the woods innit?"

"Come on, park the van up there." She points to some clear ground outside the boundary wall.

Pete couldn't call it a garden wall. No garden here for

decades by the look of it.

Geraint brings his bike to a halt, almost invisible in the gloom, watching what's going on. Six months have changed Geraint. Hormones mixed with the active life he lives have turned him into a fit young man, unlike most of his classmates who are slumped on a sofa at home. Rugby has been kind to him. Rugby, for years the preserve of the large and loutish, alongside the small and the quick. Now everyone has to be large and athletic. Including the half backs. A bit like the American Football quarter backs, the guys with the brains need to be huge now too. Coaching means weight training and bulking up as well as game skills. Geraint has built himself in the last few months.

Geraint is going fishing today, to clear his head before Monday's A Level exam. Trying to keep calm and fight off pre-exam panic. His notes are in his backpack in case he needs to check anything. Being up at the lake helps him think. No one around to bother him. His phone doesn't have a signal up there.

Now there's another reason to pass by this way. Carole. She is gorgeous! No girl anything like her in the whole Cwm Celyn area to be honest. Geraint watches the proceedings at the front of the cottage with curiosity. Or rather he watches Carole. A real babe. It was too much to hope she was single. That man with her looks like a bit of a wanker. Typical Londoner. Why do all the great girls go for the wankers?

Chapter 11: A Not So Empty House

Carole and Peter get out of the van and Sammy bounds away rooting around the frontage of the cottage.

Peter hangs back at the van, trying hard not to show what he thinks of this place. The first time here shouldn't start with a row. But, Jeez what a dump! Fuck!

Carole fishes in her bag for the keys. Oh God, did she leave them in the flat? No, here they are. She walks up to the front door and pushes the key into the lock. The key won't turn. What the hell? She can't get into her own cottage! The key won't budge. She rattles and moves the key back and forth trying to hit the magic spot.

Peter joins her at the door. "Do you want a hand with that? Don't break it!"

"It's OK." Carole manages to turn the key in the stiff door lock. Thunk. Carole tries the door, but it's jammed. She shoulder charges the door. It won't budge as if someone is leaning against the door. The wood has probably swollen over the winter.

"Let me try." Peter shoves the door which opens scuffing on the floor.

Carole smiles at Peter. "Well, are you going to carry me over the threshold?"

Peter picks up Carole and carries her into the cottage. Into the musty and untidy living room, untouched since Carole was there last. The beams of light that flood through the door and window illuminate the clouds of dust that rise as the breeze blows through the door. Peter stands in silence holding Carole before Sammy the dog bursts in. Peter puts her down and looks around in undisguised worry.

"This needs a lot of work girl. You should have had a full survey done. There's probably damp..."

Carole's heart crashes as she watches Peter walk around the room, clocking the dust, dirt and rubbish piled in the corners with distaste. He doesn't see what she sees; past the dirt to the yellow ochre walls, the beams, the fireplace. The home Pantyfedwen Cottage should be.

"Pete, I can make it really nice."

"But this needs more than a lick of paint. Rewiring? Plumbing? Furniture? Some sort of heating system? It's freezing in here."

In the cold light of this summer afternoon, Carole sees what Peter sees. Months of work. Tears well up. Carole goes into the kitchen, leaving Peter alone, concerned and apprehensive.

Peter mutters under his breath. "What have you done you crazy bitch?". How could this girl be so deluded? This needs tens of thousands of pounds of work by proper tradesmen. She can't rewire the house. Nor can he. What the hell is she thinking?

Carole stands in the kitchen watching Sammy root around. The tears let her see for the first time how the whole kitchen is caked with dirt. Years of dirt. Decades of neglect. Some of the electrical plugs in here are round. That standard went out well before she was born. Peter is right. This is going to cost thousands. Can she afford to fix this place up? The biggest decision of her life taken on a whim. A mistake. She cries silently. Dad's money, gone on this. She shivers in the cold kitchen.

Peter watches Carole through the kitchen doorway. He can see that she is crying. He steps forward to hug her but then thinks better of it. There'll be a row, and it will be his fault for being negative. He'd be right but wrong. Why do negative and realistic mean the same thing to Carole? She's changed. Life with her used to be fun.

Peter opens the other door off the living room, the bedroom door and wanders in. It's colder yet in here. And the smell hits him like a slap in the face. Oh Jeez! No air and a stench like something that died in there. Peter puts his hand to his mouth and crosses the floor towards the little sash window to try to open it. His trainers tap on the floor as he crosses but for one spot where the floor sounds hollow. Peter stands still. The floorboards creak ominously. He steps away, not wanting to fall into any rotten cellar down there. This place could be a death-trap.

He tries to open the window. Painted shut? What the hell? Who would do that? Peter struggles with the window. Nothing doing. Coughing now, the stench overpowering. Someone behind him. "Carole this window is jammed." No one there. No sign of her. He could have sworn he saw someone move in the corner of his eye.

There are pools of darkness in this room. Dark enough for someone to hide in. It must be a trick of the light. Is he actually looking for something moving in the room? There's nothing there. He'd be able to see it. Get a grip! For God's sake!

Peter heads for the door. The hollow sound as he crosses those floorboards again. What the hell? He kneels down to examine the squeaky floorboards. They look the same as all of the others. They've been there since the Ark. Someone behind him. Peter turns around. No one there again. The stench hits him, filling his lungs. Another fit of coughing. What is that stink? It's overpowering now. Peter tries to spit it out. Fuck this! He quickly leaves the room, slamming the door behind him.

Peter rushes out of the front door. Bile rising in his throat. Oh Christ! Retching. Leaning against the cottage wall to steady himself. His head reeling.

Carole hears Peter retching. She dries her eyes and follows him outside. Peter is leaning against the cottage wall coughing like an old man. That's not good. "Pete? Are you OK?"

A sound behind her on the road. That cyclist. Some young lad smiling nervously at Carole as he cycles up. "Hi."

"Hello." Carole smiles politely, turning away to hide her red eyes, grabbing Sammy who is making to chase Geraint.

Carole doesn't recognise him. Crap. Geraint rides on crest fallen. Now he can see the wanker boyfriend a more closely. Coughing up his guts outside the front of the house. Obviously not used to the clean air up here. Geraint rides off for the lake.

Peter catching his breath. "Shall we start getting this stuff off the van then? Or do you want to clear up the place a bit first?"

"Let's get the stuff inside. I'll get the kitchen box and make us a cup of tea." Carole picks up a box from the back of the van, carrying it indoors, followed by Sammy.

Peter left alone. "And I'll just hump the rest of this in, shall I?"

Sammy running around her legs. Trying to get close. He must be nervous in this unfamiliar place. Carole at the Belfast sink. She turns the tap. Very stiff, like the key in the door. Black water, then brown. Oh God! The tears well up again, but the water suddenly clears. The water now crystal as a mountain stream. Carole fills the kettle and plugs it into a newer socket. Nothing blows up. The kettle starts to heat up, making the familiar noise it does in the flat in London. Carole suddenly feeling more at home.

Filling two bowls with the cold water from the tap, one

for Sammy who is pushing himself between Carole and the
worktop and putting a plastic bottle of milk in the other to
keep it cool. No need for a fridge for now at least, it's very
chilly in here. Tea bags. A couple of mugs. Peter's Chelsea
mug. He must have had that since he was a child. Carole smiles
for the first time since she got here this time. She feels
comfortable. The whole room seems to lighten a bit. Sammy
whimpering in the corner now. "What's the matter Sammy?"
Filling the mugs with steaming water. Swirling the tea bags
around with a teaspoon. Adding the milk to both. Tossing the
two used tea bags into a plastic carrier bag. Carole picks up
the two mugs of tea and leaves the kitchen.

 Sammy watches Mari, Ifan's wife, spectral in the half-
light. Dressed in her summer dress from the turn of the last
century. The browns of the dress melding into the semi-
darkness of the kitchen. A brown shape, hardly there, but
moving now, watching Carole leave the kitchen. Sammy whimpers.
Mari's head snaps around to stare at him. Sammy runs out.

 The dog runs straight out of the front door. Carole passes
a mug of tea to Pete, who is depositing another box of stuff
in the living room. Carole sees that he has placed the bottle
of champagne on the fireplace. A gesture at last.

 "It's June and it's bloody freezing in here!"

 Carole looks for the positive. She is not going to lose
this argument. Anyway, there's no going back now. "I'll get
the fire going soon... it'll be great, you'll see…"

 "Ok, I know it's your money, but was there nowhere better
than this?"

 "I've a month before my new job starts, I could do wonders
in that time..."

 "We could, perhaps, though I doubt it. The state of this
place! I've got to get back to London tomorrow. Can you afford
to get builders in? Do they even have builders out here?"

Carole is losing the argument. "Oh Pete, please don't spoil it. I want us to be happy here. This is my first place of my very own." Oh no! The wrong thing to say.

Peter explodes. "What about the flat? You and me? Back in the real world?" The look on Carole's face tells him all he needs to know. This relationship isn't going to be fixed. Peter walks out of the cottage raging.

Carole watches him go. She's lost the argument. Maybe more. No! She can put this right! She mumbles under her breath. "It's something to remember Dad by... It's got nothing to do with you..." Mari's brown shape moves out of the kitchen behind her.

Carole picks up a framed family photograph from the box Peter has just brought in. Herself with her Father and Mother. At the place she called home. Not there for her anymore. Just like Dad.

Mari beside her, watching, feeling Carole's mood. Carole's mood softening. Tears again. For a happier time. A time she can't return to anymore.

Mari watches her intensely then something draws her attention. At the door. Fear. Mari backs away and is gone.

Chapter 12: Oppression

Peter leans on the van. Gathering his thoughts the best he can as the wind hisses through the trees. The hiss, that static clouding his mind. He is so angry and so disappointed. He knew today could be a tough day, but he always expected Carole to have chosen a cool cottage. No wonder she never showed him any photos of this place.

This all started at Christmas when she wanted to be with her family. Up here in the mountains rather than with him. Then her dad dying on the trip. Maybe it is his fault, he should have spent more time with her afterwards. Gone away somewhere. Losing your parent is something you need time to get over. He gave her time, he should have given her his time.

This can't go on. It's time to get her back to reality. Back to London. Away from here. But how to do that now she owns this... This pile of shit?

A swift movement near his feet. What's that noise? Peter crouches down and looks under the van. Sammy staring at him wide eyed and whimpering. "Hey, come here. You love me don't you feller?" Pete picks up Sammy, having to drag the dog to him. The dog is struggling, kicking in his arms. Peter puts him back down, and Sammy scuttles away back under the van. "So now you don't love me no more!" What the fuck is wrong today?

Sammy lying under the van, seeing the dark shape in the cottage doorway watching. A black shadow. Sammy backs off further, out of sight.

Peter tries to reach Sammy under the van. "Come here you little fucker!" Now there's a bad smell too. Drains? This place is a fucking tip.

Peter's mood darkening. The dark shape approaching behind him now. Peter gets to his feet. The dark shape against him. Taking the edge off Peter, blurring him and his reality.

Another whimper from that bloody dog. "Shut the fuck up will you?"

The dark shape surrounding him now. Changing his world. Oppressing him. Peter alone. Hurt. Anger and resentment flowing through him even more strongly than before.

Carole walks out of the cottage towards him, arms outstretched to hug him. "Come on hun, let's not fight."

Peter's face telling her to keep away. Peter staring at her with cold eyes.

Carole sees that his mood has not improved and goes back inside. Sammy races out from under the van to join her.

Peter is alone. Or is he? The black shadow clouding him and his mind. The hiss in the trees. That static. He shakes his head to clear it. He hasn't done that since he was a child. Trying to keep calm. Peter picks up another box from the rear of the van and heads into the cottage.

Sammy runs to the kitchen door as Peter carries the box through the living room to the bedroom. The dog sees the shadow at the front door. The black shape steps inside. It follows Peter into the bedroom.

The door slams. Peter spins around and freezes. It's definitely colder in here now. The smell getting worse. A knot of fear in Peter's stomach. Nothing to be afraid of. It's an empty room. Peter puts down the box he is carrying. Something is moving in his peripheral vision. A patch of semi-darkness like before. But different now. Circling around behind him. Just out of sight. Peter turns trying to catch sight of whatever the hell is there. He sees the room reflected in the filthy wardrobe mirror; something moves behind him. Dark. Getting closer.

Peter spins around again. The darkness is growing around him now. Peter backs up and bumps into the wardrobe. That smell is worse now. Overpowering. Filling his lungs. Ifan's reflection in the mirror beside his own. Peter's face shows terror, then mirrors Ifan's fury. Their problem the same. An understanding. Unspoken. Ifan is gone. Peter remains.

    The bedroom door edges open. Peter emerges from the bedroom. Sammy growls sensing something wrong with Peter.
    Carole comes out of the kitchen to see Peter standing silently watching her in the bedroom doorway. Sammy still growling. Snarling almost.
    Peter puts his head in his hands. "I'm confused. What's happening?"
    "What's wrong Pete?"
    Peter looks up, dark eyes hidden by the hair falling over his face. "What's wrong? It's you! I get you a great job, but you leave it. I give you a good home, but you buy this fucking place."
    "I need to get away sometimes."
    "Why do you need to get away from me?"
    "No Pete, I want you to come down here with me, away from work. I want us together. Like a family." Carole steps forward towards Peter.
    His eyes still saying, 'stay away'. "Children? Is that what you want?"
    Carole looks perplexed. What's going on in this guy's head today? "Maybe in a few years, but I'm too young yet…"
    "Too young? Mum had me when she was seventeen! You're almost twenty six!"
    "Those were different days Pete, I want to see the world, have a bit of freedom before I settle down."
    Peter explodes. "You are settled down! Crazy bitch!"
    "Pete, what's got into you?"
    Peter moves forward sharply pushing Carole out of his way. He grabs the champagne bottle and opens it swiftly, tearing out the cork. The contents jet all over Carole and the floor.

Carole watches him in shock, wiping the foam from her face. Sammy barking wildly.

Peter stares at her angrily. He walks to the front door, leaning on the doorframe staring out into the woods, swigging the bottle of champagne.

Carole is breathless with apprehension. What the hell has got into him?

Outside. He is standing in the shadows, drinking from the bottle. As Dai saw him before he saw the *Toili* at the lake. The same dark image. The angry, jealous, dangerous man.

Chapter 13: History Haunts Us

Smoke rises from the chimney through the pine trees and into the clear sunset sky up there above the forest. A fire in the old hearth for the first time this year. The white hire van is more prominent in the half-light than the cottage, which has learned to hide itself back in the shadows of the trees. Silence except for the hiss of the wind through the pines. And the clicking sound of a bike freewheeling down the road.

Geraint rides out of the gloom on his way back from the lake. He brings his bike to a halt. The sun is setting now; twilight. '*Rhwng dau olau*' in Welsh: between the two lights.

Geraint standing there between two thoughts. Weighing up what to do. To go home with the fish for supper or wait and see more of Carole.

A shape walking directly through the trees. *Through* the trees like it's the trees that are not there. Making for the cottage like a column of light mist. A white shape, formless as yet. Moving swiftly up behind Geraint.

As the form leaves the treeline it becomes clearer; a lad about Geraint's age. As he becomes more prominent the trees slip away. Gone in the changing of the light. Behind him are open fields, the nearby lake and the grove of trees up on the hill pale in the gloaming. The lad watching the cottage. New, on open ground, no van, no Geraint, no forestry. Firelight shining from the cottage window and smoke rising from the chimney into the cloudless June air. June 1904.

The lad, Owain, heads stealthily towards the cottage. Climbing silently over the garden wall, moving in the shadows towards the window.

The forest returns. The van too. The hiss of the wind in

the trees. Geraint has made up his mind. He stows his bike, fishing gear and rucksack in the trees. He follows Owain's path over the wall towards the cottage and to the window. Staying in the darkness, out of the fire light from the cottage window. Watching, listening.

    Carole is sitting on the new mattress laid out on the floor in front of the hearth. She stokes the fire she has made from some of the huge amount of rubbish in this room alone. The room is now warmer, and smoky which hides that smell a little. Sammy lies beside her.
    The empty champagne bottle lies on its side. Peter sits with his back to Carole, leaning against the wall, his face in shadow. He is drinking from a wine bottle. Drunk. Peter doesn't do drunk. Not since Carole's known him. And it's not friendly drunk. What's got into him? Not a word for half an hour at least.
    "I don't want you here on your own. This is the middle of nowhere..."
    "I'll be ok. I've got Sammy here."
    "Right. Proper little guard dog. And look at you! You don't belong here. You live in the flat. In London. With me!"
    "Hey, I'm not your property Pete!"
    "No?" Peter is on his feet snarling at Carole.
    Carole backs away, on her feet too in a flash. Frightened. She hasn't seen this before. "Pete, you're scaring me!"
    Peter pushes Carole backwards. She falls onto a pile of boxes. Peter stands watching her, drinking the bottle of wine.
    Carole sits there in shock. Shaking. Sammy barking.
    Peter's face hardens and makes a fist to strike Carole. "No!!!!" Carole grabs him by the wrist. "Pete! Stop it!"
    Peter stops, confused. Not himself. He pulls himself free from Carole's grip and walks way. Eyes closed, leaning on the bedroom door. Breathing heavily.

Carole gets quietly to her feet and backs away into the kitchen. Terrified.

Geraint outside, watching in disbelief. He makes to leave. He has seen enough. He shouldn't get involved. Or should he knock on the door? Why? What would he say? No, it'll make things worse. But it's Carole. Shit! Geraint stays in his hiding place watching Peter leaning against the bedroom door, shaking with rage.

Carole close to tears, backing into the unfamiliar kitchen. Trying to get away. Bumping into something; the Belfast sink. She turns around in alarm. Her face is reflected in the near darkness of the kitchen window. Is that a double reflection or is there someone watching her? Someone with long dark hair. Dressed in an old brown dress. Mari. Carole gasps. Mari watching her. Understanding. Carole is held in awe, as Mari smiles. Mari is gone. Carole remains.

Peter still seething in rage, leaning on the bedroom door.

Behind him Carole emerges from the kitchen. Calm, loving, sexy. "Come on now... let's be friends..." Carole crosses to Peter holding his shoulders, turning him around, kissing him passionately.

Geraint watches in disbelief as Carole and Peter kiss in the firelight. Increasingly passionately. Anger meeting lust. Lust winning.

Peter's hands running up Carole's spine, her hands clawing his back. Taking off Carole's top. Tongues entwining, naked skin exposed. Unhooking Carole's bra. Her hands pulling open the sailor's shirt, running all over his chest. Hands grabbling at her bum through the brown dress. Mari's face appears over Peter's shoulder. Whispering in his ear. Ifan biting Mari's neck. Opening her dress exposing her naked body beneath. Owain watching transfixed from outside the window.

Ifan pulls away. Mari smiles at him, half naked in the firelight. Ifan looks puritanically shocked by Mari's behaviour. Shock turns to fury. Mari cries out in alarm "Ifan? Na!"

Peter viciously slaps Carole, pushing her away in disgust. "Whore!"

Carole stunned. Covering herself in disbelief. Carole furiously strikes out at Peter who easily parries the blow, throwing Carole backwards, knocking her into a heap on the mattress in front of the fire.

Ifan towers over Mari in drunken fury. He draws something from his britches pocket. A poppet. A home-made toy doll. Or is it? Human hair, clothes made from a piece of rag. A piece of Owain's shirt. "Witch! What is this?"

Mari looks up at him in terror.

Ifan raises his fist bringing it down on Mari's face. She screams as he beats her. Owain watches helpless at the window. Owain moves away, disappearing into the gloom outside as Ifan's shouts and Mari's screams continue. Owain runs off across the open fields towards the lights of a nearby cottage.

Geraint still in his hiding place, unable to watch any more. The sounds of Carole crying out and Peter shouting haunting him as he runs, panic stricken to his bike, collecting his rod and bag, and rides away into the darkening forest.

The firelight plays shadows across the room. The filthy room Carole has bought from Phillips. More of the debris of Phillips' life on the fire keeping her warm at least. And the smoke hiding the smell.

Peter drunkenly asleep on the mattress.

Carole standing by the fire, wrapped in a blanket, watching him tearfully. Her nose is still bleeding. It won't stop. Her face and nose feeling like she has just been on a bad trip to the dentist.

Carole glances at the framed photograph of her with her parents. Her tears blur her vision. Reflected in the photograph in her place is Mari, crying, beaten.

Chapter 14: Hangover

The dawn sun illuminates the forestry. Lighting up the tops of the trees. Even in midsummer the sun is too puny, unable to penetrate down within the trees.

A couple of hours later the light is bringing the cottage out of shadows and back into the world. Slowly the sunlight creeps through the window across the living room.

Carole wakes with a start. Dishevelled huddled in front of the dead fire. Why didn't she sleep in the bedroom so she could get away from him? The smell in there was too much. The smell seems to be everywhere now. In here too.

Peter is still asleep on the mattress. Snoring quietly.

Carole feels around her slightly bruised face. It feels like she has tooth ache. Nagging in her head. Unshakable. Not letting her forget what happened.

He hit her. Never in a million years did she expect that. In the two years together they never really had a fight. There was the not speaking period after Dad died. Which has become the no sex period. But how has it come to this?

Carole gets up, desperately trying not to make a sound. Behind Carole, in the shadows a grey mass. Phillips shouting inaudibly at her. Angry at these people in his house.

Carole enters the squalid bathroom, wiping some of the dirt off the mirror to see her reflection. She looks bedraggled, face puffy from crying, with slight bruising and dried blood in her nose. Whispering, partly in fear, partly in anger. "Bastard!"

She begins to clean up her bloodied nose. She winces, and tears well in her eyes once more.

In the living room, Phillips stands glowering over Peter.

Phillips' electronic watch beeps. Peter snaps awake. What the fuck was that? Movement somewhere in the gloom. Peter sits up. Where is he? Oh God his head! It feels like he's been kicked. The champagne and wine bottles on the floor. Seriously? He doesn't drink like that.

Carole is creeping back into the room.

"What time is it?"

Carole jumps in alarm. Nervous. No scared is more like it. "About ten I think."

Peter staggers to his feet. "What!?! Why didn't you wake me? You know I've got to get back home this morning!"

"Sorry. You were sleeping. I didn't want to disturb you…"

"I don't believe this! The fucking day is gone!"

Carole backs away from him towards the light from the window. The bruising and redness on her skin becoming more apparent.

"What happened to your face?"

"It's… it's ok Pete."

Peter's whole world reels. "Did I hit you?"

Peter comes crashing out through the front door bedraggled and confused. He unlocks the van and throws his phone and bag inside. He looks around for a place to turn the van. No chance out here. Single track road, no verge, just trees. "Fuck!"

Carole at the door cottage door now. "You should stay until you've had a coffee and something to eat. We need to talk."

Peter turns to her aggressively. "Talk? Yeah? We haven't talked all year. Let me tell you something. I've never hit a girl. Never in my fucking life! Look what you've done to me! I help you, I give you a fucking life and you spit it all back in my face! I've got to get the hell away from here, and the hell away from you, you evil witch!"

"Pete, please... what's the matter with you?"

Peter gets into the van, fires the engine, the tyres scrapping on the earth as the van gets back onto the road. Peter powers the van angrily away, down the narrow road towards the lake. Carole feels the rage coming from the van.

She watches the van disappear out of sight.

The lake, tranquil but for the hiss of the breeze through the trees. The roar of an engine. Peter's van barrels down to the empty car park. An angry three-point turn, and it shoots off the way it came. A rush of wind through the trees and its sound is buried again.

Carole standing on the opposite side of the road from the cottage, the driver's side, waiting for Pete to return. The roar of the engine somewhere in the hiss of the wind through the trees. Getting closer. Headlights in the gloom. Approaching fast. Carole standing waiting, apprehensive but she has to talk to him.

The van approaching at speed. Showing no sign of stopping. The reflection on the windscreen hiding the driver. The driver? Pete surely? Who else would it be? Is it him? The reflections make it seem like someone else. Darker. The van roars passed Carole, almost hitting her, and speeds off down the road. Gone. Carole left alone.

The van rises angrily out of Cwm Celyn, leaving the forestry behind crunching through the broken glass on the brow of the hill. Roaring off across the mountain top road heading east. Driving blindly. The clear blue sky now reflecting on the windows. Peter at the wheel. Confusion and anger lining his face. What the hell happened with Carole last night?

The same emotions on Carole's face as she contemplates throwing herself into work. It's the best medicine. Filling your mind with busyness to block out the hard realities of life.

She can start by cleaning the kitchen. The fridge needs to be condemned. Good thing she at least brought the kettle and the microwave. The filth in here. Mould. Horrible. It's all horrible.

Everything has gone to hell in hours. What is wrong with Pete? What he did was unforgivable. Carole picks up Peter's Chelsea mug and smashes it against the wall. She bursts into tears. Letting all that emotion go. Tears that hurt. Her nose running, but not with blood this time. Sammy watching her from the doorway. Whining as Carole cries herself out as something else comes in. A brown form moves in the room.

Carole in the bathroom. As much of a mission to get clean as the kitchen. Come on girl, face it, as much as the rest of the entire cottage! Carole at the wash basin leaning forward, putting her face under the running tap. Mari reflected in the mirror now. Carole stands up straight, a new spark in her eyes. "Good riddance!"

Peter out there on the mountains. Not recognising this road. Passing an abandoned chapel on the mountainside. How did he get here? He doesn't remember this. It's not the right road. Where's the sat nav? Ok, let's find a place to stop and set it up. Getting lost is not what you need right now on these single-track winding roads with high hedges. The road twisting, rising up over another valley edge. No trees here at least. Quite a view if that is your thing. A pull-in up ahead, outside a house.

Peter pulls up in the van outside the ruin of a burnt-out cottage. Not at all unlike Carole's cottage. Same single storey style. But the roof, windows and doors gone. Two eyes and nose and hair blackened like some character from a horror movie he saw as a kid. It scares him.

Peter turns off the van and gets out. The whole place still smells like a barbecue. Woodsmoke. Pretty recent. Police cordon tape. Was this on the radio yesterday? Peter stares at the building. "What the fuck happened here?"

Ifan reflected in the van windscreen.

Chapter 15: You Are Never Alone

The kitchen is airless. Fetid. The fragments of Peter's shattered mug on the floor. Why did she do that? She wraps the pieces in a newspaper from 1973. *The Sun*. A naked girl smiling at her through faded newsprint. This probably kept that old guy happy, which is why he didn't throw it away. Sad mind you.

Trying to open the sash window. Stuck solid. It looks like it's been painted shut. Why would someone do that? The room needs air. A bit of life. OK. She tries the back door. The large iron key is jammed in the lock. Not safe to leave a key in a door when someone outside could see it, break the glass and open the door.

First job of the day. Open the back door, get the key working. Spraying lubricating oil, trying to turn the key. Snap! The lock turns. But the door won't open. Ah. A bolt. Likewise jammed. Rusted in place. This door hasn't opened in years. More lubricating oil and few more minutes tapping the bolt head with a hammer and the bolt slides back, millimetre by millimetre. The back door opens. Hinges creaking like hell. She sprays more oil onto the hinges which have not seen movement in some time, until the door opens silently. Now at least there is air moving in the kitchen.

Sammy not going outside to play around. Mind you the garden is completely overgrown on this side of the cottage. Brambles have long since taken over what may yet be a nice garden.

Sammy doesn't seem to want to go out there. Lying in the corner of the kitchen watching. Watching what though? Not her. "Go outside you silly dog!" Oh boy.

The next job. Much bigger. Cleaning out the kitchen. This is big. Best done in little chunks. Methodically. Emptying the first cupboard of maybe fifty empty whiskey bottles. Never washed out by the smell of them. Some have been there so long the design of the label has changed. Two packing boxes filled with the empty bottles, as the weight of the glass would split the rubbish bags.

Cleaning out the shelves where the bottles were stored. Black with dirt between where the bottles had been. 1950s Ideal Home white Formica beneath. Cupboard doors and drawers which seem grey are actually blue once the degreaser had done its job. There was a woman's touch here, maybe fifty or sixty years ago. It must have been nice. Once. And it will be again, OK?

Buckets of black water poured down the toilet to try to help clear the pipes. The black water foaming like beer. Most of a bottle of bleach as a chaser after the gallons of dark foamy water swallowed by the cesspit. Wherever that is.

Sammy hasn't moved all morning. Still lying in the corner of the kitchen watching something. Lunch. A can of dog food and a ready meal. She was glad she brought a few of these. The microwave will have to do as the only means of cooking for at least another day or so. God knows once it's cleaned if the electric cooker will work. Rusted to hell to be honest. Another expense. Oh crap.

By late afternoon the cupboards, Belfast sink and worktops are cleaned. Even the fridge is now pristine and buzzing annoyingly in the corner. Rubbish sacks breeding like big black rats filling the kitchen floor. Somewhere behind them lies Sammy, still skulking.

New crockery and cutlery are put in their places, and the provisions are stacked in the cupboards. A lot done for a first day.

One last drawer filled with clutter to deal with. Empty match boxes, string, bits of paper. All kinds of nonsense. It's been a long day. Enough. Carole tips the drawer into a rubbish sack. Wait a minute. What's that covered in dust? On top of the items in the bin bag is a very old wooden doll with blonde hair. Carved from a piece of wood. Dark stained in places. Dressed in a piece of rag. Looking up at her with oversized black eyes. There were kids here? This looks homemade. The first sign of love in this house. Shame to throw it away.

Carole picks the doll out of the rubbish bag. Blowing the dust off it. Hang on. This is definitely a boy doll. What a weird thing to give to kids. Even here in the country and allowing for different times. Ah well. There's a place for it on the windowsill.

The poppet watches her with those black eyes as she wraps up the last of the rubbish bags for the day.

Carole dumps the last of the day's rubbish sacks outside the garden wall. Rubbish collections are on Wednesday apparently. Mrs. Jones promised to tell the bin men that she will be there so the collections will start. The bin men will be busy with the amount of rubbish to come out of Pantyfedwen.

Wait a minute. This is new. Sammy following her around as if afraid to be left alone. The sky is reddening above the trees. The day has gone. Her first day at her cottage. A better one than yesterday. Shame to miss the sunset.

"Come on Sammy, it's high time we got some fresh air."

She pops indoors for the essentials; phone and keys. Carole locks the doors and heads off down the road towards the lake. Sammy waddling along in bored pursuit. What is the matter with this dog? Carole starts to jog down the road. "Sammy, come on!"

Sammy turns back for the cottage but stops. Seeing something. Something unexpected. Yelping, the dog turns around and runs off after Carole. He is still chasing her as she disappears around the bend.

The hiss of the wind. The sun dipping moves the cottage into half-light. There but being swallowed by the gloom. A shape approaching on the road from the village. Walking to the cottage. Stopping. Calling out without sound. Any sound would be taken away by the trees, but the figure is not there. Gone.

Open country like a century and more ago all around. The cottage, the road, the lake and the grove under a sunset sky. The shape, forming now as a man, walking towards the cottage's front door. Something large and low coming out to meet him, jumping up. A large dog. The bloodhound. Ebenezer, the dog owner, telling his dog to lay down. Entering the cottage through the open door. Silence. Then a scream.

Chapter 16: Ghosts at Sunset

Carole jogs along the road through the darkening forestry with Sammy running beside her. The sky is changing to reds and mauves above. The wind drops: the only sounds are Carole's footfalls and the panting of the dog. In a couple of minutes they are running down the slope to the clearing that visitors and fishermen use for a car park at the edge Llyn Celyn.

No one here this evening to see the golden colours of the sunset reflected on the mirrored surface of the water. No one but her and her best friend. The sun moments away from dipping over the horizon. Silence. Carole crouches down and whispers to Sammy. "Sammy. Look at that! Isn't it beautiful?"

Carole wanders over to the standing stone. Remembering how her father had told her that it had been there longer than anyone could remember. Centuries. Millennia. Who knows. How forestry workers had refused to move it, despite being threatened with being fired for leaving it there. How one of the workers brought a shotgun to work to ensure it wasn't moved.

Carole leans against a stone which may have stood there for thousands of years. Who put it there or why, lost in time. Watching the sun on the horizon that is heating the stone, now as it has done for all of that time. The stone feeling warm, alive. The trees around the lake shimmering and getting lost in the glare of the sun as if they are not there at all. Carole can see a different landscape, one that is suddenly very familiar, open land with that ancient grove of trees on the hilltop silhouetted against the light.

Sammy watching her. Confused. Something is changing in the dying light. Carole's dirty blonde hair appearing black. Her body different. Slimmer. Carole's clothes seeming to hang on her for a moment. Confusion in the dog's mind. He barks.

"Sammy! Want to play?" Carole again. Picking up a piece of

wood lying nearby. Waving it around Sammy's head. Sammy jumping up trying to grab it, barking.

Fifty yards away Geraint is fishing from amongst the trees along the lakeshore, but really reading. Revising. A major exam at school tomorrow. He is immersed in his notes on *Wuthering Heights*. That book had really surprised him. He thought it would be some romantic trash. How wrong could he be? Dark. Haunting. A doomed love story. Real emotions. People he sort of recognised. Like many of the people he meets at the shop. Set in a place not unlike the high country of Cwm Celyn. It may have been written well over a century and a half ago, but he can totally relate... The barking of a dog snaps him out of his notes.

Geraint sees Carole. How long has she been there? Alone apart from her dog by the standing stone. Lit by the setting sun. God she is sooo gorgeous! He starts to get up to go to speak to her but remembers she didn't recognise him yesterday. Best stay put? He can't exactly talk about what happened in the cottage last night. But there won't be a better time to talk to her than now. She's on her own. He can't call to see her at the cottage. That would be weird. Geraint is torn. He watches Carole play with her dog trying to make up his mind what to do.

Carole tosses the stick into the lake. Sammy fetches. Swimming out and rushing back to the shore. Sammy runs back out of the water to Carole. He drops the stick at Carole's feet. Carole crouches down to pick it up. Sammy shakes himself, spraying Carole with cold water. She screams in laughter and throws the stick as far as she can into the lake. A puckish look in her eye. Sammy races in after the stick. Carole begins to take off her clothes. Silhouetted against the setting sun her body is slimmer, her long black hair falling down her back, taking off her T shirt, shoes, jeans, bra, knickers and rushing naked into the water.

Geraint looks on in amazement fumbling for his phone as Carole dives into the water, coming up screaming because of the cold. She starts swimming out from the shore, with fast strong strokes. Sammy getting out of the water, lying on the shore with the stick. The sound of Carole splashing echoing around the lake.

Geraint watching in stunned amazement, screwing up his eyes against the glare of the setting sun. Thank you God! Watching Carole's head disappear and reappear on the lake as she swims. Her dirty blonde hair is now black on the surface of the lake.

She comes to a halt some way out from shore and treads water. Alone in the cold but soothing water. The water holding up her, hugging her with its cold hands against its cold body. She feels safe. She looks at the splendour of the sun setting over the trees. This place is her's. Her's alone. She catches her breath and drops beneath the surface of the lake. Swimming downwards seeing the bottom of the lake not too far away. Mari's long hair flowing behind her, her more girl-like figure catching the light. She turns for the surface.

Peter's unshaven face rises out of the bath. Hair covering his eyes. The bathroom filled with steam. Peter gets out of the bath and dries himself in a bath towel. The bathroom mirror is steamed up. Peter gets closer, his head leaning against his own reflection. Or is it his reflection? "You witch… I could kill you…" A dark face glowering in the steamed up bathroom mirror.

Carole swims for the shore. Geraint watches enthralled as she walks gingerly to the shore, more concerned about the sharp stones at her feet than her nakedness. Geraint zooms in as far as he can with his smartphone camera. Snap, snap, snap, his hands shaking so much, hoping to God she can't hear the sound of the camera nor his heavy breathing.

Carole suddenly realises that the is standing naked at the lake shore. She covers herself, pulling on her T shirt and jeans. She looks around - no one to be seen. Thank God! What the hell was she thinking? She's alone up here! Anyone could have been out there! Better get back to the cottage. She is jogging back up the road in moments with Sammy trotting behind.

Geraint lies back on the lake shore and closes his eyes — he simply can't believe what he has just seen. He views the photos on his phone. Blurred, shaky. Carole's black hair covering her face. Is it Carole at all? He can't recognise her. But who cares! Oh my God!!!

The sun dips over the horizon. A rush of cold wind. A chill on a June evening chasing the trees from sight. The whole area now lightly forested. The trees shrunk back to a time when they were planted in the early 1950s. The open country just visible in the twilight beyond.

Two figures dressed in dour post-war 1950's clothes walk along the lakeshore, hand in hand. Their pale complexions as one with the rapidly dimming light. Mr. Phillips it seems has always been colourless, even as a young man; a grey suit like a character from a cheap American film, slicked down hair. His wife, dressed in a faded dress, her face showing signs of recent tears, but she is smiling watching the brilliant colours of the sunset sky.

Mrs Phillips leans on the standing stone at the shore with her back to Mr Phillips. He is suddenly larger now, well built, filling out Phillip's slim suit. He stealthily crouches to pick up a rock, sneaking up on Mrs Phillips. He raises the rock high above his head.

Mrs Phillips leaning on the standing stone starting to sing a tune. Whack!!! The wistful smile on her face turning to surprise as blood starts to flow from her nose. Tears in her eyes again. She falls into the shallow water of the lake. Young Mr. Phillips drops the bloodied rock with a thump with a look of alarm on his face. Did he just do that? Blood floats around Mrs. Phillip's head in the water.

   Geraint sits up with a start at the sound of the splash. What the hell was that? There are ripples in the water from a disturbance by the standing stone. It's a bit misty there. What the hell?
   Geraint slightly spooked, picks up his fishing tackle and books. He carries his bike back to the car park. Nothing to be seen anywhere, except for that weird mist offshore near the standing stone. What is that? Geraint rides off hoping Carole will not be around when he rides passed the cottage. God that would be embarrassing.

   The mist near the standing stone: Mr. Phillips dragging his wife's body into the lake in the fading light. He, the mist and the ripples disappear as the cold wind blows across the surface of the lake.

Chapter 17: Missed Calls

The sun has gone. The forest has darkened to a sort of grey invisibly in front of her eyes. It's like the forest, the cottage and Carole are being covered by a black cloth. Holes in the weave of the cloth show the stars above. Thousands upon thousands of them becoming visible in the small piece of sky that the trees allow her to see. This darkness allowing her to see the starlight above. You never see the night sky in London's orange glow.

Carole didn't see this amazing star scape last night. Last night is strangely like another lifetime now. What's changed? The feeling inside her. She is somehow more at home here. Like it has always been her home.

But something is making her feel uncomfortable. Something; someone in the shadows of the cottage behind her. Unnerving yet welcoming. It's putting Carole both at ease and on edge.

The darkness of the forest, the oppressive silence. The lack of sensory stimulation driving Carole into her own mind. Her own thoughts. Her own insecurities. What was she doing swimming naked up at the lake? Anyone could have seen her! Luckily there was no one there, right? Wait! Something just moved in the gloom on the road coming back from the lake. No, now she's getting paranoid. It's her eyes playing tricks on her. There's no one there. For goodness sake!

Carole has learned from living in London that paranoia is useful. It keeps you on your toes. Riding the tube trains. Walking home after dark. You get a sixth sense if someone is watching you. Meaning you harm, or maybe something else. A vital animal instinct in one of the world's largest cities. Men are still animals. OK, people are still animals. She noticed Peter by the way he watched her when she wasn't looking. It started off being uncomfortable: then, something else.

Still, what possessed her earlier on at the lake? In one day here, she's let down her guard too far. She's relaxed. But isn't that the point of being here? Christ, she'll be having a holiday romance soon! She's almost forgotten about the outside world. About the fight with Peter. About what maybe the end of the first proper relationship of her life.

Carole looks at her phone. It has a signal. No missed calls. So, nothing from Peter. That's ominous. It's gone ten pm, he should have been home late afternoon. Why hasn't he called to tell her that he's home? To ask if she is OK? To apologise! What could he say to apologise for what he did? Why is she thinking about phoning him?

Why? Because life will go on when she gets back to London. When he comes to fetch her. When he takes her back to their flat. When she goes to work alone, for someone else. Not going to work with Pete anymore. Maybe moving out of the flat. Not living with Pete anymore. Is that what's happening?

Carole paces nervously outside the cottage. She selects Contacts on the phone. She taps the contact for 'Flat'. Carole takes a deep breath, not even sure what to say. The phone rings six times, the pause between each ring getting longer, and then the answer phone cuts in.

Pete's voice on the answerphone. Clear, strong, friendly. The Pete she thought she knew. "Hi, Peter and Carole aren't in, so please leave a message after the tone."

Carole stumbles over the words. She should have practiced these lines and not just thought about what to say if Pete had picked up. "Hi Pete... I thought you'd be home by now..." God, what to say next?

Carole's voice is coming over the answerphone speaker. Fighting against the loud techno filling the room. Peter sitting nursing a glass of whiskey in one hand ignoring the message. He is engrossed in an article on his iPad on his lap.

Carole's voice continues as the techno track reaches the drop. "It's almost ten o'clock... I'll try to call you on your mobile... 'Bye." The message ends.

Peter takes another sip of whiskey. The article he is reading on the BBC News website, the Wales section is entitled, 'Welsh Holiday Home Arson Attacks Intensify.' Peter scrolls on, engrossed. His phone is switched off on the table.

"Hello. This is Peter. Please leave a message. Thanks." Carole waits a moment, the old Pete flashing in front of her eyes. She blanks. Can't think of anything to say. "Hi Pete. Call me." She hangs up. The red mist descends as she walks back into the cottage, slamming the door.

Geraint grabs his chance. He thought she'd be out there all night! He rides by quietly, no lights in the gloom, heading quickly passed the cottage and on up the road towards the village. Oh God, he still can't believe what he saw tonight. He's still shaking.

Carole puts a match to rubbish in the fireplace, watching as the flames start grow. Burning the rubbish from the previous owner of the house. Making the place her own. Making a warm welcome. She needs the warmth, still feeling the lake's cold embrace. She sits in front of the fire alone. Sammy wanders over and lies down beside her. She looks at the phone. Still a signal, but still no call from Pete.

Peter is asleep on the couch, the empty whiskey bottle on the table. The lights still on. Behind him the never full bookcase has been emptied of books. There are gaps where there were ornaments and photographs on shelves. The place already feels unlived in. Visible signs that Carole has left. Peter doesn't do possessions. Everything he needs is on his phone or computer. Music, photos, videos. Why have them here when you can take them with you everywhere you go?

Peter's eyes darting around under closed eyelids as he dreams. Dark hair falling over his face.

Everything moving. Rising and falling. Sound crashing all around him. An earthquake? No, a ship. A ship being slammed by huge waves. Water rushing across the deck. He loses his footing, his legs being dragged away by the receding wave. The slam on the back of his head. Seeing stars. Tasting salt water as it rushes over him. He can't breathe. The water filling his nose and mouth. Gasping. Reaching for anything. Someone calling him as the water pulls him across the deck. "Ifan!!!"

Carole asleep on the mattress in the fire light. Sammy watching, growling. On guard. The firelight darting light and shadow across the room. Shadows. One of the shadows isn't a shadow.

Mari sits in the firelight. She is making the poppet - wrapping Owain's hair around the carved wooden body. She smiles as she knots the hair. She whispers like a sigh "Fy machgen i..." Repeating over and over as she makes the knot time after time in a loop, never completing the task. Making, making, making. Making him her boy.

There is another sound. Beyond Mari in the bedroom...

The bedroom door swings slowly open. The sound gets louder: the firelight illuminates the rope is hanging from the rafter. The noose.

Ifan watches as the tearful, confused Young Mr. Phillips puts his head in the noose for the first time. He looks at the wedding photograph of himself and Mrs. Phillips beside the empty bed. He turns to Ifan and screams. "Pam y diawl? Why?"

Ifan glowers.

Young Mr. Phillips drops. He gasps. Hanging helplessly in mid-air. Young Mr. Phillips swings, gasping, coughing legs kicking at the air. Hanging there. Ifan looking deeply into his eyes. Young Mr. Phillips struggling in the noose, forcing his head backwards. He drops to the ground with a bang.

Carole wakes with a start. Nothing there but shadows in the firelight. Sammy cowering beside her. Something in the fire light, smoking slightly. Carole reaches out and picks up the poppet from the hearth. How did that get there? She holds its warm body in her hands, staring into its black eyes.

Chapter 18: Signs and Shadows

The summer sunshine breaks through the heavy foliage of the pine trees. Fighting its way through every branch and every pine needle to the next. It has built up enough strength by eight o'clock in the morning to light up the front of the cottage.

Light pours through the living room window, falling on Carole's face as she sleeps in front of the long dead fire. Carole wakes up with a start. Sammy and the poppet staring at her in the bright sunshine. She yawns and looks at the poppet. Those black eyes stare back at her. She smiles, half remembering a dream. What was it?

Peter wakes on the sofa. Dead eyed, unshaven, unkempt. He sits up and then feels the pain in his head and his guts simultaneously. The empty whiskey bottle on the table. A bottle in one night? He never did that even when he was a student! The iPad beside it. The Welsh arsonists. Yeah. Memories are forming through the throb of the hangover.

Peter staggers to his feet and switches on his phone. He carries it to the kitchen and puts on the kettle. He pours a load of instant coffee into a mug straight from the jar. Milk on top. The brown mess turns his stomach.

His mobile phone rings. Answerphone. Who the fuck is that? Peter answers the call. He catches sight of himself reflected in the aluminium splashboard. Jesus! He looks awful. Truly awful.

The voice on the handset tells him he has one message. A familiar voice. Not one he wants to hear right now. Bitch. "Hi Pete. Call me." Peter deletes the message.

He puts down the phone and heads off to the toilet to be sick.

Carole lying on the mattress, studying the poppet. Processing it in her mind. It's becoming familiar now. The body. The appendage. That's rude. No, important. No, very important. This feels like a lost memory. But is it her's? It's becoming her's. It comes with the cottage maybe? Maybe. She places the poppet on the table beside the photo of her with her family.

Carole fills the kettle and puts a teabag in the mug. Green tea. Tea to cleanse the system. Clear out the old Carole and the toxins of London.

Washing her hair in the sink, the cold water pouring over her like it did in the lake. The water taking her head in its cold grasp.

Sammy is waiting for her in the kitchen. By the back door. Nervous. Carole fills his bowl with water and looks in the store cupboard. Dog food... The last can. Crap. Already? Sammy wolfs down the dog food. She needs to get some more. She clears the kitchen worktops and heads off to the living room.

Carole rifles through her suitcase in the living room. The T-shirts, jeans and work trousers she's packed for working on the cottage. Carole pulls out a summer dress from beneath them. Light yellow cotton. Button up front. She holds it up to the light which streams through it. She pulls off her night shirt. The warmth of the sun on her skin feels good. Invigorating. She reaches for the clean underwear in the suitcase, changes her mind, and puts on the dress. She buttons up the front of the dress, pulling it tightly around herself.

Sammy watches her from the kitchen door, not entering the room. Carole picks up a shopping bag, tosses her purse and her phone into it and picks up her keys. She heads for the door.

Sammy is still watching her from the kitchen. Confused.

"Sammy! Come on Sammy! Dere..." Where did that come from? The Welsh for 'Come'. Her Dad had taught her that. Amongst only a handful of words she remembers from those years when she would come here on holiday. "Dere Sammy!"

The dog trots over to join her. She opens the door and the sunshine streams in. She is silhouetted against the light like an angel. Long dark hair, slim body beneath the summer dress which hangs loosely on her. Sammy watches her, confused. The leash snaps taught on his collar.

The wind blows the confusion away. It ruffles Carole's blonde hair. Carole sets the pace, exuberantly playing with Sammy as they walk down the road through the morning's golden sunshine. Sunshine filtered into beams of light cutting through the pervasive darkness of the forest. Not a sound except her footsteps and Sammy's panting.

Except for the hiss of the wind. That white noise. All spectrums of sound filtered by the pine trees. Carole has already got used to it; already acclimatising to the forest. This constant whisper, this hiss, has replaced that constant rumble of London which was always there so you never heard it.

Carole and Sammy turn a sharp bend in the road. The hiss rises in pitch. The wind blowing directly down the short straight in the winding forest road. A sudden chill in the air. The sense of something wrong up ahead to the left. Something not as regimented as the rest of this uniform section of the plantation. One tree missing. No that's not right. One tree: broken. The upper section above say four feet up from the ground has gone. Cut clean across, neatly. But otherwise things are not neat. The undergrowth cleaved and parted by some sort of scar on the land. That scar stretching out onto the tarmac towards Carole. A scrape a good inch deep in the road in places.

Carole stops. The chill is far more pronounced here. Something is catching the light at the foot of the broken tree. Glass reflecting the sunlight back through the undergrowth. Carole goes to take a look, walking along the length of the cleaved earth to avoid the undergrowth scratching at her legs.

The tree is scarred. Torn. Black rotted flowers in decomposing plastic are tied to the tree. A note with the flowers, black ink having run blue and red, now undecipherable. On the ground an overturned, water filled jam jar. A little burnt-out candle inside. The candle holder rusted, turning the water brown. A shrine to someone. The chill wind whistles for a moment.

By the look of the tree and the damage to the road, a car crashed here. Someone drove off the road and lost their life. The damage to the tree beneath where it's been cut is substantial. The tree is gouged and scarred. The impact must have cleaved the tree above or made it unsafe. The good part has been harvested. These trees are money. Thousands of trees. Millions of pounds. A different kind of industry scarring the countryside in this part of Wales.

Carole stands there at the shrine in the forest with the wind flapping her dress. The scrape in the road, the cleaved earth, the broken tree tells a tale of life and death. Physical signs of a raw loss from who knows how long ago. Probably not too long ago. These shrines are a pretty new thing in Britain at least. And the trees have only been here a lifetime.

The cool breeze cuts through Carole' dress. Carole pulls at Sammy and heads down the road towards the village.

Another five minutes down the road and Carole is leading Sammy into Capel Celyn. Carole's yellow dress catching the sun as she walks down the road, Sammy darting around on his leash.

Carole pulling Sammy to heel as he smells at walls, doorways and gateposts as she walks along the pavement. Sammy pulling hard on the leash. Carole looks up and realises she is standing where her father died. She hadn't even thought of this when she came down a couple of months ago to view the cottage. Now it comes back to her. Her helpless panic. Everything that she had been taught on those first aid courses at work remaining locked in the depth of her head, completely inaccessible. Completely unable to remember what to do as Dad lay there, life ebbing away. People helping. Her helpless. A waste of space. In the way. A sideshow. Tears well in Carole's eyes. "Oh Dad... I miss you. I've done what you asked. I'm going to be here often. I promise. I'll be here to remember you, Dad." Almost seeing her father's face looking back at her lifeless from the pavement.

Carole composes herself and leads Sammy across the road to the shop.

A cloud passes over the sun. Further up the street falls into shadow. People half visible. Ifan talking to another man with a huge hunting dog. A blood hound. The man, Ebenezer, exchanging the dog's leash for money from Ifan.

Ifan setting off up the street with the dog, passing where Carole's Father died. Heading off out of the village, back the way Carole has come. Man and dog on a mission pacing up the road. The padding of feet and clacking of walking stick on a road. The cloud clears the sun, sunlight lights and warms the street. The shadows are gone. An empty street in an empty village. No more ghosts.

Carole loads half a dozen cans of dog food into the plastic shopping basket. Bread and a few other items fill the basket in no time. The shop is not so big, but very well stocked. And very quiet. Sammy sniffing around the shop. There seems to be nobody home. Sammy's head snaps around. Mrs Jones appears from the rear of the shop. Sammy barks.

Carole looks around the shelves, and smiles. "Shwtmae Mrs Jones? How are you?"

Mrs Jones' smile is as broad as the shop counter as she

sweeps around to pet Sammy. "Carole bach! So, you've moved in to Pantyfedwen? Wonderful! You're looking very well."

"Diolch yn fawr. Thank you. So are you. I arrived on Saturday."

Mrs. Jones plays with Sammy. "Oh wonderful! And your Welsh is coming back? That's good. So important. Your dad would be proud."

Carole smiles, the tears from a few moments ago ready to return. "I hope so."

"Is your fancy man up there helping you with the place then?"

Someone watches Carole from the doorway between the shop and the main house. Watching the sunlight pass through Carole's dress as she stands in front of the window. How her figure fills the dress. Tight against her. Every curve. Geraint watches mesmerised. Imagining her last night at the lake... Now is a great time to talk to her. But Mam is here...

Carole shrugs her shoulders. "He's gone back to London for the week."

Mrs Jones stands up amazed. "What? And he's left you to fix up Pantyfedwen on your own? That's terrible! It's in an awful state, Carole bach! Too much for you on your own!"

Carole sighs. "Oh, I can manage."

Sammy barks at Geraint trotting behind the counter to greet him. Carole calls after the dog. "Sammy!!! Dere!"

"Geraint! Come out here. Be polite. You remember Carole?"

Geraint emerges from the back of the shop, shooing Sammy as he walks forward, careful to stay behind the counter.

Geraint smiles nervously, trying not to stare at Carole. "Yes. Of course I do. Shwtmae. I saw you've moved into Pantyfedwen."

Realisation on Carole's face. The cyclist she passed in the van on the way to the cottage. What a transformation from the boy who helped her and her parents back at Christmas time.

Taller. And bigger. Oh God... The blondish hair. Dark eyes. Just like the poppet. "You passed by on the bike on Saturday? You should have stopped to say hello. I didn't recognise you Geraint. Nice haircut by the way!"

Geraint blushes. Oh God, what to say to her. "Er, thanks... I could see you were busy…"

Mrs Jones returns to fussing over Sammy who has trotted back to her from behind the shop counter. "He's doing his exams. Almost done. Wants to go to university. He'll have time on his hands soon. It'll do him good to give you a hand with anything you need up in the cottage some afternoons Carole. It'll keep him out of mischief."

A mixture of panic and excitement in Geraint's eyes. Carole watching him. Smiling, no almost staring. Yes staring. What the...

Carole flashes a smile and thank you to Mrs. Jones. "Oh that would be really good. Thanks a lot." The stare back to Geraint who raises his eyes quickly to meet hers. "Is that OK with you Geraint?"

He has no choice. He doesn't want one. "Yes… er… no problem."

Mrs Jones picks up Carole's basket and carries it to the till. She starts scanning the groceries. "This weighs a ton, Carole bach. Geraint can bring these things up to you later on if you like. And tell him if you need him around to help with anything. He needs to keep busy, a boy of his age."

Geraint blushing again, as Carole stares and smiles. Those eyes. Watching him, running over him now. Oh God...

Carole smiles at Geraint. "Thank you. It'll be nice to have a visitor up there." Especially one this good looking. Damn. "What do I owe you for this lot Mrs Jones?"

"Twenty pounds, eighty two please."

Carole digs in her bag for her purse. The money changes hands. She pops a can of dog food into her bag. "I better take this, or my little friend here will be eating me for lunch. Thank you both. I'll see you later Geraint. Hwyl. 'Bye." She gives Geraint a sly smile, before leading Sammy away. Geraint looks away at his mother who is boxing up Carole's provisions. The doorbell chimes and she has gone.

Mrs. Jones looks at Geraint with concern. "On her own up there in Pantyfedwen. What have I done? Poor dab, Geraint. Poor dab... Keep an eye on her, OK?"

Chapter 19: Back to the Grindstone

Underground. A hundred feet down the escalators, lifts and walkways into the tube tunnels under London. Hurtling and rattling his way across from the west to the east end of the city. Crossing the Victorian centre of Empire into the docklands; transformed over a few short years from mud and decay into glass and steel by billions of pounds of investment. A new city for this new millennium. New jobs. New technology. New stress. New problems. Here every second counts. And he's over an hour late already.

Peter standing crushed in with dozens of others in the packed tube train carriage. Everybody jammed up against each other. Avoiding eye contact. Faces in their phone screens or looking at the floor or ceiling of the train compartment. Everyone too close for comfort. A sheen of mutual sweat on everyone in the airless box on wheels.

The train hums and shudders to a halt at the next stop. People fighting to get out of the carriage. An Asian couple pushing passed him, chattering away. A West London West Indian kid in his late teens, dressed like American street kid pushing up against Peter. His heavy coat in mid-summer taking up more space than needed. Space is not at a premium in here. Nor is patience.

Peter feeling the down jacket enfold him. The buzzing of the loud music in the kid's headphones as annoying as a fly by Peter's ear.

Peter closes his eyes. Stifling heat. Overpowering. A crowded market. The chatter of foreign tongues. Only black faces around him. Pushing him as they jostle in the marketplace. A young black man too close for comfort. Much too close. He readies his stick.

Screech! The tube car slams on its brakes, throwing

passengers against each other. The West Indian lad pushing
Peter hard against the support rail. Peter knocks his head. He
turns around to face the lad. Maybe seventeen. Padded out in
the sweltering car like an eskimo. Chicago Bulls baseball cap
hiding his eyes and face. Oversized headphones drowning out
the reality all around him. Peter stares down at him.

He looks up, sees Peter staring. His forehead deep
furrowed. Years of practice. "What blood?"

"What did you call me?"

The lad pulls aside his headphone. "Huh?"

Peter engages his stare. Hair falling over his eyes. Dark
eyes. Angry eyes. Bloodshot. Hating. Whiskey on his breath.

The kid staring back. The man, who seems much bigger now,
holding the stare. Looking wilder and more dangerous by the
second. The train slides into the next station. The kid breaks
off the stare, slightly alarmed, pushing his way off the
train.

He keeps his eyes locked on the lad as he goes. Following
him onto the platform. The lad strutting off up the platform.

He reaches out, pulling off the lad's hat, wrenching off
the Bluetooth headphones and tossing them under the train. The
lad turning around in fury to see the wild eyed man baring
down on him pushing him hard against the train. Murder in the
eyes behind that hair.

The lad runs. He follows, pushing and shoving along the
platform. The Platform Guard shouting at them as he chases the
lad through the commuters on the overcrowded platform.

The lad heading to the Exit. Up the stairs, the lad slowed
by his belt-less black jeans falling down. He is now limping
badly in pursuit but keeping up, dragging at the collar of the
lad's oversized parka. The lad struggling free of the coat.
The lad getting up the slippery steps to the city above. The
coat getting trampled on the stairs.

The lad running along the wrong side of the barrier on the

walkway, pushing through oncoming commuters. He follows the best he can with his limp, losing the lad now.

The lad running up the escalators. He stands at the bottom. Breathless. Snarling. People watching him. Black faces. White faces now too. The market disappearing. The tube station smell returning.

The rush of wind from the tube. Peter coming to himself. Where the hell is he? Tottenham Court Road? What? Not at his stop! Peter joins the tide of people flowing down to the trains below. The wind rushing passed Peter as he walks. Clearing his head. The limp less prominent. What was he doing? What's going on? He's already late for work. The next train east pulling onto the platform as he arrives. Straight onto train before the Platform Guard spots him.

Daylight. Canary Wharf with its massive glass and steel buildings shining light into Peter's eyes. Across the square to the huge monolith he calls work. Peter straightens up and walks purposefully through the doors.

Out of the lift and into Reception. Office Workers milling around as Peter limps towards his office. TP at the door. Looking at his watch. Fuck.

"Peter, just coming in?"

"Good morning TP. I'm a bit off colour today."

"Big week Peter. Need to see how you're getting on with that presentation at the meeting at eleven."

"Absolutely." Peter enters his office, checking his watch. 10:20. Fuck. Fuck. Fuck. Booting up his computer. Logging in. Forgetting the log in. He changed it last week. What is it? Bloody IT department. Christ, his head. A knock on the door. Now what?

Frances steps into his office. Her afro glistening around her face. Beaming. "Morning. How did it go down in Wales with

Carole?"

Peter still trying to log into the computer. "Meaning?"

Frances bristling slightly. "Meaning, good weekend Peter?"

Peter doesn't respond, finally getting the log in right. He looks up. Frances studying him. "Just a heads up. TP has been kicking off this morning already. He's as nervous as a cat with the Chinese visit this week. You remember we have a meeting at eleven, right?"

Peter puts his head in his hands. Sensing Frances moving closer. Smelling the whiskey maybe.

Smelling something, and she thinks it's unpleasant. She recoils. "Something wrong Pete?"

"Get me a black coffee Frances."

Frances expecting a joke or a smile. None. "Get your own! I'm not your negro!" Frances leaves the office.

Peter opens his presentation on the computer. He stares at the screen but can't engage. The emails. Too many. Peter takes a deep breath and wishes he hadn't. The knot in his stomach tightening.

Peter enters the Men's Toilets and catches sight of himself in the mirror. Pale, sweaty, sunken eyes. He splashes water on his face. Water gets in his eyes. He doesn't really recognise his own reflection at all now. Unshaven. Long dark hair. That's wrong. The world swimming, his guts swirling. Peter rushes into a cubicle and throws up. And again. And again. Gagging and struggling for breath. Dropping to his knees. Coughing and recovering. Breathless, but ok. He wipes his face and flushes the toilet.

Standing to wash his face at the basins. Bending over is too risky. Peter looks at his reflection. Pale and ill. Even worse in the sickly light. Peter adjusts himself, straightens his tie and jacket. "There you are TP you wanker, one servile fucker reporting for duty, sir." Peter heads back to his office. The door slams.

There is a flush. The other cubicle door opens. TP emerges, his face like thunder.

Peter is back at his desk, staring blankly at the computer screen. He snaps out of his reverie as Frances taps on the door and enters.

Frances gets that smell of something again. Unpleasant. Decay? "The meeting is in five minutes. How's that presentation coming on? Can I see it?"

"It's not ready Frances, it'll be ready by the end of the day."

"You what? What's the problem? We talked it through on Friday, remember?"

"I'll get it to you in good time."

"For fuck's sake Pete! A Good Time is now! The meeting starts in five minutes!"

Peter starts to sweat. "I'm not going." Peter back in the heat, seeing an African trader. Trying to focus on Frances. It's not working. The trader clearer in his head.

"Pete, this isn't like you. You know how important this week is for us. Bring what you have. Don't forget who is the Captain on this ship!" Frances slams the door on her way out.

Who the hell does this woman think she's talking to? Who does she think she is? Peter jumps to his feet but has to steady himself. He crosses to the window and leans against the glass, sweating profusely.

A seagull whirling around outside the window. It screams, drawing Peter's attention. The sun burning away everything outside. The reflections on the glass, on the sea. A flock of seagulls now swooping around the ship and the mast above his head. The swell rising and falling. He's having to hold onto the rail to steady himself. Leaning on his stick. The crew buzzing around. The smell of the sea. Overpowering.

The meeting convening. No one sees Peter limping out of the office and getting into the lift.

Leaving the building. Disorientated by the hubbub around and the bright sunshine. Limping away from the building and out of the direct sunlight which is killing his eyes. The seagulls swooping overhead between the mast-like buildings. Peter limping into the shadows to get out of the sun. Along walkways finding railings and pillars to hold himself steady on the rolling deck. The river ahead. Limping onwards towards the water.

Up ahead tables being put out. An open door to darkness within. Limping into the bar. Inside. Silence. Darkness. Whiskey. Taking a seat at the bar. His mobile phone rings. 'Office'. He turns it off.

Chapter 20: Detours

Carole leaves the empty village and returns into the forestry which surrounds it. Returning to the constant hiss of the pines, and the chill air. Padding along the road with Sammy in tow. Walking beside the regimented pines. Uniform. Same height. Same girth. Same space between them. Orderly rows and columns. Like an army imposing order on these wild mountains unlike any human army has ever been able to do. Stretching forever into the gloom.

Except. A gap in the pines. A gap, say two trees width wide. She hadn't noticed it on the way to the village. It heads off into the gloom of the forest and a brightness beyond. An old track? Pretty overgrown at the roadside but seeming to be clearer deeper in the forest. It's not a forestry service road. Not wide enough surely? An old farm track? It hasn't been used since God knows when.

Carole stops and looks down the track. Clear sunlight at the end of the tunnel of gloom. What's down there? What *is* down there? Familiar. Important. But she has never seen this before. What is this place? She picks up Sammy in her arms. "Come on Sammy, let's see where it goes." She carefully picks a route around the worst of the undergrowth. Around five yards in, the path is walkable. She puts down Sammy and leads him down the track.

As Carole walks along the last twenty yards or so of the forest track, a tumble down cottage comes into view. Carole finds herself in another world hidden within the forest.

A single storey cottage much like hers. Smaller, much smaller in fact. The remains of a door and a window. The roof has fallen in. The timbers rotten. The slates now light grey and shattered. Creeper and brambles over the walls. What looked like a lawn from a distance back is actually a small pond, covered in algae. Totally still.

Beyond the cottage, up the hill are the trees she saw from the lake. A grove of old trees, oak maybe, covering the hill and stretching up to the skyline. Old. Very old. A snapshot of how Cwm Celyn looked before the new trees which otherwise surround her. This place is idyllic! And also familiar. Why? Almost Deja vu. But no, she could never have been here before.

Carole remembering her Dad and Mrs. Jones chatting in the shop when she was a girl. Talking about the farms swallowed up by the forests. About their school friends and their families who lived on these farms. How the farmers sold up, and either moved into Capel Celyn village or away to South Wales to make a new life. Like the Highland Clearances in Scotland, but for trees, not sheep. Her father hated these trees.

Now for the first time in her life she could physically see why. A way of life and a community gone. Her father had seen this land change irreversibly, though still there beneath his feet. And now here beneath his daughter's feet. An entire history hidden in the trees.

Carole lets Sammy off his leash, the little dog rooting around the tumble down cottage. Carole walks over to the remains of the cottage, looking through gaps which were once windows and doors. The roof has fallen inside, but the hearth, the centre of the home still visible. Nothing else left behind. Probably the occupants didn't have much to take away to wherever they went. A little wooden sign nailed to the door. Faded. Hard to read. *Nant y Cadno*. Carole wonders what that means. 'Nant' means 'stream'. 'Y' means 'The'. 'Cadno'? No idea.

Carole looks upwards at the grove of trees. The sound of birds up there, totally missing down here in the pine forest. Birds flying overhead. The whole grove sunlit and warm. Warmth reaching down here by this old forgotten cottage too. The sun beating down in fact. Carole feeling the warmth on her skin. She finds a spot in the long grass and lies down on her back.

The long grass enfolding her. The smell of the pollen and summer flowers. The sound of the birds up above. The bright cloudless sky. And that sun, warming her. She needs to be warm. She's felt so cold lately. Carole undoes the front of her dress and lets the sun warm her naked body.

Peter is at the bar. Even though his eyes have grown accustomed to the gloom, the room is full of shadows. He is the only person here apart from the staff. Or is he? The shadows moving on the periphery of his vision. Disconcerting for a sailor in a strange bar. Watching him. Awaiting a conversation or confrontation with one of their own.

It puts him on edge. The whiskeys aren't lasting too long, so he's taken to doubles to extend the warm feeling they give him. No tobacco smoke in the air. Strange for a pub. Where are his crew? Nowhere to be seen. Miserable bastards to a man.

The cottage beneath the grove. *Nant y Cadno*. Not as it is now. A home. Bathed in the warm sunshine of a summer over a century ago. A woman hanging washing near the pond where Carole would lie asleep. Her feet trampling the grass near Carole's head, causing her to stir in her sleep.

A loud tap. Tap. Tap. A young man chopping wood in the heat of the midday sun. Once his mother has gone inside, he takes off his shirt. Feeling the sun on his back. Owain, dragging more deadfall from the copse nearby. Chopping firewood ready for the long cold winter ahead. Mari watching him from nearby within the grove. Moving down to be closer. Watching his body move and the suntan his skin. Watching. Waiting. Wanting.

Owain chopping through the last log which falls in two onto the ground. He swipes the splintered offcuts away. A piece holds fast, driving the wooden splinter deep into his hand. Owain winces. He pulls at this splinter embedded in the palm of his hand. It doesn't come free. He winces. Blood now.

A hand taking his hand. Mari. Looking deep into his eyes. Holding his hand. Drawing out the piece of bloody wood. She raises Owain's hand to her mouth and kisses it. Looking into Owain's eyes. Lustful. The boy smiling. She runs her hand through his blonde hair. A call from the house. Owain's head turning sharply, leaving a clump of hair in her hand. Mari seeing Owain's mother coming out of the cottage. Mari disappears into the shadows of the trees.

Owain pulls on his shirt, picks up the wood he has chopped and heads for the house. Mari watches him walk away. Holding his hair and the blood-soaked piece of wood in her hand. Smiling mischievously.

Carole tossing in her sleep by the ruined cottage. Sammy asleep by her long dark hair spread out on the ground.

The silence of the bar broken. Half a dozen people entering the bar, talking and laughing. Peter pays no attention, staring into his whiskey glass. A loud man ordering drinks further up the bar.

Someone beside Peter. He knows her scent before he turns his head. Those hazel eyes bright above her thrilling smile. Long black hair pulled back. Patricia. Fuck.

"I was just thinking about you."

"Oh, that's nice, considering you didn't come over to talk to me at the Christmas do." She pouts playfully.

"How are you?"

"Still a single girl. He was fun for a while, but hey. Haven't met anyone to replace you on a full-time basis yet... And you? How's that little office junior? Carole. The one you had in our bed? Is she lurking around here somewhere too?"

Ouch. Same old Patricia. "No. Gone to Wales for a while."

"What, and left you all on your own? Not nice. Little bird tells me that she left your firm too. You can't be seeing much of each other these days. Must be lonely for you."

Whatever the downside of her high maintenance personality, Peter missed her directness. The sexy bitch. "Do you want a drink, Pat?"

Patricia picks up Peter's glass and takes a sip. "I'll have a whiskey too." Running her finger up and down the glass, her smile widening. "I wonder what she could be up to down there on her own?... Dear me, the mind boggles..."

Carole is still asleep outside Nant y Cadno cottage. Her eyeballs flicking around wildly, caught up in the dream. Or is it a memory? The poppet in her hands, being shaped as it's whittled. The wood still dark with Owain's blood. The head. Arms. Body. Legs. The appendage, so big, being shaped by the knife in her hands. Mari's hands. Making the eyes with an Indian ink pen in the fire light at Pantyfedwen. Black eyes.

That boy's eyes concentrating hard here at Nant y Cadno. Owain whittling. Shaping a love spoon from a piece of birch wood. *Y Fedwen* in Welsh. Fitting for the girl from Pantyfedwen. Owain absorbed in his work. His mother shouting at him from the cottage to get back to chopping logs. Owain ignoring her. Whittling some more. An intricate pattern of leaves and branches revealed from beneath the wood shavings. A heart. The spoon. For Mari.

She is standing watching him from the grove above. Almost as one with the trees. Her thin frame and dark hair hiding her from view. Owain looks up and sees her immediately. He climbs the hill and joins her in the trees, handing her the love spoon. Mari smiles, kissing him passionately, running her hands over his body. Owain's mother calling him from the cottage below. Mari grabbing him by the hair when he tries to return to her.

Mari leads Owain further up the hill and deeper into the Grove. The hill getting steeper, the trees thicker. The smell

of the earth stronger as they climb. Panting as their feet
slip on the wet ground as they scramble upwards hand in hand.
The sun bathing them in a golden light as they climb higher,
birds singing in tops of the trees way above their heads.

Beneath them, Cwm Celyn in its summer glory. To the east,
Llyn Celyn lake glistening with its distinctive standing
stone. Capel Celyn to the west. Nant y Cadno and Pantyfedwen
to the south. Unnoticeable from this height, a figure walking
along the road between the two cottages.

Mari and Owain reach the crest of the hill and enter the
fabulous grove of ancient oaks. Wood pigeons coo softly. Mari
looks around her in wonder spinning around breathlessly, giddy
with excitement. Owain catches her and lays her on the ground.
He takes off his shirt and his breeches. Mari smiles up at
him, undoing her dress.

Ifan rushes up the track to Nant y Cadno cottage, led by
the blood hound on its leash. Ifan drags the animal to the
cottage door. He slams his walking stick into the door,
hammering away. Screaming, "Mari!! Mari!!" The door it rocks
on his hinges.

"Mari... Mari..." Owain gasping and calling out her name
as she smiles up at him. Mari rocking back and fore as Owain
pounds her wildly. Mari cries out in lust.

Patricia's cries out as she rides Peter. He grabs her and
rolls her onto her back. Wild frantic sex. Peter bites her
neck and licks Patricia's face.

Carole wakes with a start. Sammy licking her face. She is
caught for a moment between dream and reality. Aroused.
Confused. "Sammy!.... Stop it... What time is it?" She fetches
her phone from her bag. "Jeez. You must be hungry." She puts

Sammy on his leash and gets up, realising that her dress is open. As she buttons her dress, she looks up the grove on the hill above. Half remembering her dream.

    Sammy barks and starts to lead her back up the track into the trees. "OK, I'm coming. I'm so glad you're here. Good boy."

Chapter 21: Visitors at Dusk

"She thinks more of that scruffy mongrel than she does of me." Peter lies on his back in bed, Patricia with her head next to his, watching him.

"Why haven't you split up? Thrown her out?" A hint of hurt on Patricia's face. The relatively recent history behind this. Peter and her. Two short years ago. A year after moving in together. The lease on the flat came up. Carole came up. Bang! She was history. Unceremoniously dumped for an office junior. That's not happening again. Now she's taking back what's hers.

"I don't know Pat." Maybe he should have stayed with Patricia. She knows him. Knows what he wants.

"You have to move on. Pete, we should do this more often. I haven't skipped an afternoon off work, since... since we were together. I've really missed you. Like this. With me. No one knowing what we're doing." Patricia climbs onto Peter, kissing him. Kissing down his body. Peter knowing exactly what's happening next, tensing with expectation, then relaxing with it. Relaxing for the first time in months.

The time on the bedside clock reads 4pm.

Carole washes her face in the bathroom. Trying to shake off the dream that is still haunting her. The grove up on the high ground. Why was she dreaming about it? Who was there with her? A boy. What boy? She never went up there when she was here on holiday. Never had a summer romance here in Cwm Celyn. So, it's not a memory coming back to haunt her. She hardly noticed the grove. It was always one of her dad's landmarks in the valley, but too difficult to reach. Surrounded by miles of the forest with no roads leading there. Or so it seemed. Maybe now... But why?

She is getting back to reality. Looking at the mess still to be cleared in the cottage. Even the kitchen is a mess.

Hadn't she left that tidy this morning? Everything is now disorganised on the worktops. She is sure she put those things away. Strange.

She's done nothing today. A wasted day.

Carole picks up her phone. It's passed four o'clock. Signal yes. Calls no. Peter hasn't rung! Bastard! Why not? The longer this goes on, the more difficult it'll be to put right. If it should be put right. She has to deal with this. No time like now. He'll be in work. Tied to his desk as usual. He'll have to talk to her!

Carole pacing outside the cottage, on the phone, getting increasingly stressed. Growing more concerned; no actually angry as the conversation goes on. Her mind racing. What the hell is going on? "No, I haven't tried his mobile. Is...? So, he hasn't come back from lunch? At this time? OK Frances, thanks... I understand... Yes, talk soon, 'bye." Confusion on Carole's face. Something is wrong. Where the hell is he if he's not at work? Would Frances be covering for him? Would she? Christ! Has she got no friends at all anymore?

Carole dials his mobile number. It goes straight to answerphone. Fuck.

Carole dials another number. 'Flat'. Four rings. The answer phone cuts in. Peter's voice. Carole's face drops. Christ, where is he? "Peter and Carole aren't in. Please leave us a message after the tone and we'll get back to you."

Gathering her thoughts. "Hi Pete, it's me. I've been trying to get through to you... Where are you?"

Carole's voice like a ghost in the living room of the flat. Her message being recorded as the red light flashes on the answer phone. The flashing red light paling to insignificance as the sun bursts through the window drowning it out. Other sounds drowning out her shaky voice on the speaker. Rhythmic. Gasps, moans from nearby.

Patricia astride Peter on the bed. Hearing Carole's message. Groaning and crying out to drown out the sound of Carole's voice.

Carole's message continuing. "Are you ok? Frances says you haven't gone back to work this afternoon. What's wrong? We need to talk..."

Patricia smiles as she hears the stress in Carole's voice. She watches Peter beneath her, staring wildly up at her. "Come on! Fuck me, Pete!"

"Pete, are you there?" Carole faint on the answerphone.

Peter closing his eyes. It's too much. He arches in ecstasy. "You sexy bitch!"

Patricia cries out again and falls forward on Peter, grasping him tight.

"Call me back." The answerphone rumbles on.

Patricia listens. Sweet revenge on the girl who took her man. Yes, he was her man. Now he's her man again.

End of message. Beep beep, the witch is dead.

Patricia kisses Peter, their tongues entwined.

Carole pacing the cottage living room. What the hell is going on? Something is wrong! It's not like Peter to go off the grid, nor miss work. He never had a day off sick in the time they worked together. His mobile off. And he's not at the flat. He's avoiding her. He's avoiding everybody it seems. And he's a couple of hundred miles away. And she has no transport. She can't leave the cottage. Not that she could find Pete even if she wanted to, in a city with three times the population of Wales. Carole roars in frustration and flops down on the mattress in the living room, burying her face in the pillow. Tears of frustration well up.

Sammy whining nearby snaps her out of it. Bringing her back to the miserable reality she has created around herself.

Nothing to do but get on with the job of the day. Making this place a home from home. But so much to do. Maybe Mrs. Jones was right. Too much. Rubbish everywhere, even underneath the bags and boxes of stuff she has brought to rejuvenate this place. Tears blur her vision. It's all too much.

The poppet watching her with those deep dark eyes. Carole's eyes lock with it. Carole picks up the poppet to put it away somewhere. Anywhere. She doesn't want anyone seeing her like this. But it feels so warm in her hands. Alive almost. The wood feels soft. Skin-like. Carole strokes its hair, running her fingers down its warm body which swells to her touch. Oh Jeez!!! Did it move? It's still staring into her eyes. Oh God, she's losing it...

Carole puts the poppet back down and heads into the kitchen to put some water on her face. To wash away her tears and this hopeless feeling. She can feel the poppet's eyes on her. She opens a few of the buttons on the front of her dress splashing water onto her face and chest. Damn, she's hot, sweating...

Sammy barking loudly. Someone's outside. Who could that be? Carole heads for the front door.

Geraint is at the cottage gate on his bike, with a rucksack on his back. Sammy is jumping up inside the wall and barking excitedly at Geraint who is working out if he may get a bite from the dog if he steps inside the gate.

Carole stops inside the cottage door, keeping back in the shadows. Geraint. In a T-shirt and shorts. Skin tanning from the summer sun. Muscles moving under the skin. Stop it! "Sammy come here!"

Geraint is still watching Sammy a little warily. "I hope you've fed him."

Carole walks over and grabs hold of Sammy. Oh God this boy is hot...

Geraint's eyes widen as he sees Carole's dress is open. Her naked body beneath is visible as the dress falls away. Her bare body, just feet away. Jesus wept. Carole seemingly unaware of it. Or is she? Geraint blushes. Oh God!

"Sammy, stop it! Geraint, hi." Carole unable to think of anything else to say. Smiling at Geraint as she holds onto Sammy's collar. The cool breeze on her body feeling good. So good.

Geraint purposefully taking off his rucksack and looking away. "I brought your shopping."

"Thanks Geraint, it's very good of you to bring it up. I hate to be a bother."

Sammy calming down now. Tail wagging relishing the visitor. Someone else to play with.

"No bother. Where shall I put it?"

"Come inside." Carole leads the way into the cottage away from the cool breeze, inside the cottage, with its... atmosphere. It does have an atmosphere.

Geraint follows her inside, his eyes getting used to the gloom. The first thing he sees is the mattress and the suitcase with Carole's underwear. Which she clearly isn't wearing now. Oh God... "How are you settling in?"

"As you can see, it's a bit of a mess, but it's coming along... I haven't done a stroke today though... don't know what's got into me..." Carole smiles coyly, sizing up Geraint.

"Mam says starting any job is the toughest part... is there anything you could do with a hand with, now I'm here?"

"Where to start? Really. I'm not going to get much done today. Are you any good with a corkscrew Geraint?"

Geraint looks bemused. "I've not had much practice..."

"Well, there's only one way to get good at anything. Practice... but first I've got to find the thing..."

Carole heads into the kitchen. Geraint follows to the door, watching the shape of her body through her dress. Carole starts rummaging in a drawer, her dress falling away again giving Geraint a view of her cleavage.

Geraint is torn, both excited and embarrassed. He turns away as Carole looks up.

"Got it. Here we go..." Carole produces the corkscrew from the drawer. "Come on." She crouches down to get a bottle of wine from the lower cupboard. She passes both to up Geraint. 'Ok lad, let me see you do your stuff!"

Geraint struggles with the bottle & corkscrew. Geraint drives the screw into the cork and turns it slowly. Nothing seems to happen. Geraint feels Carole's eyes on him. All over him. She's checking him out. Oh God... The metal screw enters the cork and digs deep. As he turns the screw the cork rises. The cork emerges with a pop. Geraint, pleased he hasn't messed this up. He doesn't want to mess up in front of this woman. Not now. Anything could happen. Oh God, he's getting so excited. "Job done, ma'am!"

Carole claps teasingly, laughing. She puts the two glasses on the worktop, standing very close to Geraint.

Geraint's hand shakes as he fills the two glasses, maybe too full. He glances at Carole who is looking directly into his eyes.

"Have you been here before Geraint?"

A fist of fear in Geraint's stomach. Does she know he was outside the other night? Or at the lake? Oh Christ. Best to act innocent. Say something! "No... I didn't want to come here when old Mr Phillips was still alive... I was scared to death to come here. Everyone said it was a haunted house..."

Carole laughs. "What? I never heard that!"

Oh God, this is going badly. Geraint tries to back track. "No, well... It's rubbish any way, isn't it? Ghosts and things."

Carole moves closer, touching her arm against his. Geraint feeling her breath on his face. "Come on, tell me about it...

Please".

Geraint swallows. He can't look Carole in the eye. She is staring at him, with those deep brown eyes. He wants to kiss her, but he's terrified that she'll slap him. Like that girl at the school disco. Bethan. All his friends said he was in. That she was up for it. But when he asked her outside, she slapped him in front of everyone. Everyone laughed.

Geraint swallows a mouthful of wine. OK, just tell her the story. See what happens. "The story I've heard is that a bit over a hundred years ago, a woman who lived here had an affair with a local boy. Her husband was a captain of a ship. Always away from home. He came home unexpectedly and went out into the countryside to find them. He must have killed them both and then run away to sea again, because they never found any of the bodies. No one's ever seen the ghosts. It's just everyone thinks they're here. So, it's just a story." Geraint looks at Carole, still staring into his eyes. Her pupils wide, making her eyes appear black. Her mouth open, breathing softly. Her chest heaving.

"I think it's nice having ghosts..."

Carole so near him that he can feel the heat from her body. Geraint closes his eyes for a moment. His mind snaps back to the cottage. How it terrified him as a kid. How he wouldn't come here. Genuinely frightened. Not of ghosts. Of Phillips. Or rather what Phillips would become if there were no other adults around. Very dark and scary. Meaning him... harm. Geraint snaps out of the mood Carole has put him in. He's scared. This is not how women react to him. There's something wrong. "I don't. I think ghosts are all around us all of the time."

Carole moves even closer. Black eyes staring into his. Her breath in his mouth. Close. Urgent. "I wonder if there are any ghosts down at the old ruined cottage near the lake, you know, the one about a mile closer to the village..."

Geraint more scared than horny now. Not liking this one bit. "Nant-y-Cadno? I haven't been down there in years..." Carole inching closer. Running her hand through his hair. Say something! "I think that's the cottage where the lad lived in the ghost story…"

"So, they were neighbours, eh? Two lonely people in the hills... and one thing led to another?"

"Yes. Suppose so..."

"I think I'll go back down there tomorrow afternoon. Sunbathing. It's very private. I like the lake too. I like swimming. I took Sammy down there the other evening. Is that where do you go fishing?"

Geraint flinches, spilling his wine glass. "Oh, I'm sorry!" Red liquid running across the worktop.

Carole snaps out of her reverie. Oh God, what is she doing? Geraint looking down her dress. Oh no! She stiffens and buttons her dress. "It's OK Geraint. I'll clean that up." She takes the glass from his hand. "Do you want me to pour you another glass?"

Geraint is both relieved and deflated. This is more the way women normally react around him. He relaxes a bit and looks for a way out. "Thank you, no. I better be getting home. Mam asks if you want me to come back tomorrow to help you with something?"

Carole composing herself. No harm done. No use crying over spilt Rioja. Nothing got out of hand, thank God. And it would be good to have some help around here. "Yes, if that's OK... I'll need a hand moving furniture so I can clean the place up and do some painting."

OK, Geraint knows he has to come back. Maybe he should rehearse what to say next time. She is so gorgeous. And she wants him to come back here. So, he hasn't blown it. Thank God for that. "Right, OK... Shall I come by tomorrow afternoon?"

"Perfect. Thank you. And say thanks to your mum for me. Be

careful on the way home." Carole practically shoos Geraint towards the door. She's back in control, but damn, that can't happen again. She's on her own up here. She doesn't need any problems. Especially with such a cute boy. His back arching as he pulls on the rucksack.

    Carole waves to Geraint as he rides his bike up the road towards the village. He looks over his shoulder as he rides off. Carole is torn, almost crying out to him to return. He disappears from sight. Carole realises she has some of Geraint's hair between her fingers. She studies the blonde locks as she leans against the garden wall. Playing with it between her fingers. She looks up to see if he is in earshot, but too late, he's gone. Damn she wants him to come back. Carole goes back into the cottage, not bothering to close the door.
    There are shadows where she stood at the garden wall The trees seem to disappear as the light intensifies. Mari is talking to a passer-by. Owain. She tries to draw him closer, but he runs away. Mari watches him go running his hair through her fingers.

Chapter 22: Lights in the Night

Carole tosses Geraint's hair into the fireplace as she walks to the kitchen. It falls short, onto the grate and onto the poppet.

In the kitchen she wipes down the worktop, cleaning up the spilt deep red wine. It's on the floor too. The kitchen looks like a murder scene. That was expensive wine. Washing the cloth under the tap, watching the red liquid disappear like spilt blood. Blood on her hands. But no blood has been spilt. No harm done.

But what was she thinking? Why did she leave her dress open like that with an eighteen year old boy alone with her. And he's coming back. Is she leading him on? Best have a word with him tomorrow. Make sure there are no... Feelings. Complicating things with the way things are with Pete is just... Too much. She sips from her wine glass. This won't cork. She'll have to finish the bottle. On her own.

The wind through his hair should clear Geraint's head, but he is still so confused by what just happened. Riding his bike back towards the village. Hardly noticing anything around him as he goes. Freewheeling bike, freewheeling mind. Carole inviting him back. Telling him where she'll be sunbathing. Asking about him fishing at the lake. Does she know he was there when she went skinny dipping?

Geraint takes the bend, rattling over the gouge in the road where the crash happened killing Bethan, the girl who slapped him in the school disco. She went off with Gareth from the sheep farm up on the top of the mountain. He took her to the lake. No need to guess why. But they never made the bend as he was bringing her home. Old Land Rovers are very unforgiving to their passengers. The machine didn't forgive her. It killed her at the same time it died itself, nearly felling that tree that got in its way. Gareth getting away lightly with brain damage.

Hard lessons to learn when you're seventeen. Lives change on split second decisions. On who wants what, from who, and when. Decisions dictating where people end up at certain moments. Thousands of decisions a day. Not all of them good. Some very bad decisions were made that night.

Geraint stops the bike, like he's done so many times. Bethan was lovely. Now she's in the cemetery down in Llanddewi. Things could have been so different. He was quietly devastated. Crying off and on for months. As he is in danger of doing right now.

He came here to see the crash site the following night after Mam had gone to bed. He saw what the minister had warned him about in Sunday school. *Canwyll gorff*. The corpse candle held by the dead who still walk the land. A white light for a woman. It was her. No doubt. The light at the foot of the tree, so he could see her. Did she blame him for being a twat? Is that why she went off with Gareth instead to teach him a lesson? Was it all his fault? He was terrified, alone with the ghost of a newly dead girl in the dark forest. He ran home crying like a baby. Now he wouldn't go this way on his own after dark.

He'd lied to Carole earlier. Yes, there are ghosts here in the forest. He's seen them. He had to lie to Carole. That was the kind thing to do. Geraint rides on.

Carole. He can't stop thinking about Carole. She's as hot as hell. Her body. So close to him. He saw so much of her just now, and she just let him. Does she want him? Geraint brings the bike to a halt and realises he's at entrance to the narrow track; the track to Nant y Cadno. Where Carole goes to sunbathe because it's private. Oh God. Geraint takes his phone out of his pocket and watches the video he shot of Carole at the lake. The quiet sound of splashing on the video, hidden by the rising hiss of the wind in the trees. Now another sound, a car approaching fast from the village. Geraint stuffs the phone into his pocket and rides on. Up ahead the car turns up the mountain road. Geraint alone in the forest once more. Swallowed by the gloom as the sound of his freewheeling bike chain is drowned by the hiss of the wind in the trees.

The wind is rising. Hissing through the trees outside the cottage. Sending the smoke from the chimney off into the murk.
Carole has lit the fire, burning more of Mr. Phillips' memories as fuel. Old magazines and newspapers. Stuff the old man's family should have disposed of. Still, it's keeping her warm. Carole sits on the mattress, drinking the wine and watching the flames burn on the hearth. Sammy lying at her feet, asleep. Someone watching her though. She can feel eyes on her. From the hearth. From the shadows in the firelight. Stop it. There's no one there.
The poppet. Watching her from the hearth. Its hair in its eyes. No, not its hair. Geraint's hair. Carole picks up the poppet and the strands of Geraint's hair. The poppet is warm. It must be the fire. Its head a little sticky. Carole realises that the hair is attached to something black. Pitch. Sticky in the heat. She presses Geraint's hair into the pitch. It sticks, meshing with Owain's hair. Carole puts the poppet back down, further away from the fire. Somewhere cool. Somewhere that it is not watching her. But the sensation does not go away. So, what's watching her from the shadows of the firelight behind her?

A light swinging gently in the darkness. Squeaking as it moves, as the ship groans. He is lying in his bunk, his leg bound straight. In pain from his damaged leg. Sipping whiskey from a flask to take the edge off his world. Looking at the photograph of himself and Mari outside Bethlehem Chapel on their wedding day. Not a look of felicity. Rather suspicion and anger. Turning to hatred.

Mari or is it Carole in the fire light back at Pantyfedwen. Laughing. Not laughing with him. Sneering and laughing at him. Someone with her. Putting his hands over her bare chest, pulling her back into the darkness, as her laugh turns to groans of pleasure.

Peter wakes up with a start. A shooting pain in his leg. He climbs out of bed, trying to stop the leg muscle cramping. The pain searing him awake. Limping across the room, trying to find something to steady himself.

A voice in the darkness. "Pete, are you OK?"

"Carole?"

"What do you want her for? You've got me now..." Patricia pulls back the covers. "See anything you want?"

Peter still confused by his dream. That bitch. Laughing at him. Destroying his life. The pain sears through Peter's leg. He turns away and leans for support on the bedroom wall. His heart thumping in his ears. Patricia holds him from behind. Her body warm against his. Patricia smiles. "You're with me Pete. Remember?"

The wine bottle empty. The wind howling in the chimney. Carole asleep on the mattress. The fire is just embers now.

Mari smiling as she works by firelight. Binding Owain's hair and pushing it into the pitch on top of the poppet's head. Mari kisses the poppet. "Owain..."

Carole groans in her sleep. Her eyes darting beneath closed eyelids. Breathing harsh. Dreaming a wild dream.

The wind howls. Something is creaking nearby. Inside, as regular as the creak of a ship at sea. Mr. Phillips swinging from the noose in the bedroom. Eyes bulging as he realises he's about to die. At last.

Chapter 23: The Blinding Light of Day

Peter's leg hurting as he and Patricia emerge from the DLR at Canada Square. He is limping. She is clinging on to him. She was never clingy before. Maybe she's helping him walk. More likely she thinks she needs to be all over him now that she's sleeping in his bed again. Marking him as her boy. Making a point of kissing him deeply before heading off for her office. Damn she's hot. Just what the doctor ordered to help forget about her. That bitch. Carole.

Peter's head turns. The smell of fish. Billingsgate Fish Market is not too far away. The wind must have changed. Unusual for this time of year to have a wind from the north east. A good wind to have at your back in the English Channel. Peter heads south for the office, the sun in his eyes, reflections from the glass towers all around him, the limp now very pronounced.

Peter limps quickly through Reception, hoping to avoid anyone who notices that he is already running late. He closes the office door and drops into his seat. His leg is killing him. He logs in. No, he doesn't. Not again! What was the new password? Oh crap.

A click, creak and click. Frances has let herself in and closed the door behind herself. Leaning against it. Angry. Very angry. "Where the hell were you yesterday?"

The log in fails again. What the hell is it? "I had to go home. I didn't feel well…"

"Really? Why not tell me? You left your mobile off. I couldn't get hold of you. Carole called too."

Peter groans. Carole. She doesn't work here anymore. He's come to work to forget about her. Having her stuff still at the flat is rubbing salt in the open wound as it is. Now this bitch is carrying on about her. Peter gives Frances a look. No words needed.

"OK, that's between you and her, but you left TP to me yesterday. He was pissed off that I couldn't find you, and he wants you to run the presentation for him this afternoon at 3pm."

"OK." Yes! Logged in. "Thank you, Frances." Opening up the emails. Bollocks! Loads of them.

Frances stands ignored at the door. She can do sarcastic. Now is an example. "You're very welcome, Peter." Frances exits slamming the door behind her.

Carole is painting the kitchen wall. Trying to brighten up this dark room. A lighter pastel shade. This place needs a woman's touch. After a while the gloom in here is overpowering.

The bedroom door slams. Carole jumps out of her skin.

Sammy scratching at the back door desperate to get out. "Don't do that, I'm going to paint that next!" She opens the door and Sammy runs out. The dog stops and turns. Yelping, wanting her to follow. "I'll come out to play later."

Carole carries on with the painting, adding the light tone to the wall. It seems to darken in front of her eyes. A trick of the light maybe. She can still see the colour underneath. This will need a few coats. It's almost like she can't cover up that miserable old man's life here at the cottage.

The miserable old man who is standing behind her. Screaming at her. His cheap electronic watch beeps on the hour.

Carole stops in her tracks. What the hell was that sound? She feels someone behind her. Carole turns around. Nothing there. Apart from a sense of darkness. Darkness unseen. And cold. Suddenly quite cold. It raises goosebumps on her arms. And that damn smell. Stronger than ever. Turning her stomach.

Sammy barking and yelping wildly outside the door. Carole

puts down her paint brush. "OK, OK, let's go for a walk, shall we?"

Geraint serving some 'hippies' in the shop. He has less patience with them than his mother. A gawky couple. As out of place here as they probably were where they came from. English people moved out here to the middle of nowhere, selling an expensive little house in the South East of England to buy a big house or a small holding up here. Most don't last a winter. The cold. The wet. The isolation. Depression was what brought them here. It's usually what drives them away. This couple have at least tried to say his name, but still murder it. Calling him 'Grant' now. Jesus! Mercifully they leave before he needs to correct them yet again. Geraint alone again in the shop. Him and his revision notes. Not that he can concentrate for one second.

Carole is different to that lot. Hopefully she'll be staying. He can't stop thinking about her. Geraint takes out his phone and watches the video from the lake. It's a shame it's so blurred. It hardly looks like her. A trick of the light probably.

He closes his eyes. He is looking down Carole's dress again. Feeling her touch him. Watching her swimming naked in the lake. Imagining her lying in the sun at Nant y Cadno. Imagining lying beside her. His hands on her. Everywhere. Her grabbing him, but she's different now. Dark haired, thinner, desperately pulling him into her.

Geraint leaning forward on the shop counter, lost in the daydream. His reflection in the security mirror distorting. Shorter. Slighter. Blonde hair longer.

He is in the woods with this woman. A mix of arms and bodies and mouths. The woods are different. Old oaks. A mist around him and this woman writhing beneath him. Reaching up for him, crying out. But that's not his name...

"Geraint!"

What the hell? Mrs. Mathias has come in to get the paper and milk. Standing right in front of him. He never saw her. Geraint tries to focus. He was completely out of it.

Carole hasn't bothered to change out of her work jeans and T shirt. She needs to get out into the fresh air. She can't shake that atmosphere in the cottage. Cold. Morbid. Oppressive. And that smell that seems to follow her around everywhere she goes.

She needs to lighten her mood. She is carrying a rucksack with a towel, sunglasses, can of pop, her phone, headphones, keys and a book. A bit like going to the beach. Heading for her own private cove in the trees, at the ruined cottage. To catch some sun. Warm up. Clear her head. She closes the front door, locking it. Turning her back on this for now. Carole pulls on the rucksack, puts on some lightweight headphones and selects a music playlist on her phone.

The music kicks in, filling her ears with the sound of her younger summers; trance. The rhythm and repetition of the dance music immediately taking her out of her fugue. To another place. Holiday music. Sammy comes bounding around from the side of the cottage in time to the rhythm. Everything hits the beat. Carole popping the sunglasses on the top of her head. Putting Sammy on a leash and leading him off down the road.

The music driving her footsteps as she walks between the towering trees. The hiss of the forest sounding like the distant sea, taking Carole back to those brief summers in the Balearics. Drinks, pills, pools and parties. And boys. Week long relationships. Sex anywhere you could get away with it. Why hasn't she done that in so long?

Sex anywhere. Is that possible here? Yes, definitely. In the open countryside all around her. At the shore of the lake.

But best of all in the grove. Beautiful. Her private place. Where no one would find her with him...

Carole stops in her tracks. What is she thinking? The grove? The boy? These aren't her memories. The breeze passes over her, blowing her away, leaving someone else. The music carries on, clouding her thoughts. Lost in trance. The smell of the pine trees fading. Open fields in front of her closed eyes. The countryside smells from a hundred years ago. Flowers. Grass. The wind in her long dark hair.

Sammy barks. Her eyes snap open. The pines. Nothing but the pines. Carole walks on.

In a few minutes she is at the entrance of the overgrown track to Nant y Cadno. Bright sunshine there through the trees, drawing her in like a fly into a web. Walking out of the breeze and into the shade of the trees. The cool air enfolding her. Cocooned for a moment.

Breaking the tree line. Walking into the sun and the summer heat. The sun searing her face and the bare skin of her arms. She is in a different place, with a different climate, now that the pine trees are at a distance. A small vestige of what was here in Cwm Celyn before the trees came. Dragonflies buzzing around the green algae which covers the pond. Insects everywhere. Butterflies, bees. Life in the middle of the deathly forest. Everything moving in sync with the trance music in her headphones which fills her head; but is it her head?

Spreading the towel on the ground. Kicking off her shoes. Taking off her jeans, her T shirt and her knickers. Standing naked in front of the house. In front of his house. Wishing he was here, watching her. Who's house again? The boy in Geraint's story? Yes? The sun heating her skin. The wind breathing on it. The music taking her to another time.

Frances looking through Peter's office window. She dials a

number on her phone. A buzzing sound. Frances enters the
office. That weird smell is getting worse in here. The buzzing
sound is coming from Peter's desk. His mobile phone is by the
computer.

Peter's answer phone message in Frances' ear. Frances
looks around in despair. "Pete, you've done it again! Have you
got a death wish or something?"

He is at a bar, the only customer. He downs his whiskey
and heads out into daylight. It hurts his eyes. He limps off
to find another bar. Plenty here in the docks. All day to
explore them.

Geraint leaving the shop, mounting his bike and riding off
at speed.

She is lying face down on the towel in the long grass.
Insects buzzing around her naked body. Sammy lying nearby,
asleep in the sunshine. Her headphones pumping music into her
head displaces any reality outside. Her eyeballs moving around
wildly under her closed eyelids. Breathing heavily. In a
shallow sleep. Dreaming, or is it remembering?

Laughter on the trance track. Owain and Mari's laughter as
he chases her around the grove. Mari is easily caught, and she
falls to the floor pulling Owain down on top of her. The love-
spoon Geraint has made for her falls from her hand. Owain
kissing her.

Geraint rides the bike up the road heading for Carole's
cottage. He couldn't wait any more. He has to see her.
Rehearsing what to say if Carole makes a move on him again.
He's not going to mess it up this time. This is possibly a day
he's going to remember for the rest of his life.

Slowing as he reaches the path to Nant y Cadno.

Considering. She is probably at her cottage. It's only late morning. But she said she comes here and it's a glorious morning. She could be here. He stops the bike. Geraint carries his bike up the track, stowing it a few yards in. Moving quickly and quietly up the track, through the gloom towards the sunshine beyond.

His mind drifting. She's here. He knows she's here. All he can think of is Carole's body. But now it's not Carole's body. And he is not Geraint.

Kissing her in the long grass of the grove. In the shade of the ancient woodlands. Looking down at her. The dark haired girl. Not Carole. Someone else. Someone from the past. Someone wanting him with a passion. Yes. It's Carole.

Carole gasps as she lies dreaming in the sunshine. She rolls over onto her back. Laughter and breathing on the trance track. Mixing reality and dream, or is it memory?

Owain kissing Mari, opening up the front of her dress as she looks up at him smiling lustfully. Mari suddenly distracted, pushing Owain away. She sits up and looks around, listening intently. Owain looks at her questioningly. A mist flowing around them, appearing out of nowhere. Muffled sounds. The mist killing any echo so the sound could be coming from anywhere. Breathing. Footfalls. Thumps.

Mari's face fearful. She knows. She knows something is coming for her. The snap of a twig and the growl of a dog. A bark!

Carole sits up to the sound of Sammy barking. She looks around in surprise, still half asleep.

Geraint is twenty feet away, on his knees, desperately trying to keep the dog quiet.
Carole stands up, making no attempt to cover herself.

Geraint is completely caught out, watching her with surprise which turns to lust and embarrassment. Carole is coming closer, walking naked through the long grass. Carole is silhouetted against the sun. The sun so bright that he can't make out her features. She looks slimmer, with long dark hair like the girl in his head today. But that makes no sense. How to explain his way out of this hopeless situation? "I was on my way to see you at your cottage. But I thought you might be here... Sorry."

"Sorry for what?"

"For disturbing you."

"I told you I'd be here. Maybe I want you to disturb me." Carole has reached him. Inches away.

He can smell her, almost taste her in the breeze. This can't be happening. Geraint watches Carole almost warily. She reaches out suddenly. Geraint prepares for a slap. Instead, she runs her hand through his hair.

"Come on." She takes him by the hand and leads him to the towel on the ground. He awkwardly kisses her, hands by his sides. "What's the matter?"

Geraint is still in turmoil. What if he is reading this wrong? What if she shouts or screams? What if she tells his mother? What if... "It's my first time…"

Carole smiles. "So, enjoy me."

Excitement overcomes him. It's like someone else is in control now.

Carole kisses Geraint deeply. Undoing the belt of his trousers was his hands tentatively explore her body. She yanks down his trousers and pulls him down with her to the ground. Wrapping her legs around his back, pulling him out of sight into the long grass.

Exploring each other. Kissing. Entwining. Holding each other as the pine trees blur away. Focussing on nothing but each other. The oaks in the grove up above seeming to reach down to enfold them in a different place and a different time. The sun sears them, obscuring everything.

Chapter 24: Afterglow

No clouds. A clear blue sky. Jet trails crossing westwards towards America. The thin trails spreading out to wide ribbons of white cloud tens of thousands of feet above them. The little silver shapes creating them shining as they catch the sunlight. When this cottage was built, the only way to travel those distances was by ship. A journey of weeks. Not hours. The sailors making those trips would not be home for months at a time. The world is a smaller place now. You are only hours away from anywhere. Even here.

Carole is waking up. Waking up to a new situation. Geraint who she saw grow up as a schoolboy when she was here on her holidays is asleep beside her. Naked like her in the long grass. What has she done? What got into him? What got into her?

The sun blazes down and Carole falls back to sleep to the distant sound of a jet engine rumbling above the quiet hiss of the wind in the pines.

The roar of engines. Rush hour. Misnomer. All day is rush hour. Millions of people trying to get around a convoluted city. He is navigating by the sun, at least when he can see it between the high buildings. Right now on this road alone, thousands of people trying to get home through grid lock. No rush. Just building frustration.

He is trying not to lose his way beneath a leaden sky. Dark clouds rolling in overhead. A dark cloud of diesel smoke engulfs him from a passing red double decker bus. An old tourist bus. Not the new 'cleaner than thou' buses that seem to be the norm now. He coughs as the noisy smoky machine passes by.

Constant traffic crawling by and coming to a halt. Now he is moving faster than these machines, even with his limp.

Passing the bus, moving up the line of traffic. Passing bored faces behind steel and glass. Cut off from the reality outside. But still mindlessly performing their functions in this Devil's Ant Hill.

He prefers the company of sailors. And them as drunk as he is now. Their emotions clear for all to see. Raw. Vital. Not like these faceless bastards he passes on his way home.

Home. The flat. What was that to him now? His wife gone. Rather, not his wife. She wouldn't take a ring on her finger. The heathen bitch, up to something in his absence. Something sinful no doubt, back there in the forests. He has to find her. Correct her. God will tell him what to do. God will know how to deal with her.

She looks up at Geraint above her. Sweat on his face from the exertion. Sun in her eyes. He looks different, the curls in his blonde hair more pronounced. They are both breathless. Spent. He lies down on her, she holding him close.

A large bird with a pronounced forked tail circling above. Watching them.

"What kind of bird is that?"

Geraint screws up his eyes as he looks into the sky. "A Red Kite."

"I've never seen a bird of prey that big."

"They were almost extinct. Now you often see them up on the open mountain. I've not seen one here before though. The trees are too thick for them to hunt here."

The bird wheels off on the breeze and glides into the trees of the grove up above. The grove. Resplendent in the sunshine. Different from everywhere around. And old. Very old. "I've never been up there on the hill. Have you?"

"Where? Gelli Dywyll? No, I've never been there either."

"Let's go up there. Another day."

The late afternoon sun finding the angle between the trees to fill the forestry road with light. Carole and Geraint walking back through the late afternoon light. Walking out of the sun. Sunlight searing their forms. He pushes his bike. His laughter pealing out like a bell. She thinner and darker holding him. The sun dips behind a cloud. Instant shadow. A change of light.

Carole climbs onto Geraint's bike, and he pedals them both up the road. Sammy running behind. In a couple of minutes, they arrive at her cottage.

Carole unlocks the cottage door but holds Geraint back at the threshold. "Wait there. I'm just going to fetch something." Carole emerges with a bottle of wine and the corkscrew which she pops into her ruck sack. "Come on."

He stands in the flat holding a plastic supermarket bag. Surveying the scene. Near empty shelves where she has taken her things away. He doesn't miss the things. But these things are just the tip of the iceberg. She's taking something bigger away from him. She's taking away everything he's worked for. Everything.

He looks in the mirror, not really recognising himself anymore. Face grey and sullen. Long dark hair in his eyes. When did he last have long hair? What's going on?

Falling onto the sofa. Clonk. The bottle in the shopping bag hitting the floor hard. Careful. He mustn't break it. It helps him to focus.

That bitch. She is causing this. It must be witchcraft. There in her hovel in the mountains. A place that feels like it's in another century. But maybe that was a simpler time. Black and white. Right and wrong. A time when you could burn a witch.

The iPad on the table. He reaches for it. Opening up the web browser on the last page he looked at. The Welsh Holiday

Home Arson campaign. The page updates. New weblinks. Another fire. Today! "The attack has been linked to the current campaign of arson attacks on rural cottages owned as second homes in the Welsh speaking heartlands. The First Minister of the Welsh Assembly...".

Crazy bitch. She's out there in a cottage alone in a place where these houses are being burnt down all around. Very remote. No neighbours. No transport. All alone. Anything could happen.

More weblinks to explore. Politicians distancing themselves from this popular movement. Just as they did before Brexit. Spineless self-serving bastards.

In moments he's asleep. Holding back a big dog. A cottage behind him. Not somewhere he recognises. The dog pulling him now as fast as his damaged leg can go. Pulling him upwards to that woodland up on this hill. Taking him to somewhere where something is happening, he doesn't want to see.

Carole and Geraint sitting in the trees at the lakeside. At Geraint's favourite fishing spot. Hidden from view, but with the view out over the lake, the grove up above, and the sun now dipping behind it. The wine bottle half empty. Sharing the earphones connected to Carole's phone. Trance music mixing with the light wind in the trees and rippling of the little waves on the lake shore. Her head on his shoulder. Half awake.

He hoping she doesn't realise he could have been there when she went swimming a couple of nights ago. Things are happening so fast. It's incredible. "You're so gorgeous."

Carole smiles at him, kissing him. "No, I'm just an ordinary lass..." She puts the other earpiece in Geraint's other ear. She pulls off her shoes and jeans and wades into the water, gasping as the cold water grabs her. Once she is up to her waist, she ducks under. The water pulling her T shirt tight against her body. Slimmer. Her hair dark down her back.

She swims out into the lake. Geraint sits on the shore watching her for a moment. He undresses quickly and wades into the lake after her.

Peter asleep on the sofa. Being pulled through the woodland by the powerful dog. His leg buckling, having to use the stick to support himself as the dog pulls him onwards. Climbing the steep hill into the trees. Into the grey mist that is descending. No bird song. A bird of prey way overhead, circling. Quickly obscured by the mist that's falling fast. The mist deadening the sound of the dog panting and the sound of fornication nearby. The dog pulling him towards it. Losing his balance. Stepping on a branch. Snap! Everything stops. Seeing them in the mist. Turning the dog loose... It doesn't bark. It buzzes.

The dog buzzing, fading as it runs towards the naked couple. Everything disappearing except for the buzzing. He opens his eyes. Dusk. A long continual annoying buzz. The intercom. Who the hell is that? Peter staggers over to the door and views the tiny CCTV screen. Patricia at the door. Peter presses the access button. Patricia steps inside.

He opens the flat's front door. Patricia coming up the stairs. "What do you want?"

"Charming! I thought you'd be glad to see me." Patricia reaches the apartment door, and Peter pulls her inside. He throws her across the room onto the sofa. Walking towards her slowly. Patricia gasps. "What are you going to do to me?"

Peter's hair covers his black eyes.

"You're quite the gentleman. Walking me home like this." Carole kisses Geraint in the doorway of the cottage.

"I aim to please. Same time tomorrow?"

Carole looks slightly perplexed. Where is this going? She loves it but...

Geraint seeing the worried look on her face. "Don't worry, I'll be here tomorrow afternoon, right after I run out of excuses not to come here…"

"Bad boy. On your way!" Carole gives Geraint a playful push.

Geraint rides his bike away down the road towards the village. His lights fade into the gloom of the forest. Carole watches him disappear from view and turns the key in the door. She opens the cottage door, and the atmosphere hits her.

Patricia reels from the blow, sobbing. She pulls his hair, he wrenches free. She hits him with the whiskey bottle, spilling the contents everywhere. The bottle bounces off across the floor, pouring the whiskey on the white rug. He reaches for the bottle and Patricia gets away from him. She grabs her clothes from the sofa and backs towards the door. He rights the whiskey bottle. placing it carefully on the table.

"You bastard! What the hell possessed you? Do you want to hurt me?" She pulls on her blouse and skirt.

He looks at her from behind the long dark hair with those angry dark eyes. He gets to his feet. Taking his belt out of his trousers. Coming towards her. Raising the belt.

Patricia watching in disbelief. Backing away. Getting through the door and slamming it. Standing there in the hallway half dressed. Scared. Checking her pockets. Has she got her keys and her phone and her money? Yes.

Fuck! Yes, that's what they did. Fuck. No endearment. He used her and then he hit her.

Silence for a moment. Click. Patricia jumps backwards. The door opening inch by inch. The face in the door. Not really Peter. What the hell?

"Ast!"

Patricia stands in shock. "What did you just call me?"

The door flies open. Smack! He lashes her with his belt.

Patricia cries out and runs off down the stairway. Out of the building. Into the square. Down the road towards the main road. Then realising that she is still half dressed. Making herself presentable as possible she runs off out of the square.

He calmly closes the door to the apartment. Closing out the world outside. Crossing over to the sofa, picking up the whiskey bottle on his way. Sipping from it. Picking up the iPad. Clicking on the Photos app. Pictures of Carole smiling at him. His hair in his eyes. He spits out the word which has come into his head from somewhere... "Ast!"

"Ast!"

Mrs. Phillips cowers on the cottage kitchen floor, crying.

Mr. Phillips, the younger Mr. Phillips, stands over her threateningly, belt in hand. The slight grey man in his early twenties is shaking with the same rage as his older incarnation. Time would never let those shakes go away.

"John, stop, please. We work together in the same school. It's normal we meet to discuss matters after work. I have to talk with him. But very well. I promise I'll come home directly school is over in future."

He stands over her, looping the belt back around his trousers. "That's all I ask. People talk. I won't have people talking about you... us..." Mr Phillips reaches out his hand to his wife, and helps her up, giving her an awkward hug.

Mrs Phillips whispers conspiratorially in his ear. "We have to get out of this house John. Everything was good until we moved here."

Mr. Phillips nods. "Let's go out for a while. Down to the lake. Clear our heads."

Mrs. Phillips walks into the living room. Phillips watches her go, his hair falling over his eyes. He limps into the living the room following Mrs Phillips out through the front door. It slams.

What was that? Carole wakes up with a start. "Pete?" Carole lies back on the mattress. She hugs her pillow. Trying to shake the nightmare she was having. Pete hitting her with a belt! Christ! She could feel it.

A rhythmic squeaking sound comes from somewhere in the house. What the hell is that? She looks at her phone. 3am. She's not going looking for that noise at this time. Carole puts the pillow over her head like a scared child. The swinging belt, the creaking sound repeating over and over. Carole screws her eyes shut.

In the bedroom Mr. Phillips swings in the noose.

Chapter 25: Cleaning House

Carole in the kitchen, looking at the wall she painted yesterday. The smell of new paint masking the 'atmosphere' in here at least. The wall is now lighter, but she can still see the original colour deep beneath. It may take another couple of coats of paint and a bit of time, but she's not going to let this beat her. She will make this cottage hers. Why is she even thinking this way? As if there is a battle going on between her and... Who?

Geraint in the shop. Totally distracted. Watching the second hand on the old plastic electric powered clock turn. Too slowly. His exam revision work on the counter in front of him not registering. The buzz of the fluorescent light. The hum of the fridges. The sound of his breathing. Dying to get out of here. Dying to be with her. Listening to her breathing. Her gasping his name. Her crying out.

The painting in the kitchen redone. But already there's a bit of the darkness showing through from beneath. The back door propped open to help dry the paint but also to let in the fresh air and to drive out the 'atmosphere' that's still here. The smell is always there somehow.

Carole in the living room now, washing down the painted walls. Readying them for repainting too. She needs to brighten up the entire place. Bring a woman's touch to this place once more. Lighter. More feminine. Welcoming for Christ's sake.

The sugar soap in the water hardening her hands. The odd rough patch of plaster chaffing them. The dirt of decades in that bucket of water at her feet. It has turned as black as the devil in no time. Pitch black and foaming. It looks malignant. This dirt needs to go. Right now. Out with it!

Carole carries the bucket out through the open front door

and across the road. She throws the filth away into the trees. The darkness can stay out here in the forest, not in her house. Her house is going to be her sanctuary.

She looks at her cottage in the woods. Still looking forlorn. A lot of work to do yet. The front door slams hard startling her. The wind. You can be in places where you don't notice the wind. Pantyfedwen isn't one of them. It's always hissing, occasionally howling, like some sort of angered animal. Of course, she left the back door in the kitchen open to dry the paint more quickly and to get rid of the smell. Maybe she should prop the doors open. Stop that happening again. Carole crosses the road back to the cottage. She feels someone watching her. That city paranoia stopping her in her tracks.

The cottage watches her with a sad face. Two black eyes for windows. The eyes are the windows to the soul. Why did that just come into her head? And a shut mouth. Saying nothing about what has happened here. Not confessing anything. Something watching her from within the left eye. To her right. The bedroom. With such a strong reflection on the glass, it's hard to see anything within. It's like looking into a dark mirror. Is that her reflected? That pale face watching her? It must be her. But it must be!

Carole tries to open the door, but it doesn't budge. She shoves it with her shoulder. Solid. But then giving slightly, like someone pushing against it, keeping her out. One more time. A hard shove. The door gives. She nearly falls into the house. The bedroom door slams! What the hell? The front door slams behind her. The kitchen door slams. Sammy barking wildly. What the fuck! "Hello?"

Sammy still barking madly in the kitchen. She's scaring herself now. 'Hello'. Like anyone is going to answer. Pull yourself together girl. There's no one here.

But wait a minute. The bedroom door slammed. She's not

been in that room since she got here. The door was closed. She's sure it was.

Only four rooms in the entire cottage and she has not been in there since she arrived. Why would that be? Something telling her not to go there? Maybe Frances seeing a shape in her photo of the room had more of an effect on her than she realised? That was spooky. But. Oh, come on girl! Don't be silly.

She opens the door into the bedroom. The door opens with a creak. The smell really hits her. Carole coughs. Oh God! It smells like something died in here. Maybe this is what the 'atmosphere' is.

Carole steps into the bedroom. True her eyes are still adjusting from having been outside. It's murky. The dark wood abandoned furniture from the previous owner, the wardrobe and that mirror and the box Peter brought in. And the bed. They could have at least taken away the mattress! Maybe that's what the smell is. Jesus Christ! Did Mr. Phillips die on that? Carole retches.

Even walking across this room sounds different. The floor is bare boards in here, not solid like the other rooms. Newspapers and assorted rubbish scattered around on the floor getting kicked as she walks. Dirt everywhere that you can see, even in this low light. The old man's family could have least made an effort to clean the place. A butterfly caught in a cobweb. This is disgusting.

But to look on the bright side. This room could be nice. What were once white walls are faded to a discoloured grey. At least repainting won't be a chore. Oh God, the smell though. Carole pulls back the tattered curtains. Dead flies on the windowsill. Hundreds of them. Dying trying to leave this room. Why did she think that? Some more light just shows the dust hanging in the air. You can see it move, forming patterns against the light in the middle of the room. Not beautiful.

Weirdly unnatural somehow. Kind of human in shape.

Carole is coughing harder now. That smell is awful. She tries to open the window. Stuck. Carole pushes the sash up with all her might. It moves, but not enough to clear the wooden frame. Carole fights with it to open the window further. She wins. An inch at a time. Still coughing until the forest air flows in. A victory. Damn. But the dust does not go out. Carole heads back into the living room to find a broom, dustpan and brush. The cloud of dust follows her as far as the door. Watching her.

He sits at his desk staring at an email. From Mr. Radcliffe. Where does he know that name? Oh, by God! Radcliffe! He's found him. Wishing his attendance on that damned ship no doubt. The same ship which almost spoke for his leg. The limp he will always bear, but he will not receive any settlement as the Captain swore he was drunk on duty. Can't that devil leave him alone? Surely Radcliffe must consider the contract of service terminated after all this time?

He hits 'Reply' and types quickly. 'Mr. Radcliffe. I have no doubt you think ill of me. Let me explain the facts of the situation to you sir, in my defence. I did not attend to sail that night because matters are pressing at home. The Lord tells us in Exodus, 'Thou shalt not suffer a witch to live.' God is my master for eternity. You are but my master whilst I remain in your employ on this mortal coil. You tasked me with taking coal to Marseilles, sailing under ballast to Odessa, taking grain to Rotterdam and returning to Cardiff. That, sir, would take too much of God's precious time. The witch has to die. As a matter of urgency. When my task is done I shall report to your offices and shall be as ever, at your disposal. Your obedient servant...' Damn! What is my name?

"Peter."

No, that's not it. It doesn't sit on him right now. Who

said that? That negress again. What does she want?

She stands at the doorway looking vexed. "Can I ask you something?"

She seems haughty. She needs to remember her place. Her name is Frances, isn't it? "Can it wait Frances?"

"Why? Are you actually in danger of doing something?"

Peter raises his head. How dare she? Talking to him like that!

"Have you talked to Carole?"

"That's not a work issue, is it?".

"Yes, it's a work issue if you're distracted, and if you're jeopardising projects we've been working on for months. Yes, I'd say it is a bloody work issue Pete! Work and life. You can't separate them because they make you what you are. They are two sides of the same coin. Sort out your problems with Carole, she's a great kid. Then you'll get a grip on your work here."

Peter stands up sharply and moves his head threateningly close to Frances.

She recoils, frightened, but stands her ground. "Oh, now you're going to hit me? At this rate, I'll only be on your side because I'm paid to be." She coughs. Unable to breathe.

He looks at Frances with dark eyes beneath the mop of hair. He sneers.

Fear wins over. "Pete, what's got into you?" Frances leaves the office, slamming the door.

He sits down and hits 'Send' on the email. He needs a drink. He gets up and limps out. The leg playing up badly today. The limp nearly crippling him in agony as he crosses reception. No sign of Frances. To the lift then. No way he can manage the stairs.

Geraint riding his bike slowly up the road through the village. No one much around, but he needs to be careful.

Mustn't be seen to be rushing off to see her. To talk to her. To have her. Geraint has not been so excited in his entire life. Knowing that when he gets there, she'll want him. No more awkwardness. Just sex. And with a woman he's fancied since he was a boy. And now she's made him a man.

Geraint gets to the edge of the village and pedals hard. Heart racing, blood coursing through his body. Legs pumping hard. Breathing heavy. Only thinking of one thing. Carole.

Carole has finished sweeping the bedroom floor. A couple of dead mice. Hundreds of flies. Newspapers back to the 1950s. Dust and dirt. Another rubbish bag full of the remnants of Phillips. How could anyone live like this? Next it needs a wash down. The floorboards are black. Maybe she'll hire an industrial sander, sand them down, stain and revarnish.

Time to get the mattress out. Back to the kitchen to get the washing up gloves. It seems so disgusting, she can't bear touch it with her bare hands. But it has to be done. Get it the hell out of here. Reclaim the cottage as her own. Move her own mattress onto the bed. It should have been the first thing she thought of on getting here. Why has she not dealt with this? Pulling off the dirty sheet and pillows. Filling more rubbish bags. Out with them. Putting them against the garden wall ready for the refuse collection.

The front door slamming behind her again. No way! She'd propped it open! Enough! Carole pushes hard against the door, and it opens. She's angry now. She storms back for the bedroom. She can still see the dust in the air, just standing there. She grabs the mattress. It weighs a bloody ton. Surely it can't be this heavy? Dragging it off the bed. Struggling. It slams onto the floor with a crash, almost like there's someone lying on it. Dragging it across the floor to the bedroom door takes all of her strength.

Stuck. It won't get through the door. Having to stand it

up. It stinks. Pulling it upright is almost impossible, like having to roll a body off it. Where it touches her, it leaves marks on her T shirt, hurting her nipples as it rubs hard against her. Carole is furious, dragging at it, pull by pull forcing it through the door.

Into the living room. She can't stop it flopping back flat on the floor. Dragging its deadweight towards the front door. Trying to open the door. It won't budge again. What the fuck is wrong with this door? Dragging the door open, her foot against the door making sure it doesn't slam again. Gripping the mattress, dragging it through the gap, the dust covering her. Coughing hard. The mattress hurting her chest as it rubs against her. Battling it through the door.

A hand on her shoulder. Carole screams!

"Sorry!" Geraint backs away holding up his hands defensively.

"Oh, Jesus Christ, you scared me!" Carole gets her breath back. "Give me a hand with this please."

"Let me do it." Geraint drags the mattress out of the house. Fighting to keep it upright. He manhandles it out of the gate and dumps it against the garden wall with the rubbish bags. He is covered in the dust and dirt. He coughs to clear his lungs.

Carole watches him move. The muscles. The strength. She looks at the dirt on his shirt over that chest. "Your clothes are all dirty. Let me wash them for you."

Geraint laughs. "Have you seen yours?" He turns to Carole. She is staring at him. Her hair darker somehow. She takes off her dirty T shirt. Her body glistening with sweat in the sunshine. She kicks off her shoes. She undoes her jeans. Pulls down her knickers. She stands there naked, staring at Geraint. He stands there breathless. Speechless. The blood rushing from his head. She goes inside the cottage, out of sight. Geraint follows.

Chapter 26: English Girls

Phillips raging as Carole and Geraint make love on the mattress in front of the fireplace. In his house!

This is what he knew was happening just before he came home to find his wife with the schoolteacher that evening. He found them in the kitchen, drinking tea. As innocent as you like. But something had got into his wife. He was often told that women wanted men. But there was no sign of that with Rachel. Until they moved to Pantyfedwen.

Rachel. An English girl from Hereford. Not a great distance away from here, but a different country. Aware of Welsh, but never able to say a word. Hadn't tried. It was expected that if someone married a non-Welsh speaker, the couple and their children and indeed the entire family would only speak English from that point onwards. That was the way of things. Englishness establishing itself over the Welsh language in a way that the forces of Empire had never quite managed.

And now another English girl in his house ignoring him as his wife had done. Leading astray a local man as his wife had done. Breaking her vows. Phillips slams the front door.

He stands in middle of the road near the turning for the mountains. Waiting for her to come home from the school. Making sure she doesn't go off with him over the mountains to the towns in the south. But where is she tonight? Where is Rachel?

She's wearing a clean T shirt and shorts which hang loose on her. Her black hair running down her back. Bringing in two sets of clothes from the washing line, which have dried in a couple of hours in the breeze. She has hung the washing line around the bedroom side of the cottage where it is very difficult to see from the road. Not wanting anyone knowing the boy is here with her lest Ifan be told about it.

Carole stops in her tracks. What???? What did she just think? Carole takes a breath. She walks back to the cottage watching her own reflection in the window. Definitely her. Why wouldn't it be? What's going on? What the hell was she thinking just now?

First thing this morning her mind was clear. Her task to clean the place out. Out with the old, in with the new. The boy comes back, and she loses her mind again. She is not in control of her own thoughts nor actions. Enjoying every second with him. But this is crazy. Not wrong exactly, but...

Geraint stretched out naked on her mattress. Her bed. He's asleep. Teenagers sleep for hours. Let him sleep. She puts his clean clothes on the mattress. Think girl. What are you going to do about this situation?

The wind is picking up. She opens the front door, propping it open. Allowing the wind to blow through the house. Cleansing it of the atmosphere she hopes. She has been here for a few days, and she's not done anything like what she planned to do with the place in that time. A deep clean. Clear out the rubbish. Repaint. Then see what needs to be done by tradesmen. So far only one room done, and that was on the first day. Since then, nothing finished.

But is it more important that she has fun? With this boy? Fixing up this place is not the priority. It's fixing herself after Pete. After Pete... There, she's said it. Carole stands in the doorway to feel the breeze flowing past her. Hopefully blowing away whatever fugue is getting into her here. The wind whistles and moans.

"That wind, it's spooky even in daylight. It's like the trees are talking." Geraint hugs her from behind. Strong arms. Naked.

Carole fighting it. No, she's not going to lose control. She has to be strong. Think of Dad. The reason she came here.

"My dad used to call the trees the English Army of Occupation. That used to upset my Mum, being an English girl. He remembered Cwm Celyn as open country when he was a boy. He never really told me why he never moved back though. Probably because the place had changed so much."

"There were pictures in the pub before it closed last year. They showed what Cwm Celyn used to be like. Open country. The Government bought up all the farms and planted these trees after the war. People thought it would bring work. But it's poisoned the earth. The soil is very acidic now an old farmer told me. No one will be able to farm here for generations, if ever again. The only work for my friends around here is cutting the things down."

"You're a very articulate young man. University will do you good. It might even stop you being scared of the wind in a haunted house."

"That's not fair! This place scared the hell out of us when we were kids." Damn. He'd promised himself not to talk about this. The last thing he wants to do is to scare Carole away.

"So tell me more about this Mr Phillips who lived here. I only met him once in your shop. Oh, and out on the road. I nearly ran him over."

Old Man Phillips. Geraint hated him. "Few people would have been sorry if you had run him down. He was an odd bugger! He used to stand in the middle of the road. They said he was waiting for his wife to come home. But she had been dead for decades."

Carole remembers almost running over Phillips in the middle of the road. He had made no attempt to get out of the way. Like he had a death wish.

"They say he went strange around the time his wife drowned. People say he killed her, but no one could prove it. I believe it though because he was really nasty."

Carole's mind suddenly clicks into overdrive. The seaman killed his wife. Phillips may have killed his wife. No wonder there's a bloody atmosphere in the cottage! Bad enough that the old man had killed himself here. No wonder this place was selling cheap! Why didn't anybody say anything about this? "Let's get out of here."

"Where would you like to go? To the lake?"

"No. When we were down at the ruined cottage yesterday. The high land, above the forestry."

"The oak trees? Gelli Dywyll?".

"Yes. What does that mean?"

"The Dark Grove. Why do you want to go up there?"

The flat. Silent. Blinds drawn. The unpleasant smell. Cocooned from the city outside. A blue glow in the living room. A figure sitting on the sofa sipping from another whiskey bottle. Long hair falling across his face. The business suit he wears is full. Stretching with the strength of the man who is wearing it. He is slumped, staring at the picture of Carole on the iPad. Muttering under his breath. "Exodus. Chapter 22. Verse 18. 'Thou shalt not suffer a witch to live.'"

Chapter 27: The Dark Grove

Carole & Geraint walking westwards along the road. Sammy trotting behind them. The wind hissing through the trees. Big white clouds rolling over them in the sky above, but up ahead, hill fog. Not burnt off by the summer sunshine today. Unusual.

Geraint puts his arm around Carole's waist, but she shrugs it off. She is going to keep control. Everything on her terms now. After this morning and yesterday, she has to let the boy down gently. He's genuinely nice. What makes it worse is she will be seeing him every Christmas and summer she comes down here until he leaves university. Then like everybody else here, he will probably have to move away. Educated out of his square mile.

This afternoon she'll try to reset the gauge. Friends yes. Lovers no. Without breaking the lad's heart. That is quite an ask. She needs to be gentle. Carole takes Geraint by the hand.

The smile returning to Geraint's face. That was odd. Did he cross the line? No one can see them out here together. And now she's holding his hand again. He can't work Carole out. It's like she is a different girl every minute.

"You know I have a boyfriend?"

Here goes. The knot in Geraint's stomach tightens. "You've mentioned him. I've never seen him." He's lying. Keep your story straight and it'll be OK. Never even hint at what you've seen. So, this is the time to fight his corner. Be a man. How can he compete with that bastard? What can he do? All he can do is play the nice guy. "So why did this boyfriend leave you here on your own?"

"We had a fight the first night I was here. He left in the morning. But really things have been going wrong for a while. Things just came to a head I suppose."

"When is he coming back?" Feeling the sting of tears at the back of his eyes. Keep it together. Play the grown up. How long does he have to keep this up before she lets the bastard go?

"I don't know. He won't return my calls or texts. He hasn't phoned me at all." Carole weighing this up in her mind. Yes. The evidence is there. Peter and her are no longer an item. That's huge. That's fucking huge. The flat... Shit!

"So, are you going to leave him?"

A simple question, and perhaps fair enough. But things can't get more complicated with this boy. Keep control. "I could... now. It takes years to build trust, but you can lose it in a moment. And if you break someone's trust, it doesn't come back."

"So, it was a bad argument?" Damn! Don't push things. 'If someone has wounds don't scratch them' as Mam says.

"I saw a side of him I'd never seen before. It went on for hours. It was the worst argument we ever had. By a long way. It's strange I can't really remember what we were like together before the fight. It cancelled out everything we had built for three years in one evening. I tried to stop it, but he was drunk. He said and did things I couldn't believe. And I never really thought about this. I can't forgive him." Carole stops in her tracks. Raw.

She hugs Geraint. Holding him tight. Face in his chest.

"He was my first serious boyfriend after university. I met him shortly after I was looking for a job in the city after university. We met. He took me out... He put me forward for a job at the company where he works... I got the job, and that's when I found out he was living with a girl... I honestly had no idea. They split up and she left the company. All my fault but I knew nothing I swear! It explains why I never really made any friends at work. They were all her friends."

"I heard London is a dog-eat-dog sort of place."

"It is. Sometimes you have to take what you want in this world. But I'm not that kind of person. I work hard. I earn my way. I was shocked by what he had done, but he said it was all because he loved me. He was so nice to me. I believed him."

"So, were you going to get married?"

Were. Already it's in the past. "We got a place together. My mum and dad were expecting that we would. But he never asked, and I didn't push. I think I just assumed we would."

"Sounds like he made you totally dependent on him. He had you needing him for everything."

Carole pulls her face out of Geraint's chest and looks up at him. "You're very astute for your age."

"Just because I'm your toy boy doesn't mean I'm immature."

Carole laughs. "Wise beyond your years young man."

Geraint leans forward to kiss Carole, but she lets him go and turns away. She leads him by the hand further down the road.

Confusion clouding Geraint's mind again. What does this woman want? Now she's holding his hand but won't kiss him. An hour ago, she was riding him like a pornstar in her cottage. What the hell is going on here? Is she leading him up the garden path? Should he be angry? Should he play it cool? Is she having PMT? That's what the boys at rugby say when their girlfriends go nuts. Or is she genuinely nuts? Fuck! What's going on?

The mist rolls in over Capel Celyn and the forest.

They head off down the overgrown path to Nant y Cadno. Carole lets go of Geraint's hand. She leads the way, stepping quickly and urgently through the undergrowth. Geraint watches her. She's not acknowledging him now. Looking straight ahead. Seemingly detached. In her own world. Stopping at the tree line. Watching the abandoned cottage. Hiding slightly in the trees. Hiding from what?

Geraint watches, a little scared. Why is she behaving this way? "Carole?"

She doesn't respond. Like he's not there. Like she is in another time. Seeing something else. She moves off quickly within the trees. Geraint makes to follow, but she's disappeared. Gone. What the hell is she playing at?

Geraint steps out into the sunlight and walks in the general direction she went. Towards the foot of the little hill on which stands the grove. Gelli Dywyll. Looking dark even in the sunshine. Probably how it got its name.

Still no sign of Carole. "Carole!?!" Sammy running around his feet, having also lost track of her.

Geraint looks at the cottage in the sunshine. Vague images in his mind. Sitting in front of a fire. An older woman crying. Him crying. Someone has died. The chill of recognition of that feeling. A deep connection. His dad dying when he was a boy. A lump in Geraint's throat.

Hands over his eyes. "Carole?". She removes her hands. "Where did you go?" She smiles provocatively, taking him by the hand and leading him up the hill into the grove.

Pulling him by the hand up the steep slope. Already the trees here are different. The space between the trees is natural, not regimented. Hardwoods. Leafy. The sun's rays reaching through the leaves to the ground. Warming everything. Bird song. Life. She leads him climbing towards the top of the hill. A light mist rolling in up there. Sammy barks from somewhere nearby.

She runs off ahead entering a circular clearing amongst the trees as if she knew it was there. She spins around in the sunshine, and the circling leafy skyline above her head becomes like a kaleidoscope. She laughs like a child.

He looks on, seeing the thin figure spin and dance against the sky. Long dark hair flying, catching the light. He steps closer. She grabs him, wrapping her arms around him. Spinning him around. Falling to the ground. Rolling on the mossy earth. Over and over. His blonde locks entwining with her dark hair as they roll.

She pulls off his shirt straddling him. Kissing him. Biting him. Undoing breeches. Pulling them off. The mist rolling down the hillside engulfing them. Black hair on blonde as they kiss. He pulls open her dress. Cries as their bodies entwine. Moans and gasps deadened by the mist as it flows down the hillside.

A sound nearby. She stops moving. Pushing her finger to the boy's lips. He looks at her questioningly. The sound of barking in the mist now. Distant. But getting closer. Mari sits up, she pushes Owain's away. "Ssshhh!!" She looks around desperately into the mist as the barking of the dog gets louder. A branch snaps. Ifan's dark figure appears in the mist with the dog. "Ifan!"

Carole snaps back to her senses. Pushing Geraint away. Climbing to her feet. Pulling on her clothes. Confused. Looking around desperately for the source of the barking.

"What's wrong?" Geraint shaking his head to clear it.

Carole trying to get some focus. Oh God, she was having sex with Geraint again. What the hell was she thinking? This had to stop. But it's too late! "He's here!"

"Who?"

"Him! We've got to get out of here!"

The barking gets closer, it could be from anywhere in the disorienting mist.

"It's only Sammy barking…"

"Get dressed! We have to go NOW!" Carole drags on the rest of her clothes, shaking, looking desperately into the mist. Then she sees them. The ghosts.

She steps back, against a tree, dragging Geraint with her. Holding him tight. She is Carole. This is Geraint. She is not going to be a part of this!!!! She is watching from the side lines now. No longer a part of this thing. Rather watching it play out. Watching helplessly.

A shape approaching, fast and low. The blood hound sees its quarry. Owain sees Ebenezer's dog close on him too late. Crying out as the dog latches onto his throat. Grasping at the dog but his jaw has locked. Owain looking in panic to Mari for help.

Mari standing naked, screaming watching as the dog rips out her lover's throat.

Carole screaming. Now she sees a figure limp out of the mist. Ifan.

Geraint looks at her watching something that he doesn't see. Something that's not there. But he can feel it. He feels the fear. The electric in the air. Something bad is happening. He wants to run. He pulls on his clothes.

Ifan is carrying his stick which he flips around and holds like a club.

"Ifan! Na!" Mari drops to her knees in abject terror.

"Thou shall not suffer a witch to live." Ifan brings the stick down with sickening force on Mari's head.

Carole screaming!

The light goes out in Mari's eyes. She falls to the ground. Dark blood running from her nose. Ifan raises the stick again and again. Smashing it down on Mari's head. Blood splatters everywhere.

Carole holds Geraint in terror, hugging him close.

Ifan's face and clothing splattered with Mari's blood. She has long since stopped moving. He drops his stick. The stick lands beside the love-spoon Owain has made for Mari. Ifan throws the love-spoon away into the trees in fury. It distracts the blood hound. It moves away from Owain, its maw covered in gore. Owain lies dead, his throat torn out.

Carole retches. Geraint looks on in concern. "Carole?"

Ifan picks up Owain's body, dropping it into a gully amongst the trees nearby. He returns for Mari's body. He pulls her by the hair along the ground and kicks her down the same gully. He looks down at the two dead naked bodies entwined in death. He averts his eyes. He throws their discarded clothes on top of them, as if to make them look decent.

He forages around for rocks, dropping them down the gully too. And branches. Fallen leaves. Anything he can find. Furiously covering the gully with debris until there is no sign of the two bodies. Ifan screams in anguish.

He freezes, knowing someone is watching. Ifan looks up. Straight at Carole. Fear in his eyes. Seeing a ghost.

Carole and Ifan lock eyes.

Carole runs. Dragging Geraint behind her. Racing down the hill, bounding, out of control, hitting a tree, keeping her feet, losing Geraint's hand.

Geraint following her running wildly down the steep hill. Slipping. Losing his footing, sliding on his back down the slope.

Geraint gets to his feet, shaken. Carole runs back, grabs him by the hand. "Come on!!!!"

They both run passed the abandoned cottage of Nant y Cadno. Back down the forestry track. Not looking back.

Behind them the grove is enfolded by the wall of mist rolling in. In seconds the grove is hidden from view, the mist descending towards the cottage before swallowing it also.

A dog's running feet behind them in the undergrowth. Carole desperately glances back to see Sammy running behind them. She lets out a sigh of relief.

She runs out onto the road, heading back towards the cottage. Geraint and Sammy following. The mist at their backs.

Chapter 28: Remorse

Ifan looks around for any sign of the apparition he saw returning to torment him further. A woman in the woods. Dressed as a man. Screaming at him and crying. Looking at him accusingly. Sent by the Lord to punish him? But he was doing the Lord's work!

So, it must be witchcraft. A spell Mari cast as she died. Or something Mari's cohorts, those whores of Satan have done to frighten him. Or is the Lord testing him even after he has completed His work?

Ifan is shaken. He falls forward to his knees and to the ground. Prone. His sobs echo eerily around the trees of the grove as they are swallowed by the mist. This place he knew as a playground as a child. As did his forefathers. Unchanged for centuries. Untouched by human hand while the other trees of the valley were cleared centuries ago so that the people of Cwm Celyn could farm God's land.

This dark grove has been considered a sacred grove by the people of Cwm Celyn for generations. Celyn. Holly. Christ's Thorn. Sacred to God. So he was told. That was what the local vicar had said when he was a child. But the same man also said that he should keep away. Once the grove had been sacred to something else. Sacred to beliefs older than Christ. Should he have heeded that advice today? The advice of a man of God? Kept away? Avoiding the work God had told him to do?

This is where Mari was doing her worst! He needed to carry out the will of the Lord! To end this witch, his adulterous wife.

So, what was it he saw? Who *was* that woman dressed as a man? How will he find her to silence her from bearing witness to his act? Because the Law of the Land never fully corresponds to the Law of God. They should be one and the same. Sometimes, like now, they are not. If the bodies are found, he may hang.

Ifan produces his Bible for support. Psalms. Songs to the Lord. These are what are required now. His spirit needs to be uplifted. He turns to the Book of Psalms for an appropriate psalm. Many he has taught himself by rote. But not all. Scanning the tiny black text. His eye falls on one. Psalm 11, verse 5.

'The Lord trieth the righteous: but the wicked and him that loveth violence his soul hateth.'

Ifan feels a cold hand on his heart. He reads the text again. Again. Again. Rubbing his eyes. He has been tried. He has been righteous. He is not wicked. But his soul is a violent one. Since boyhood. Could it be God is telling him that he has done wrong? But, 'Thou shalt not suffer a witch to live.' He did the right thing! Surely?

Doubt wracks Ifan. God's words to support his actions. God's words to make him doubt those same actions. He wipes the tears from his eyes. He needs guidance. What is wrong? What has he done to displease the Lord?

A preacher's words ring in his ears. All are children of God. Even those heathens he meets in the ports of the world. So, are not this witch who he took into his own home and her adulterous lover from the farm next door, are they also not the children of God? Should he say a word over their grave, so they do not return to haunt his dreams? Is that what the Lord is telling him? Showing him spirits so he does not bring more upon himself in his moments of darkness and doubt? Should he ensure their entry into the Kingdom of Heaven by praying for them? Should he now be the greater man and do this? Yes! Yes, he should.

He has done his best. But as Jesus said, no one is good but God. In the Gospel according to Luke. Yes. Ifan turns to the New Testament to find the passage. To strengthen his resolve.

Ifan staggers to his feet, standing over the grave he has created for his wife, and this young boy. Words to rebuke Mari for her evil ways. Breaking God's commandments. 'Thou knowest the commandments, Do not commit adultery, Do not kill, Do not...'

In the same passage. *Mari's* sin. *His* sin. Bound in the words of Jesus. Ifan's hands begin to shake. The Bible moving too much in the murk of the fog to read clearly. He pockets the Bible and takes out his hip flask. He pours the remaining contents into his mouth. The shock on his throat making him cough and clouding his mind further. Standing in a fog of confusion. Has he done right? Has he done wrong?

Tears cloud Ifan's eyes. The fog rolls thick. Barking nearby. Ebenezer's blood hound bounds out of the mist. Its maw still red with blood. Ifan looks down at the animal. It has just killed a man but is barking at him like a pet asking for a reward. He takes the dog's lead in hand, picks up his stick and walks away back down the hill. The blood on his stick is still warm. His dead wife's blood. Covering his hand as he uses it to support him over the rough ground.

Ifan is swallowed by the mist.

Chapter 29: Trying to Burn the Past

The thick mist follows Carole and Geraint back towards the cottage. Moving through the trees more smoothly than the wind. Enfolding. Swallowing everything behind them. Closing on them. Sammy running to keep ahead of its cold grasp. Far above them the yellow sun unable to burn through, losing its power. Unable to save them from the encroaching darkness and the cold.

The fog enfolds them. Carole shivers, pulling Geraint close. Geraint as confused as ever. He is going to bed with one person and waking up with another. It's like there are two Caroles. This could get scary. What if she has a split personality or something? "Are you OK Carole?"

"I don't know. I'm frightened. What did I see up there?"

"I didn't see anything. One moment we were making love and the next..."

"We have to end this Geraint. I've got a really bad feeling about this. I don't think you should be around me. It's not your fault. I don't know. I..." Carole looks up at Geraint. Tears rolling down her face.

The knot is back in the pit of his stomach. So are the tears welling in his eyes. Shit! What did he do? Just what she wanted. That's all. And now she's crying. "Why?"

"Geraint. I'm afraid for you."

"That makes no sense. I can look after myself."

The fog rolling passed the cottage, only yards ahead but already disappearing in the encroaching gloom.

"Come inside. I'll explain."

Carole leads Geraint by the hand to the cottage door. She unlocks it. She lets Geraint in, shoos Sammy after him and slams the door behind her.

The fog rolls over the cottage. In moments the cottage is as invisible as the forest around it. No sound. Not even the wind to tie the cottage to the real world anymore.

The fog is getting through the bedroom window which has been left open to let the 'atmosphere' out. Carole is beginning to understand that just opening a window will not solve that problem. This is something deeper. Something existentially tied to the cottage. And that maybe what she has seen this afternoon is the opening of a door to understanding it.

This is now her cottage. So she is tied to the cottage. She is becoming a part of the history of the cottage. And if that's the case, that's not good.

The kettle's whistle snaps her out of her fugue. Pouring boiling water into two mugs of instant coffee. Milk. Normality after the madness in the grove. Geraint standing behind her in the doorway to the living room. She never noticed. She has to notice him. Look after him. He's the innocent in all this. She hands him his mug of coffee. "Come sit down."

Sitting on her mattress on the floor with Geraint. The chairs in here are broken. They need to go out ready to be carted away or burnt, along with that stinking mattress. Maybe she should throw out all of the furniture. Why hasn't she done this? She was distracted. More than distracted maybe.

"OK, I'll tell you what I saw up there in the grove. We were... We were making love. But it wasn't us Geraint."

"What do you mean?"

Carole trying to articulate this. Not only for a younger guy. Not only for a lover. But for herself. How to put this? "I wasn't myself. I'm often not myself when you're around. I behave like someone I'm not. I'm not a girl who takes a younger man off to the woods. But that's what's happening. It's like I'm watching myself doing it. It's not me who is making love to you Geraint. I think it's the woman who used to live here."

What the fuck? Geraint considers. That's so mad. But it

explains how he's feeling too. He's felt outside himself when he's making love to Carole. When he was watching her before they met properly. Watching her with her bastard boyfriend. "I've been feeling strange for a couple of days. Like I'm not in control. But I think it's because I'm in love with you."

Carole's eyes close. She was afraid of this.

Geraint watching her closely. "But if you're right... Does it mean we're being haunted?" That's a better thing than being mad. "Maybe possessed. It happens, my mother told me." He remembers his mother talking to the preacher about ghosts in Cwm Celyn. How the religious establishment view has changed. Acceptance of ghosts and spirits. But there would be no role for her in her chapel, despite the fact she is so devout.

Carole's face has turned white. "Possessed? By demons?"

"No, influenced by ghosts. Ghosts are usually unhappy. They create a bad atmosphere in places that were important to them. She says ghosts are only dangerous when they see something in you that they recognise. They can bring their world into yours."

Yes, that makes sense! "Peter and I fought on our first night here. It went far further than any fight we had before. The ghosts were here they saw a couple fighting, just like they did I suppose. And maybe the man left after a fight. Leaving the woman alone. To find a lover because she was so lonely. Maybe that's what is happening again. History repeating itself."

"My mother says that's what ghosts do. Repeat history over and over until the cycle is broken. But why did you see ghosts in the grove?"

"The sea captain, the wife and the lover... the murder must have happened there. That's what I was seeing."

"It's all over now." He puts a protective arm around Carole. She shrugs it off.

"I think we are in danger. I think you should leave."

"But are you going to be OK on your own? Seriously, I'm worried about leaving you here on your own, Carole."

"I'll be fine." Carole kisses him on the cheek, chastely. She gets up and leads him by the hand to the front door. "Honestly, I'll be fine." She opens the door. Geraint steps outside into the thick mist. "Goodnight Geraint. Take care in the fog, OK?" The cottage door closes on him.

Geraint is torn, not wanting to leave her. But there is no option allowing him stay here with this crazy woman. Or is she haunted? So is he haunted? He gets his bike.

It hits him. She threw him out. Anger starts to build. He stands there on his bike getting over the shock. What a bitch!

The mist is very thick. He can only just see the cottage from outside the gate, a dozen feet away. Door closed. Closing him out. Outside, alone, confused in a world obscured by a thick silent fog.

Maybe not silent. A regular sharp tapping sound somewhere in front of him coming his way. Tap. Tap. Tap. Muffled footsteps but not regular. Panting. A bark. Not Sammy. A bigger dog. A roaring angry bark. Just up ahead. The clinking of a chain. The overpowering smell of dog. And whiskey. And a man's sweat. Geraint rides away into the misty gloom as fast as he can.

Carole watching from the window. He's gone. She's on her own. That's for the best. Hopefully the lad won't be too hurt. Best get on with the reason she's here. Making this cottage her own.

Beep beep! The sound of an electronic watch. She's got to find that. It's freaking her out.

She is using the fog to hide the smoke and any problems that may come from setting a fire in the forest. She is outside the bedroom side of the cottage. Where there's just rough grass. Not the jungle of brambles on the kitchen side.

Setting fire to the mattress. Burning it in her garden. Yes, *her* garden. Getting rid of the smell. The atmosphere. The feel of someone else in her cottage. Putting the rubbish sacks of old newspapers and other clutter on the flames. The smoke merging with the mist. Sparks flying up and burning out in the dank air. No one will see this. No one will know she is burning the cottage's past.

Dragging the broken seating out of the cottage. Putting that on the fire too. She stinks of smoke. Tastes it in her mouth. It burns her eyes. Who cares? This is therapeutic. The roar of the fire in place of the hiss of the wind. Warmth in the chill air.

The flames rising higher. Carole afraid for a moment. Realising, though she can't see it, that she is surrounded by forestry for miles in every direction. Oh God! The cottage! Fetching a bucket of water in case of emergency, but there is no need. The flames die down.

Back inside. Into the bedroom. Smelling of smoke now. That's a pleasant change, but she closes the window. The bed comes apart quickly once she has turned it onto its side. Breaking the thin pieces of timber holding it together.

The bedroom door slamming behind her. As if to stop her taking anything else out of the room. She's not having that! Dragging out one half of the bed. Then the other.

Dragging them outside and dropping them onto the fire. She's engulfed in the smoke. Tears rolling down Carole's face. Not from the smoke. Good tears. Tears of freedom. Shaking off the ghosts in that room. Making the place hers.

She goes back inside her cottage. Back to the bedroom. Standing in front of the mirror. That wardrobe is too heavy to move. She looks at herself in the mirror. Face blackened by the smoke. Covered in dirt. She wedges the wardrobe door open.

Hiding the mirror. The only other thing left, a little chest of drawers. She opens the drawers. Old clothes. That smell again. A drawer at a time onto the fire. Not even bothering to go through the contents. Then the frame. All gone. Up in smoke.

Carole watches the flames die. Burning off just about everything the past owner left behind. The smoke dies. She pours the bucket of water on the embers. Carole goes inside her cottage.

In the bath, freezing because the heater is not very good. Washing the day away. The things she's burnt. And Geraint.

She falls naked on her mattress. Crying. Letting the stress out. Head in her pillow. Sammy lying down nearby. Things will look better in the morning. Carole falls asleep.

Bang!!! The front door flies open. Carole wakes with a start. The smell of dog. Not Sammy. Sammy growling and barking wildly in the darkness. The fog drifting into the living room. The bedroom door swinging open.

Carole rushes to the front door to slam it shut, remembering she is naked only when she gets there. The fog still there, as thick as ever. The smell of smoke remains. Night has fallen. What time is it? She shuts the door, locking it. She puts on the light and finds her phone. Just before 3am. What the hell? Sammy still barking wildly.

Wind blowing in from the bedroom. Carole goes to shut the door. A strong breeze coming through. Where's the light switch? Screw it.

Carole walks across the floorboards, bare feet on the dark wood. Solid floorboards but here they creak. Passing the bed on the way to the window. The bed??? She burnt the bed. Didn't she burn the bed? It's not the floorboards creaking now. Something else creaking. Carole pushes the window shut.

Wake up girl! The bed must be a trick of your mind. So

what the hell is that noise?

Carole turns around. The wardrobe. The dressing table. The bed. A woman asleep in it. A man standing at the foot of the bed. Not paying any attention to the woman in bed, nor Carole. Looking across the room. Looking at what's creaking.

Ifan. Dead, hanging from a noose. Glazed eyes. Creaking as he swings slowly from side to side.

Carole stands staring in abject fear. Breath steaming in front of her. Shivering with the cold and the fear. She puts her hand over her mouth to stifle a scream.

Ifan's eyes open. Looking directly at Carole. Recognition.

Mr. Phillips' head turns, watching her too.

Carole runs passed the apparitions, out of the room, slamming the door behind her. Breathless. Terrified. There's no key for this room. She stands there holding the door handle. Holding the door closed.

Feeling something turning the knob. Pulling on the door. Trying to wrench it from her grasp.

The sound of movement on the other side of the door. Beep beep! Carole screams.

Chapter 30: A Little Prayer

Carole stands outside the cottage. It's a little after first light. She is bagging up what's left of Mr. Phillips' belongings after they have been burnt. Breaking up the burnt remnants of the furniture and mattress with a branch. Smashing up the burnt material. Anger turning to fatigue. Stuffing the remnants into black refuse bags. Putting the bags outside the garden wall. Apparently today is bin day in Cwm Celyn.

All that's left now is just a black patch of ground and some black soot on the garden wall. She throws a bucket of water over the soot. It doesn't come off that easily.

So is the cottage clear of the ghosts after burning everything? After last night obviously not. In fact, it's worse. Right from Frances' reaction to the photo of the bedroom those months ago, she was half aware something was wrong. Not that she admitted it to herself. Not even with the slamming doors and the 'atmosphere' did she admit there was a 'problem' here.

Now she has seen a second ghost couple, and the man who must be the sea captain in the house. Shortly after she's seen him murder his wife and her lover up in the grove. And the way he looked at her. Hanging there in the noose. Watching her. Recognising her. The creaking of him hanging there. She'd heard that creaking before. And that fucking beeping watch! Before she wouldn't admit something was wrong. Now she has no choice. Carole shivers.

What was it Geraint said? Something like ghosts being dangerous when they see something in you that they recognise? When they can see you, they bring their world into yours?

Who can she talk to about this? Not Geraint. Best avoided. His mother though. At least she's approachable. OK, that's the plan. Down to the shop at opening time. She looks at her phone. Five am. It's at least a couple of hours before the shop opens. Maybe more. This is hardly the centre of civilisation. Life is slow.

Carole goes back into the cottage. She checks that the bedroom door is firmly shut. She hasn't slept. She lies down on her mattress.

Sammy barking. Orange flashing lights. The throb of a heavy engine. Carole wakes up with a start. What the hell is going on? Shouting outside. She rushes to the window. A refuse truck. Loading up the last of her rubbish bags. Roaring off up the road towards the lake. Probably the only place to turn around a truck of that size. What time is it? Just before half past seven. Life goes on. She must go on.

Walking down the road. Yesterday's fog gone. The sun already burning off what mist remains. Sammy trotting beside her. A buzz in her pocket. Her phone. Pete! Oh God!

Carole takes the phone out of her pocket. 'Dad & Mum.' Oh. Another ghost. She never got around to changing the label to the number. Mum. She hasn't phoned her since the night before she travelled down. "Hi Mum."

"Carole? Is that you? Why haven't you phoned? I've been worried sick!"

Ten minutes later the call ends. Time spent putting her mother's mind at rest that everything is going well. Peter and her are renovating the cottage, and yes, she can see it later in the summer when it's finished. And yes, she'll be coming home soon. Job done. And at least she's touched base with the outside world. The real world where there are no ghosts.

Carole walks into the village. A couple of Land Rovers have driven passed her on their way down from the mountain. Now a school bus is picking up a dozen school children from outside the shop up ahead. Is that Geraint? Oh God, he still has his exams!

Carole hangs back until the bus has gone, then walks along the road lined with emptied bins. A couple of cars driving off. All leaving Capel Celyn. Leaving it to its ghosts and the haunted girl on the Main Street.

Carole stops at the shop doorway. Looking through to see Mrs. Jones buzzing around. Carole goes inside.

"Carole bach! How are you settling in? Has Geraint done something useful up there at Pantyfedwen?" Mrs Jones is all smiles.

"Yes, thanks very much. He's a nice boy. Very intelligent."

"If he was a few years older maybe?" Mrs Jones winks.

Carole smiles awkwardly. Oh God this is difficult enough. "I need to ask you a bit of a strange question. Geraint mentioned you may know something about... Ghosts."

Mrs Jones goes pale. "Ghosts at Pantyfedwen? Oh no... Carole bach. I'm sorry! I should never have mentioned that place to you." She puts her hand over her mouth. Trying to regroup. It's all her fault. Carole is such a nice girl. Dai's daughter for God's sake. She was only trying to help her. If Phillips had died a natural death well, things would be different. Oh God no. Now there's more trouble.

"You believe me?"

Think woman. Say something. Something to placate her. "This whole valley is full of ghosts. There was a real community up on the mountains before the forestry was planted."

"I know about the farms in the woods. I've been to Nant y... Cadno?"

What the hell is she on about? Nant y Cadno? What about Pantyfedwen? There's always been trouble at Pantyfedwen. "What's happened Carole bach?"

"I've seen the sailor and his wife."

Mrs Jones puts her hand over her mouth again. Oh my God! Oh my God!

"And a young couple who lived there too."

Oh Jesus wept! And she thought that Carole was a level headed girl. Living there in London. Surely she'd put up with no nonsense? "Oh good God Carole, you've seen them?" She is Dai's daughter after all. He saw things. Damn she never considered that. How stupid is she getting in her old age?

"I think it's worse. I think I was, I am... Affected by the woman. The sailor's wife."

The blood which has drained from Mrs. Jones' face is followed by the blood from her mind too. She's speechless. How could this be happening? Carole hasn't been there more than a few days! People still told stories about that couple when she was a child. He devoutly religious, but a drunk. Going off to sea. She becoming the local wise woman. Old magic. Misunderstood, no, reviled back then. More accepted now, at least by the English who move in here. But she herself was always in two minds about it. Natural magic is one thing. Dark magic is another. A dangerous thing. Dangerous things make people dangerous. "Affected? Possessed?"

"I think so..."

She has to protect Carole from this woman. The witch of Pantyfedwen. "Ghosts are usually sad people who can't move on when they die. Sometimes they are nasty people. Nasty people make nasty ghosts Carole. But all they need is a little help to move on. Don't worry, ghosts never hurt anyone." Well not in a physical sense anyway. She thinks about Phillips. Was he always a nasty piece of work or did something make him that way? Way back before she knew him, was he ever a nice man?

"Don't I need a priest?"

"No, a blessing maybe. Move the woman on. Exorcising, that's more Church and Catholic. Demons and whatnot. A different thing entirely. These ghosts are chapel people.

Puritanical even. A priest will mean nothing to them. No, they just need help to move on. They need to be put to rest. Prayers are enough. If you're willing, I could come up there. Say a few words. It's the least I could do." Indeed it is. Time to put things right. Her fault, her place to right the fault.

"If you think it will help".

"I'll take you back up to Pantyfedwen right now. Half a mo. I'll fetch my Bible." Mrs. Jones pops behind the counter and into the house.

TP, Patricia and Frances looking at Peter's computer screen in his office. The IT guy opening up yet another email.

Patricia points angrily. "Yes, this one."

The Sent Email opens. "Why do you pursue me? You are banished from my house. As the Lord says, 'She is now in the streets, now in the squares, And lurks by every corner.' Die the death of a sodomite you whore."

TP takes a sharp intake of breath. "OK Patricia, come with me. Let's discuss what can be done." TP ushers Patricia out of the office. He whispers to Frances. "Contact his GP. Send a couple of the lads around to his flat." TP heads out.

Frances takes a deep breath. "I think we should call the police." But TP is gone. The IT man is preparing to close the account. "Wait a minute. Would you open that one please?" An email to Carole's work email.

"Witch. You cannot hide your adultery from me. Read your Bible. Deuteronomy teaches, 'If a man be found lying with a woman married to a husband, then they shall both of them die, both the man that lay with the woman, and the woman.'"

Frances swallows hard.

Mrs Jones' little red Japanese car is parked up outside Pantyfedwen. The breeze whispering this morning. Not hissing.

Calm.

A calm inside the cottage. Mrs Jones stands at the centre of the living room. Bible in hand. Eyes closed. She is finishing a prayer in Welsh. "Yn Enw'r Tad. Amen."

"Amen." Carole stands there. As if expecting something to happen. Another gust of wind slamming doors as the ghosts leave or something. She opens her eyes. "Mrs Jones, do you think this prayer will have ended my problem here?"

Mrs Jones nods, smiling. "There's only the slightest veil between the world of the living and the world of the dead. You could say history is actually alive all around us and constantly repeating itself. Her spirit should be at rest now. She shouldn't bother you again."

"I feel I've shaken her off since I saw her being murdered."

Mrs Jones still feeling as guilty for all this. But glad she has been able to put it to rest. "That must have been awful Carole. But you felt that she did not have any power over you after that?"

Carole nods. "I feel like myself again."

"Good. I'm so glad that's over and done with. I hadn't thought. Your father, bless him, he would see some things when he was a boy."

"He did. Up to the end. He told me he saw a... a doily?"

Oh God no. "A Toili? A ghostly funeral?"

"Yes. By the lake. The day he died."

Is she doing the right thing, letting Dai's girl think that she's safe from ghosts? She is never going to be safe from ghosts, just like her father was always troubled. Time to give advice. "You should be alright now, but please, you need to be careful Carole bach. Ghosts may haunt a place, but really they need people to haunt. So they are drawn to people like you. If they can see you behaving in a way they the ghost recognises, the ghosts get confused. They think they are you.

That is what has happened to you, poor dab."

She hadn't expected that. A warning. What she was after was closure. An end to this. "So ghosts can travel around with people? They could follow me?"

"If the people they are haunting travel, I expect so."

"So ghosts have free will?"

"No. They haunt. What they are doing is replaying their lives over and over. They are hurting themselves. But they could end up hurting you in the process." Oh, the soothing words are not coming out as she planned. Time to wrap this all up. "Make sure that she's gone. If you find a relic of this woman, throw it out or better burn it. Photographs especially. Throw out anything to do with these people. Clear the house."

Mrs Jones looks around. The living room now cleared. The kitchen tidy, though in need of repainting. The bedroom. The wardrobe and mirror. Otherwise clear. "I'll send Geraint up a little later to move this wardrobe out for you. Old mirrors are not a good thing to keep."

"No need, I'll manage."

"No you won't Carole bach. That thing is really heavy." She returns to the living room. "Carole, where did you get this?" Alarm in her voice.

Carole draws her eyes from the empty bedroom. Mrs Jones is holding the poppet. "I found it here. It's nice to know there were children here."

"There were never children in Pantyfedwen Carole. And this isn't a child's doll. In years gone by women up here in the hills who used to make these. It's called a poppet in English. They were a charm. Magic if you will. Used to bring people home safely from the sea or to make people fall in love with them."

"Or to hurt people. Like voodoo?" Why has she been so obsessed with that thing. It looks ugly and frightening in Mrs. Jones' hands, where it was warm, sexy in her hands.

"I don't think so. But it's a traditional magic thing. There's still witchcraft in these hills. In the nineteenth century the church and government tried to kill the old beliefs and the Welsh language. But they did neither."

"Is it valuable?"

"You should throw it out." Mrs Jones walks for the door. She crosses the garden and crosses the road trying not to look into this thing's deep black eyes. Trying not to notice how soft and warm the poppet is. How the hair wraps itself around her fingers. She closes her eyes, mutters a prayer and throws the poppet into the woods.

She re-enters the cottage looking relieved. She picks up her Bible. "I'll send Geraint up here to help you this afternoon."

Chapter 31: Regression / Possession

Semi darkness. Daylight fighting its way through the blinds on the windows. Not enough to stir him. He's still deeply asleep on the couch holding something tightly to his bare chest.

The place probably smells like it did some forty years ago when it was a squat. Funky. In the original sense of the word. Sweaty. Airless. Bad. But now it probably smells worse.

A buzz. He stirs. Another buzz. What the hell? A third long, continuous buzz. Peter opens his eyes. He sits up with difficulty, retching a bit. The object he has been holding tightly to his chest falls to the floor. A Bible.

The buzzing ends. Peter taps his iPad to check the time. Mid morning. Who the hell is that mid morning on a work day? He picks up the Bible and reopens it to The Old Testament. The good part. The guidance to deal with the shit life throws at you. Like that bitch of a... Not even a wife. He lies back down on the couch. The room stops spinning. What is he going to do about her? Follow the instructions within.

Another long loud buzz. Peter staggers to his feet, over to the door and the entry camera screen. Two of the office juniors. What the hell are they doing here? How do they know where he lives? Peter unlocks the door and heads out onto the landing, staggering dangerously down the stairs, limping to the front door. He throws it open. The two office juniors step back down the steps onto the pavement in alarm.

"Roberto. Jimmy. You are disturbing me in prayer."

"Sorry Peter." The lad's voice is shaking. What the hell is this? The clean-cut guy from work standing there in stinking jogging gear. No shirt. Unshaven. And you can smell the whiskey. Hair over his wild eyes. Grasping the Bible in his hand for grim life, whilst the other hand steadies him on the whitewashed pillar outside the door. "Frances said we should bring you with us to the office."

"Ensuring my attendance? Tell that negress I shall not attend. I have other matters which need my urgent attention. She and you can go to hell." Peter disappears inside and slams the door.

Painting the walls of the living room has been a better experience than doing that kitchen wall. With the dirt of ages gone, the emulsion lies thick on the walls. No bleed from the colour of the paint beneath. The walls shining and rapidly drying to a beautiful clean matt. The room changing its tone and its smell with the fresh paint. Carole lost in her playlist of trance music on her iPhone. The earbuds blocking out the hiss of the wind as it blows through the cottage, blowing away any remaining 'atmosphere' now Mrs. Jones has done her Exorcist stuff. OK, her nice gentle 'helping the spirit move on' stuff. Seeing off that girl who used to live here and died up in that grove of trees all those years ago. History now. Gone. Soon to be completely forgotten, lost in time.

Carole shudders remembering the violence of the death she had 'seen'. Just in the same way her Dad had described how he 'saw' things when he was younger. Understanding now at last why Dad never spoke about it, even in the days when she thought it was cool. Not a gift. Not at all. More of a curse.

The trance music takes her mind as she dips the roller in the paint and continues working down the wall towards the front door. The music stops. Her phone is ringing. Carole wipes some stray paint off her hands and fishes the phone out of her jeans pocket. 'Work'. Meaning her old work. Peter? Oh fuck!

"Pete?"

"Hi Carole, no it's Frances. Sorry to bother you. Listen, this is urgent. Has Pete been in touch with you?"

"Frances, hi. Er no, I haven't heard from him since

Sunday. I've been phoning but he hasn't been answering my calls. Oh God, is something wrong? Has he been in an accident?"

A moment of silence at the other end of the phone. "No, nothing like that. He's been very flaky in work, Carole. Now he is skipping work completely..."

"That's not like him. Is he sick?"

"Maybe. We found some of his emails. Disturbing. Some are very threatening."

"What? Threatening to who?"

"You, amongst others..."

"But I haven't had any emails from him".

"They went to your work email account. That's been suspended since you left. Carole, I sent a couple of the office lads around to find him. At your flat. Apparently, he was in a hell of a state."

"Oh my God! You mean he was sick? What are you going to do?"

"He was drunk Carole. Rolling drunk at eleven in the morning. Not much we can do. But it may be too late. He's really screwed things up with some of our clients with these emails he's sent." A long pause. "I'm just letting you know that all is not well. Should you speak."

Carole stands in silence, not knowing what to think. How can he have gone downhill this fast? He was here a few days ago. But never so angry. Never ever violent like on that night. Her first night in this cottage. Their first...

"Carole?"

Carole snaps out of it. "Thanks. Thanks for letting me know."

"One more thing. It's not my business I know. Do you have a new boyfriend?"

What the hell? How could she know about Geraint? Oh God! "No."

"OK. Take care yeah?"

"Thanks Frances. I will."

The line goes dead. Carole stares at the phone. What the hell's going on with Pete? Something moves in the daylight outside. She looks up. A tall figure silhouetted against the light. She drops her phone in shock, suppressing a cry. The figure from last night? No. "Pete?"

"Hi."

Geraint. Filling the doorway. Looking older than his years until he steps inside where she can see him clearly. A young kid really. What the hell had she been thinking this week? Oh God.

Geraint stands in the doorway. Unsure of how this crazy woman is going to react. He's going to play things very... Professional. "Mam said you wanted me to come up here and help move some furniture."

"Hi Geraint. Thanks for coming up. I bet it's very difficult for you coming here."

What the hell does that mean?

"I'm glad you're here. I'm glad we're still friends. Your mum sent the spirit of the young woman away. The one haunting me. I guess they've all gone. Including yours. If you think the young lad is having an influence on you, let her know. I feel so much better after her blessing, I can't tell you."

Oh no! Religion meets hippy shit. She is bonkers. Don't get drawn into it. "What do you need me to do Carole?"

"I like you. But we can't be anything other than that anymore. Just friends. In case they come back. It's too dangerous."

Oh Christ, it's not working. She is so bloody gorgeous. Geraint feels the now familiar knot in his stomach. "Why dangerous?"

"Last night. In the middle of the night. There were sounds from the bedroom." She's beside Geraint now, frightened like a little girl. Taking his arm. "There were ghosts. I saw them. But I know your mum sorted it. She told me to get the last of the furniture out of there. The last of the things of the past. So I can burn them. Can you help me?"

Geraint nods.

"Thanks Geraint." She leads him by the arm to the bedroom. She opens the door.

The 'atmosphere' is still here. Curtains flapping in the gentle breeze moving through the room now the door is open. "It was horrible. The man was hanging just over there. I really don't want to be in here."

"So you want the wardrobe moved?" Geraint trying not to get drawn in again. To get hurt again. But it's not working.

"Get it out of my house!"

"Anything else I may be good for? Or shall I go home then?"

Oh no. "I never meant to hurt you Geraint. And I do care for you. The point is we're not puppets replaying the lives of old flames who haven't moved on from this place. We are our own people. We've got to end this. You and I, we both need to shake off these ghosts."

He limps along the pavement. Orange hazard lights flash. He drops into the Porsche. Tossing a holdall bag onto the passenger seat. Strapping himself into the body-hugging driver's seat. A seat a little bit tighter around him than usual. His hooded top filled by a bigger build. Hair rubbing against the convertible roof. Dropping the seat as far as it can go. Adjusting the rear-view mirror. Hair hiding his face.

Ignition. The engine throbs. He feels cocooned in this throbbing machine. The machine roaring as he pulls away, pushing him hard in the small of his back. Exhilarating like a ship in full sail suddenly catching the wind. Braking hard and being pushed back into the seat. Man and machine joining the traffic at the main road at the exit from the square. Aggressively pushing into the flow of traffic westwards. Turning up the music to drown out the voice in his head. The voice saying "No. No. No. No. No."

The Porsche prowling like an angry animal through the traffic. Soon on the dual carriageway heading west. Tall buildings towering on either side of the motorway. Figures in the windows working indoors on this lovely day. Clerks counting the money when honest sailors like him risk their lives to colour their balance sheets.

Huge televised billboards lining the roadside. Two lanes of traffic becoming three. Three lines of sparse traffic leaving the city heading west. On the other carriageway thousands of cars standing still, queuing to enter the city.

The sat-nav view opening out showing the motorway stretching out forever. The Porsche moves effortlessly into the outside lane. Travelling in a fast moving convoy of cars, up to over 80 miles per hour then coming to a stop, then starting again. No apparent reason for the ebb and flow. Soon the road will be clearer. Soon.

Ahead above the motorway a line of planes with lights on seem to hang in the sky. Bringing thousands more people every minute into this city.

But he is leaving now. Heading back to the cottage he built with his bare hands in one night. To the piece of land he claimed by throwing his axe at dawn. All of it done for his cheating wife. Time to correct his mistake.

He is heading for the open fields of the Celyn Valley. Home. The traffic comes to a halt again. He types Capel Celyn into the sat nav.

Chapter 32: Beneath

"It's bloody freezing in here." Is he really talking to himself or to the other person in this room? Geraint's skin is covered in goosebumps. Checking behind him. He can feel someone watching him. Close. Angry. But there is no one to be seen.

The scream of the kettle boiling in the kitchen. Geraint jumps. Jeez, he's really nervous. He sees the hairs standing up on his forearms.

Geraint works on dismantling the wardrobe. And the sooner he can get that done the better. He came here very nervous about being around Carole after the way she just broke up with him. Carole has been all consuming this week. Screw his exams, he hasn't been able to think about anything else. A rollercoaster ride doesn't start to describe it. And now he has reverted to his childhood fear of this place.

He and his friends used to ride their bikes as fast as possible past the cottage on their way to the lake. His father had told him to keep away from the place because of the ghosts, but obviously it was to keep away from Phillips.

Geraint had seen music documentaries on the BBC about ageing punks. Some of them reminded him of Phillips, even if he was twenty years older than them. They seemed to be difficult, hard men. Maybe they were in part, but it was really an act. But Phillips didn't act. He was. He would have been the town bogeyman if there was a town, and if there were bogeymen.

Bogeymen are not monsters. They are people. So they are far more frightening than monsters anybody made up. They don't disappear when the sun comes up. They are always there. Always a menace. Somehow most kids naturally understand this. And horror films remind the rest.

Once Phillips took a boy hostage for a few hours, for

spying on him. Forty years or more ago, long before he was born. Those were different times his dad had said. The police were called. Nothing happened to the boy, so nothing was done so nothing was said. That was that. Except all the children were told to keep away from the haunted cottage. And so by implication from Phillips. The bogeyman.

If he'd kept away from the haunted cottage this week maybe he wouldn't be feeling as hurt, angry and confused as he does now. Wound up and wanting to lash out. But that isn't down to Phillips. No. It is down to her.

The last of the screws come out. The mirrored wardrobe door comes loose. Geraint gently lowers it. Something reflected moving behind him. Geraint drops the mirror in surprise. He spins around. Carole with his coffee.

"Careful! That could have been seven years bad luck!". Carole holds out Geraint's mug of coffee.

"I'll drink that outside if you don't mind." Geraint picks up the heavy mirrored door and carries it out of the room, leaving Carole holding his coffee.

The mirror leans beside the front door. Two half drunk coffee cups in front of it. Carole and Geraint reflected in it, carrying some of the remaining parts of the wardrobe to the place where she lit the fire last night.

Geraint drops his pile of wood and walks away, leaving Carole pointedly alone. Geraint marches off wordlessly into the cottage. Carole watches him go, partly exasperated, partly sympathetic. Noticing the way his head is tilted forward and his shoulders sag. Hurt. Totally different body language to Pete who was wound up tight in his anger at her on Sunday morning. Was it really only Sunday morning? She follows Geraint inside.

Geraint stomps from the living room into the bedroom. The

sound of his footsteps turning from pats on the solid earth floor to the more percussive floorboards as he crosses the bedroom towards the remains of the bed. Stepping on floorboards that groan and give under his feet. Geraint stops in his tracks.

These floorboards look the same as the others. Geraint taps on the surrounding floorboards. Then the four in this section of floor. These sound hollow. A little play in them. They actually bow when he stands on them. Why? And why should he care?

"What's the matter?"

Geraint looks up at Carole with a scowl. What's the matter? You've broken my heart you bitch! You've changed me. But what do you care? "These floorboards. It's like there's something hollow beneath them. Is there a cellar?"

"I wouldn't think so. This cottage is pretty basic."

"You're probably right. It's a *Ty Un Nos*. A one night house. If someone could build a house in one night on Common Land it was theirs. And the land around it too as far as the builder could throw an axe. Nant y Cadno is a *Ty Un Nos* too."

Carole can't help but smile. An old head on a young body. "How do you know this stuff?"

"School project." Her smile. It breaks Geraint's scowl. "Most of them, like *Nant y Cadno* are buried in the forestry now. Our primary school teacher brought a few of us up here to see if Phillips would let us do a project on this cottage." Geraint smirks.

"What happened?"

"Phillips told her to fuck off in front of the whole class. We'd whisper 'fuck off' in an old man's voice behind her back all the time after that." Her laugh. Oh God... "So why do these sound hollow?"

"We just need to nail them down properly."

"Do you mind if I take a look?"

"You don't know what can of worms you might be opening up there." But why not? The boy is doing her a favour and if it helps get them back on better terms. "There's a er... claw hammer in the kitchen drawer. Second one down. That might get the nails out."

Geraint heads off to the kitchen. Carole gets on her knees and taps the floorboards. He's right. This bunch sound very different. Could there be something underneath? Should she leave it alone? No, she needs this place to give up its past. Out with the old...

Geraint stands behind her. Hammer in hand. Looking down at her. At the back of her head. The weight of the hammer making his arm feel strong. At one with the hammer. His mind racing out of control. The lust that turned to love that turned to hate that has turned to anger that is turning to rage. The hammer arm starts to swing. Beep beep.

"Did you hear that?" Carole turns around and takes the hammer from Geraint. "That beeping. It's like someone's watch. But where is it?"

Geraint coming back to himself. "Yes, I heard it."

Carole hooks the claw side of the hammer down the side of the floorboard and tries to wrench it free. It lifts a little, the two old nails holding it down raising with the old wood.

"Let me." Geraint uses the hammer claw to remove the two nails. A whiff of mildewed air. He coughs. "Carole, look, there's definitely a space under this." Geraint begins work on the other end of the board, freeing it, pulling out the nails. He flips over the floorboard to reveal what's beneath.

There is no cellar, rather a shallow hole. The joist on which the floorboards lie has been knocked aside to make room for an old sail-cloth bag, discoloured to black by damp mould. The release of mildew and fungus forcing Geraint to his feet in a fit of coughing.

It hits Carole. The 'atmosphere'. Overpowering. Like a

wave breaking over her. Carole choking on her words. "What the hell is that thing?"

"A bag I think." Geraint loosens the next floorboard. In a moment it's up too. Lying beneath, the bag is around six feet long and quite broad. Tied with rope. Bag and rope once white are now mouldy and black.

"Why is it buried in the cottage?"

"It must be valuable to be hidden away like this." Geraint positions himself kneeling over the bag, ready to lift it, taking the strain as he was taught in weight training. The bag flies out of the hole, not as heavy as it looked. It thumps onto the floorboards. The ropes are just wrapped around the bag to keep it closed. As the wrap comes apart, white dust from the bag whitens his hands. "This dust… it's lime…"

"It doesn't smell like limes."

"Lime. Farmers put it on land that's acidic to help things grow."

Geraint struggles to open one end of the bag. Something beneath the coating of lime. Geraint brushes the lime away and snaps back his hand. A human skull.

The sunlight suddenly white hot and blinding him. The dust filling his mouth and nose, burning and choking. Stinging his blinded eyes. He can't breathe. The car veers sharply to the left across two lanes of traffic on the motorway. Car horns and the screech of brakes of fast moving vehicles nearby. The Porsche's powerful brakes pulling it to a halt on the hard shoulder. Whooshes as huge trucks whizz past inches away. He rubs the dust from his eyes, squinting against the blinding light. Coughing the dust from his lungs. He is as white as a ghost. Gasping for breath. What happened?

Geraint is shaking. Near panic. Why the hell did he come here today? His brain spinning. Talking to help keep it all together. "Lime is an alkaline. It used to be put on dead bodies." He retches.

Carole puts her arms around him, hugging him from behind. Looking down at the two eye sockets staring back at her. The sockets getting deeper, and the teeth being revealed as the breeze blows the lime off the face. "What are we going to do?"

The folded sailcloth is falling away. The lime dust revealing a dark coat. Nineteenth century probably. The once white shirt is now grey black, stained by the decomposed body beneath. Something in the jacket pocket. A piece of paper or card. Geraint snatches it quickly, not wanting to touch the body. The card is folded in two.

"What's that?"

Geraint unfolds the card. A photograph, Covered in dust. He blows away the dust. Two figures outside a chapel. "That's Bethlehem. The chapel in Capel Celyn. It's just been rebuilt. See the date? 1904."

Carole stares in horror. Recognising the faces. The couple from the cottage. The man and the woman he killed up at the Dark Grove. "The sea captain and his wife. This is the sea captain. They never found him, remember? So why is his body here?"

"You said you saw him hanging? If he killed himself, he wouldn't have been given a proper burial. Being a murderer and a suicide, he couldn't be buried on holy ground."

"Oh God, he has been here all the time. He's caused all this. I want this murdering bastard out of my house!" Tears start to roll from Carole's eyes. She begins to cry. To sob. Her whole body shaking. Her dreams of a place to remember her father turning into a horror show. Her relationship in tatters. Her boyfriend losing his mind back in London. And her young lover in her arms. But he's not her lover anymore.

Geraint unwraps her arms from around him. He helps her to her feet and leads her out of the room. Out of the cottage.

Sammy trotting over to see what's wrong. Carole sitting on the ground, leaning against the garden wall cuddling her dog. The photograph still in her hand. Geraint watching all this reflected in Phillips' mirror, hoping he has no more part to play in this. He walks over to the pile of firewood which was the wardrobe. He sets fire lighters amongst the remains of Phillips' furniture and strikes a match.

Hidden by the sound of the crackling flames and the shattering of the mirror in the fire, the creaking starts again. Ifan hanging from the rope in the bedroom. Swinging slowly. Dead eyed. The barking of the blood hound thudding like a slow heartbeat. Ebenezer looking on. Eye to eye with the corpse. Closing Ifan's eyes with his fingers. Cutting Ifan down. Rolling him in the sail cloth. Covering him with lime. Raising the floorboards. Rolling him into the floor. Replacing the floorboards. Ritual without ritual.

Leaving the cottage leading the dog. Sammy barking wildly.

Carole gets to her feet and joins Geraint who is looking into the flames of the fire, consuming what's left of Phillips' possessions. "People used to believe that photographs captured people's souls." She tosses the picture of Ifan and Mari into the flames. "Let's set them free. Good riddance." The picture crinkles up and is devoured by the flames.

Chapter 33: Within the Woods

The car has made good time across England. Before it stretches a long open bridge across the massive tidal river. The biggest tidal range in Europe, surges and currents he once knew well. Across the bridge, signs of welcome in his own language to his own country. This world has changed, or has it? Soon he swings the car north into the heartland.

A turreted fairy tale castle he only previously saw through smoke. Castell Coch. The Red Castle. A romantic reworking of a building created to control his people by the richest man in the world. A man who took this wealth from deep within the heart of this land. A man whose coal he used to ship away from the ports which that same man had built in Cardiff for that very purpose. His own place in this cycle of exploitation makes him as guilty and as helpless as any other Welshman who dug or carted away the riches of his land for such masters.

The fast moving traffic taking him in moments passed places he once had to travail by train or coach. No smoke in the air now. Just a landscape long since stripped of trees to feed industry. Now stripped of industry. Open mountain now. Bare. Bleak under leaden skies that remind him of the smoke that used to hang over this land.

Smoke disappearing into the gloom of the trees. The flames have died, leaving only charred and burnt wood, turning to ash in the wind in front of his eyes. The embers of the last of Phillips' possessions. Closure. For her at least.

The photograph of Ifan and Mari now also ash in the wind drifting into these dark pines which have overrun their land. A place that newlywed couple would not recognise now. That place they knew is now hidden beneath these trees. Living trees which have sucked the life from this valley, creating a desert on this once fertile farmland.

Geraint empties a bucket of water over the embers. He turns to return the bucket to the cottage. Carole is standing in the doorway. "Is the fire out properly?"

Geraint nods. "Did you phone the police yet?"

Carole shakes her head. "I think we should go up to the Dark Grove, to see if we can find the bodies of his wife and the boy."

"Why? What good would that do?"

"It would put their souls to rest. It's the right thing to do. I can get my life back." A pause. "We can get our lives back Geraint."

So, he is forever an afterthought. Screw this. "Leave it to the police." Geraint puts down the bucket and walks out of the gate.

"Please Geraint. Come with me. What if the police can't find their bodies? This might go on and on."

"How do you know where to find them?"

"I saw what he did with the bodies. I know where they are in the grove." Carole looks pleading. "Come on. You and I can put an end to this."

Geraint picks up his bike leaning outside the garden wall. Carole runs after him with Sammy following. She grabs his arm. She won't let him leave. He throws the bike back down. Defeated. She is going to have her way. He pulls his arm away and buries his hands in his pockets. "Come on then. Let's get on with it."

Not a word spoken as they walk. Geraint keeping his distance from her. Cold and angry. The very air is getting cold around Carole. The sky whitening up ahead. The weather can change so quickly up here. The trees seem to blot out everything including any sense that you are in the foothills of the mountains. Quite high up. The whiteness up ahead is low cloud. Soon to be fog. It can be cold here even at the warmest time of year. And Carole feels very cold and lonely on this narrow forest track right now.

Would this really work? Exhuming the bodies? Getting them taken away. Would there be a burial? A service to put them to rest? Would that work anyway?

Mrs. Jones' little exorcism was for the Sea Captain's Wife. Not for the Sea Captain. Nor the boy. How could she not have thought of that? No sign of her ghost since Mrs Jones had been there. But the Sea Captain? Has she thought this through? Oh God. And the one person she could talk this through with, is walking silently and sullenly a little distance in front of her.

Geraint peels off into the trees. Damn, she almost missed the pathway to Nant y Cadno. Geraint wordlessly leading off down the overgrown path towards the light beyond. Carole and Sammy follow. Breaking the treeline. Crossing the open ground to the tumble-down cottage of Nant y Cadno. Its history as a place built in one night to claim a stake on this land, now buried and forgotten in the forest. It's taken sixty or more years for the cottage to begin its fall back into the earth. Its walls are strong. It will probably still be standing here within the woods when her days are over.

Up ahead the Dark Grove. Black against the white sky. A rumble nearby. Low, continuous. Thunder? No. Moving away now.

Geraint is already climbing the slopes. Carole runs to catch up with him.

Carole slipping on the wet ground. Geraint reaching down to help her up. The smell changing, from faint pine to strong earth. Grass. The scent of flowers. Geraint pulling her into another world within the world of the forest. The trees older. Thicker. Having been here for centuries. Moss underfoot now. Her feet bouncing on it as she and Geraint and climb the hill hand in hand. Sammy scampering behind them.

It's getting darker now under the canopy of the trees, broken up with patches of sunlight through the breaks in the boughs.

Geraint turns to look at her for the first time since they left the cottage. "So where are we going?"

Suddenly she is not sure. "Let's keep climbing." The trees are not the same, irregular, and she can't remember any detail. Oh God, she has only been here once. What if she can't find the place she saw the Sea Captain dump the lovers' bodies?

Carole and Geraint walk into the circular clearing. Everything comes flooding back. Their bodies entwined. The fog drifting in. Pleasure. Abandon. Fear. Fear that they were not themselves. Fear that they are not alone. Fear that someone was coming. Coming through the trees. Coming with murder on his mind.

"This is the place." Geraint looking around. Recognising the place where they were making love when she freaked out and dragged him away screaming. A mix of emotions as he looks at Carole in the dappled light. The girl he wanted, he had and had now rejected him. All in the space of a few days. The confusion and anger rising again.

"Yes. This is the place." Carole looking around. Trying to remember where Ifan took the two blood covered bodies. Only half remembered now, like a dream. Relived so clearly, and then, bang, it's gone. What's the word for it? A phantasm. She saw ghosts. But it wasn't a fantasy. Come on, think...

"So where are the bodies?" He wants to get away. Fetch his bike and go home. Go back to his room and let this flood of emotion out where no one can see him. Especially her.

Carole starts walking towards Geraint, concentrating hard. Geraint steps back and slips. He falls into a hollow in the ground. Knee deep. Filled with stones and debris.

Carole shaking. "Here."

Geraint scrambles out of the hole in alarm. He's not ready to come face to face with dead people again.

Carole crouches down. The floor of the hollow is wet moss, covering loose stones beneath. She tosses the moss aside and sets about removing the stones, one by one. "Give me a hand."

Geraint reluctantly helps removing the stones. He pulls aside some more moss. Pulling up debris, moving the stones aside. Not really wanting to find anything but getting this over and done with. The sooner this is done, the sooner he can get his bike from the cottage and get away from her.

Carole working frantically beside him. Her fingers brush something too smooth to be a rock. Very smooth. Round. But cracked like a broken pot. A deep round hole. Then another. A skull. "Oh God."

Carole looks down at the skull, cracked on one side from Ifan's blows. Mari. Tears well in Carole's eyes. "We've found them. She pulls away at the stones and debris around. Two skeletons under the rotted remains of their discarded clothes. Lying side by side. Revealed after a century and more of being hidden in a ditch in a wood, yards from where they died.

Geraint is shaken. Not expecting Carole's madness to be based on any reality. "OK, we've found them. Call the police."

Carole reaches for her phone in the back pocket of her jeans. It's not there. "I've left my phone at the cottage."

Geraint sighs in disbelief. He produces his phone. "I have no signal. I can't stay here." Geraint walks back across the clearing and down the hill.

Carole looks down at the remains of Mari and Owain. Two lovers murdered here over a hundred years ago. She and Geraint have been swept up in the story. Now it should come to an end. No more tragedies.

The mist starts to swirl through the grove. Carole turns around to speak to Geraint. She is alone. Geraint is gone.

Phillips standing in the mist. Standing in the road as he has always done when that devil drives him from his home. Standing motionless. Emotionless.

Standing emotionless at her funeral. Decades ago. The people of Capel Celyn there at Bethlehem in numbers as his wife is laid to rest. Sympathetic faces. Suspicious faces. A couple of police. Watching him for emotion. But they won't see it.

Emotion on another face though. That of the red eyed school teacher she took to his home. The police should be watching him. He heard that the police had interviewed him, but he had an alibi for the time that his wife fell into the lake and drowned.

Phillips is the only one without an alibi. But nothing can be proven. Nothing will be proven. Rachel left the house alone to go to the lake for a walk. She must have slipped and fallen into the lake. She couldn't swim. Nothing unusual there. A tragic accident. Phillips had found her at first light when he went out to search for her. The hair falls over Phillips' face as he steps forward and looks down at her coffin deep in the grave.

Phillips standing emotionless looking down at the body lying in his dead wife's garden. The school teacher. It's taken weeks of waiting at the cottage door. Drinking whiskey and waiting. Waiting for him to pass alone. Striking up a conversation this evening. Reaching out to his wife's former colleague. Her lover. Driving the knife home repeatedly. A frenzy of anger unleashed on the man who caused him to kill his wife.

Digging in the freshly dug earth where the cess pit has been installed. A shallow grave for a shallow man. No one will notice the ground disturbed. Phillips covers the body in her garden at Pantyfedwen. She won't care. She won't be using it again.

Chapter 34: Coming Home

"Geraint, wait!" Geraint is pacing off across the open ground beside the ruin of Nant y Cadno. High stepping through the tangled long grass which would trip him if he tried to run. Sammy scampering at his feet.

Carole is slipping and sliding down the mossy lower reaches of the hill from the Dark Grove. Behind her the mist is looming over the hillside. Carole reaches the level ground at the foot of the hill and runs after Geraint. Not wanting to be alone here in a place of ruin and death.

Geraint leaving. Getting the hell out of here. Going as fast as he can away from this place with two dead bodies to where he left his bike. Only one dead body there. Rotting in a bag under the floor for over a hundred years. Tainting the place. Making it foul. Making it a bad place. And he knew that it was a bad place. So why did he get involved in all this? Carole. Who took advantage of him. He has to get away from her, but she grabs him by the arm.

"Wait for me. Please Geraint." She pulls him to a halt and hugs him. "I was right. It'll all be over now. You'll see. Once we talk to the police."

"Once you talk to the police. Leave me out of this."

Carole looks up. Geraint's face hard. Angry. A child-man. Not a man yet. A good boy, but unable to cope with this.

Was she really able to cope with this? The aftermath of a century old murder-suicide. How to explain this to the police? Regardless, she has to finish this. Shake off the ghosts, put them to rest, and get back to her life. Here and in London. And there's still Peter to resolve. "You're right. OK, I'll deal with this once I get back to the cottage. You go home. Don't mention this to anyone."

Geraint nods. Carole leads him off through the trees, down the overgrown pathway to the road. Out on the roadway Carole lets Geraint go, expecting him to head back to Capel Celyn. But he turns with her and heads back towards the cottage. His bike. Of course.

Carole and Geraint continue up the road, wordlessly. The mist rolling in fast now, descending and thickening. In a couple of minutes they are walking through thick fog, the only sound their footsteps and Sammy panting as he trots beside them. The deadened sounds amplifying Geraint's silence. Still angry. Still very hurt. Carole reaching for something to say. Not finding anything.

The mist cools them, their clothes now wet against their bodies. Carol shivering, wishing for a hug that is not coming. The dampness on her face could be mistaken for tears.

The tall shadows of the trees looming over them, just visible through this low cloud. The gloom and the trees. Enclosing them, oppressing them. And then the break in the trees on the right. Her cottage. It will be truly hers once that body is gone. Strange, the swirling mist looks like smoke rising from the chimney. The light playing tricks on her. She thinks she can even smell the smoke. It must be the remains of the bonfire.

Sammy bounding forward, barking, and trotting excitedly through the open door, tail wagging. The open door? She shut it, surely? Locked it? No, she doesn't have her keys nor her phone. Leaving her house unlocked? City living had taught her never to do that. She'd never have done that today unless she was so obsessed with closure. Finding the bodies.

Why would the door be open? Could that body have got up and walked away? What a stupid idea. "Sammy?" She can hear the dog barking excitedly inside. A growl. Carol stops at the gate. The same growl Sammy made when they first got here. Something's wrong.

Geraint is getting on his bike, wordlessly, with his back

pointedly to Carole.

"Geraint. The door wasn't open when we left."

Geraint looks at her quizzically. "Really?"

Sammy barking. Angry growls now. Then a yelp and a whine. Then nothing.

Geraint gets off his bike, and sweeps passed Carole into the cottage. Into a foggy gloom with fire light. A fire in the hearth. "Sammy?" His eyes taking a second to adjust light in here. The dog lying on the floor in the middle of the living room. Neck at an unusual angle. Sammy looking asleep but broken. What the? A smack to the back to his head. Blood in his nose and mouth. Stars in his eyes. The floor rushing up to meet him, but he doesn't feel the impact.

Carole hears the thud, and the silence. No more barking. Silence. No wind in the trees. Nothing. "Geraint?" No reply. "Geraint, what's wrong?" Silence. Should she run away? Why? Because her dog and her boyfriend... Her friend aren't making any sound? Geraint was in no mood for games. Would he jump out and scare her to get back at her? He's very hurt, and very angry. Anything could be going on in his head.

Fear rises in her stomach. Fight or flight? No, she's not bloody running away, not after digging up bodies. What could be worse than that? "Geraint!?!"

Carole rushes towards the cottage. Firelight in the gloom. Oh God! Things on the floor, taking shape. SLAM!!! The door closes behind her. The 'atmosphere', very strong now. And a different smell. Familiar, evocative and suddenly very frightening. Petrol.

Carole spins around. A figure wearing a hoodie blocks the door. Oh Jesus Christ! The arsonists!

She takes everything in. Her dog. Dead at her feet. Neck snapped. Who would do that to an animal?

Geraint, lying on the floor. Face away from her, blood on the top of his head. A holdall bag and a petrol can nearby.

Clang! A tyre iron hits the stone floor. Carole jumps out of her skin.

The figure in the doorway looks at her angrily. Face red in the fire light. Peter. But it can't be! He's... Bigger. Darker. With dark angry eyes. Not the man she knows.

Carole's mouth dry with fear. She can hardly speak. "Oh my God Pete, you've killed him!!"

Peter smiles, which turns into a sneer. "Good! Practice makes perfect, don't it?" He turns the key in the door behind it. It snaps locked.

Carole runs into the kitchen and tries the back door. Locked. She searches around desperately for the key. She turns around. Peter stands in the doorway, holding the back door key in his hand.

"You think I'm fucking stupid? Running away from me. Ruining me. Hiding up here in the mountains with some local kid. I bet he fancied a big city girl, eh?"

"Pete, it's not like that." Or is it? It could look that way. She looks around desperately. The knife block. Empty. Oh God, he's thought of everything!

"You've done me a big favour here. I was all set to torch this place, with you in it. Arsonists would get the blame. Perfect."

An emptied bleach bottle in there Belfast sink. He has thought of everything. Oh Christ! "Pete. Please don't…"

"Shut up, I'm thinking. This is beautiful... B plan. Lone woman in a remote cottage, attacked by the local rapist. He kills her. Her boyfriend turns up unexpectedly, finds the geezer still in the house, and kills the bastard in the struggle. Any jury would let me walk. Simples." That frightening smile again. Carole has never seen it before. He's not himself. Like she wasn't herself. Oh God...

"Pete listen to me… I know it's not you doing this… please Pete, fight it… I shook off the ghost of the girl. Shake him off Pete. Don't let him control you! This isn't you. Fight him!"

A moment of doubt crosses Peter's face. Carole rushes him, slamming into him with all of her might, knocking him backwards. She loses her footing and falls hard on the living room floor. Peter lands beside her, face to face with her on the floor. Or is it Peter?

"Ast!!! Putain!!!"

Not Peter's voice. Words in Welsh Carole half knows. Female dog. Bitch. The other one, similar to Spanish maybe? How does Pete know these words? Carole looks Peter in the eyes. Those darker eyes. Partly hidden under Peter's hair.

"You killed your wife and her lover… isn't that enough? Why Mr Phillips' wife? Why me?"

"You are all whores. The ruin of honest men. Homed and fed, but unfaithful. Biting the hand that feeds you."

"Oh no. You're wrong, and these are different times. I'm my own woman. Peter and me aren't married. I own this house. Me! Times have changed, and your time has passed. Move on! Let Peter go. Leave us in peace. Get out of my house!"

He lunges at Carole, who rolls out of the way kicking out at him. He recoils, hurt. Carole jumps to her feet and turns on him, kicking him time after time to the head, then the body. He rolls over to shield his head from the reign of blows. He stops moving.

Carole stands over him panting. The panting turning to gasps, turning to sobs. "Oh God Pete. He's got into you!" She sees her dead dog and tears flow. Nearby Geraint lies motionless on the ground. She drops to her knees beside Geraint. "Geraint can you hear me?" She shakes Geraint who does not stir. "Geraint!!!" She shakes him again. Oh God, how could things have come to this?

The stench takes her breath away just as two strong hands grab Carole around the throat, pulling her back into his arms.

She tries to get her hands beneath his. He's bigger and stronger than Peter. And angry. Pressing harder. She can't speak. Can't breathe. Can't struggle. The darkness intensifies around her. Masking the world. Her arms fall away.

His breathing as harsh as hers as he whispers in her ear. "Why did you betray me? I gave you everything!"

Carole's eyes close. She falls limp in his arms.

Chapter 35: Passing

He looks down at her lying on the floor. Tears in his dark eyes. "Why Carole? I gave you everything!" He glances across at the body of the teenager with whom she had betrayed him within just days up here in the mountains.

He tenses. His body expanding. Hair falling across his eyes. "Ast!" He gets to his feet, distancing himself from her body. Their bodies.

Time to get on with the plan that has distilled and matured in the darkness of his mind all week. He picks up the petrol can and heads for the bedroom. He opens the door. The air is stifling. Dead, or worse. The room now empty of furniture, desolate. A hole in the floorboards. White lime dust spread all around on the black floorboards. The canvas bag open on the floor. The body visible within. His body. Dried and rotten. His clothes perished. His face gone leaving his skull. His time over.

His body quakes with a shudder. He covers his mouth to stifle a scream. They say if you die in your dreams, you die in real life. This is not a dream. This is real. Too real. Shattering. Remembering his coat splashed with their blood. His waistcoat. His shirt. Trousers. Boots. All there. Bloody and muddy from the deed done.

Ifan sways. Reality hitting him in waves. Something is not the same. Where is the picture of Mari and him on their wedding day? No sign of it. He tucked it in his waistcoat pocket. His memory of a better day. Before her witchcraft. Before her infidelity. Before her fornication. A day when perhaps they really did love each other.

He drops the petrol can and crosses to the body. His body. Coming face to face with himself. He drops to his knees. Dark eyes filling with tears. The waistcoat pocket is turned inside out. No image to soothe him. Just the reality of his death filling his senses.

He releases a roar of inner pain at the death of himself. Ifan recalls the passage of testament where Jesus had called to God from his cross. "O Dduw, pam wyt wedi fy ngadael?" Why has he been forsaken? He weeps bitter tears in this desolate room. Emptying his soul from this body. Wishing to return to his own body. The one lying here before him. But how? He should be with God. But how? So many Commandments broken even though he has tried to find a better way. How can there be Redemption now?

Mari used to say a ghost was just someone who did not realise they were dead. He now realises. And it's overwhelming.

The room spinning away. Faces from his childhood at Capel Celyn. Friends. Open fields. Summer streams. Half remembered conversations with friends long gone. Seeing Mari like an angel beside him. Ships. So many ships. Other lands. Storms. Pain. Whiskey blunting his mind. Inspirational preachers. The Bible which suddenly meant so much. The memories washing away now. A life lived and forgotten. A wave rises. His vessel drops. Ifan lets go. Ifan is gone.

Peter's eyes snap open. A skull stares back at him. Peter pushes back in shock. Confused. Waking from a dream he doesn't remember. What the fuck is going on?

He climbs to his feet, backing away from the long dead body wrapped in some kind of bag. In an empty room. Where the fuck is he? Familiar, but... Fog outside the window. Shit, is he still asleep? A can of petrol nearby. What's going on? What did he do with the car? He staggers to the door.

A fire in the grate. Sammy the dog. Still and his neck at a strange angle. Dead. A flash of recollection. The dog barking at him angrily like it didn't recognise him. Grabbing the dog to silence it. Forever.

Carole! Oh God! His voice comes out hoarse, like he's been straining his voice. "Babe?" No reaction. "Babe!?! Carole!!!" Remembering a snippet of the dream. Strangling the life out of the love of his life.

Another body. Some lad. A teenager. What the hell is going on?

Then the paranoia returns. Her alone with some man in the woods. The arsonists. The chance to be rid of her. And here he is in the middle of it. Half done. Maybe more than half done. He's killed two people, and an animal. He's not a killer. What the fuck has happened here? Peter puts his head in his hands. "Oh my God. What have I done?"

How to get out of this? There is no way out of this! Prison for something he did not do. Or did he? Is this what it's like to lose your mind? And then to lose everything you've ever loved? And then your life? Fuck. Fuck. Fuck!

She has driven him to this, and now he has had his revenge. But the joke is on him. It's the end of his life too. Best take control of that at least. She's not going to win.

Peter staggers around the bodies to his holdall, carrying it into the bedroom.

Peter fishes in the holdall bag and produces a length of rope. It was supposed to tie her up. Too late for that now. Peter had never been in the Boy Scouts. Not coming from that sort of neighbourhood. So is that memory working his fingers? Or is it someone else's memory? The first attempt unravels. The second works. A noose. Peter stands on the holdall so he can feed the rope around the beam in the bedroom. The beam both Ifan and Phillips have used in the past. He ties off the rope. The noose hangs in front of his nose. High enough. He galvanises himself. Pushing his chin through the noose. Tightening it at the back of his head. He looks around the desolate room. The body in a bag. What a fucking dismal place to end it all. He kicks away the holdall and swings free.

The creaking sound fills the cottage.

Huge pressure on Peter's neck. He can't breathe. Gasping now. No room to take in breath. His throat stretched and crushed. Trying to stay calm. Letting go.
But something else now. The will to survive. He claws at this throat, reaching up to the beam, but there's not enough purchase. He can't get enough of a grip to take his weight. His gasping getting more laboured. His eyes clouding.
A figure in front of him. Smelling familiar. Very familiar. Hugging him now. Sounds. Unfocussed. The pressure off his throat. He snatches a breath or two. Moving upwards and coming down with a crash, banging his head. Stars. Black. Nothing. For a moment.

Carole removes the noose from Peter's neck. Her voice hoarse, bruising showing around her neck. "I thought you were stronger than that Pete! I thought you had a mind of your own."
She punches Peter in the chest with all of her might. Peter flinches at the blow and coughs, clearing the liquid in his windpipe. Clearing his throat so he can breathe.
"Pete?!?" Carole pushes the hair away from Peter's face. Blue eyes. Not dark. Coughing. "That's it Pete, breathe! Come on!"
Geraint stands in the doorway, a look of confusion on his face. "What are you doing? He tried to kill us!"
Peter turns to Geraint. Hoarse. Strained. "No. Not me." He drops into a fit of coughing again.
"Why aren't you calling the police Carole?" Geraint wobbling on his feet.
"Pete wasn't in his right mind, Geraint."

"He's killed your dog!"

"Sorry. So sorry." A hoarse whisper. Tears in Peter's eyes. "I'm so sorry."

"So what are you going to do? With him? With that body?" Geraint wiping his eyes in pain.

"We need to move on too. Now we have to deal with the body. It's what's been causing all of this. The whole history of this place, everything that's gone on between all of us. We need to get his body away from here. End this nightmare."

Peter whispers grabbing Carole by the wrist. "How can I help?"

Chapter 36: Burial

"And how do I explain this Geraint? Two sets of bodies from the last century in two different places. It's too much of a coincidence for there not to be suspicion. Difficult questions. And it will bring the police here. And they'll look into what's happened here today. Yes I'll tell the police about the bodies in the woods, but we have to deal with this one ourselves." Carole stares at Ifan's body, whose presence and influence has nearly cost her life, and that of the young lad who is still watching Peter warily from the doorway.

Peter is losing his patience. "Let's just get it the hell out of here. Bury it in the woods."

Geraint bares his teeth as he speaks to Peter. Still very raw from what's happened in the last half hour. "Why would that work any better than him being buried in here?"

"OK, bury him in a graveyard. I passed an abandoned one a few miles away up in the mountains."

"He can't be buried on sacred land. He's a suicide."

"Alright son, you got a better idea? Do you? Let's hear it!"

Geraint leaves the room.

Carole gives Peter a withering stare.

Geraint is raging, heading for the door. He almost kicks Sammy's broken body on the floor. He stops, tenderly picking up the little dog and carries it to the front door. He unlocks the door letting before heading out into the murk outside.

Geraint carries the dog's dead body around to the far side of the cottage, the garden side, outside the kitchen. Away from those two arguing in the bedroom.

A few rusty gardening tools have been left to rot against the wall. Grass growing over them. Phillips' tools. More likely his wife's. This garden hasn't been touched for years.

It's overgrown. Overrun with brambles. Impenetrable to be fair. He lays Sammy's body down by the back door. A good place for the dog to be. Protecting the house. Geraint wrestles a small hand spade free from the long grass, starting to dig the dog's grave outside the back door.

"He's right. We can't bury it, and we can't dump the body."

Peter thinks hard. "So where would this body be at rest?"

"He's a sailor. We could bury him at sea."

"That's what, a couple of hours from here?"

"There's the lake."

"It's not too far, is it?"

Carole ponders. "A five minute walk. There'll be no one out there in this fog. No one will see us."

"Do we need a priest or something?"

"This is Non-Conformist country. Not so hot on ordained priests. Geraint will know some prayers."

"Him? Seriously?"

"Yes, his mother is a lay-preacher." Carole momentarily thinks of phoning Mrs. Jones. Not a good idea. Real dead bodies now. No longer just 'an atmosphere' in P*antyfedwen* that can be shooed away by good intentions.

This is real. Real life crime. This is no longer a romantic ghost story to tell her friends on a winter's night. The dark secret of what happened to the Sea Captain, his wife and her lover is finally uncovered. It's a story of obsession, witchcraft and death which should be shut. Put away. Forgotten. Untold. The fewer people know about this the better.

Carole nods. "Yes, let's take him to the lake."

This is good soil. Deep, dark, peaty. Very rich. The smell is overpowering. Just like up at the Dark Grove. Too rich to have softwoods planted in it, as they have been everywhere else in Cwm Celyn. Those trees ruining the soil, making it acidic and poisoned. A shocking waste of God's earth. The whole of Cwm Celyn is ruined. And this little square of it which is unaffected will now be a grave.

Geraint has dug a good foot down into the earth in very little time. He's hit a rock. That's as deep as the hole will go. He places Sammy's body in the hole. A cute little animal, much too innocent and trusting. Killed by a larger dangerous animal. One it trusted. One it thought it knew and who loved it. One which wasn't itself anymore.

Geraint peers through the glass of the back door. He can see Carole sitting on the floor of the bedroom, still speaking to that bastard. All seems calm, so all must be well.

Geraint walks over to a section of the dry stone wall backing onto the trees. One section is loose. A few stones falling. He selects a long thin stone, solid, smooth sided, but not too heavy. Perfect for the job in hand.

"I'll be gone by the time you get back to the flat." Peter sitting on the floor. Huddled up, hugging himself. Working out the details of the end of their relationship in his head. "You'll have to be gone by the end of July. That's the notice period. And we're paid up until then."

Carole nods, resigned to these changes. They have become inevitable. Her life in London is changing. No more Peter. No more living together. No more flat in a month. A new start. A new job. Changes. Opportunities. Everything is happening at once.

Peter gets to his feet. "We better get on with this, I should get going before dark."

Geraint taps the stone down onto the compacted earth. Keeping Sammy safe beneath. His stone doubling as a step from the garden into Pantyfedwen.

Geraint hears the front door open and close. He carries on with bedding in the stone. Carole and Peter appear from the frontage of the cottage. Geraint doesn't look up, still working on his knees.

Carole looks at him with surprise. "What are you doing?"

"I buried Sammy." Geraint gives Peter a look before finishing bedding in the stone.

Carole starts to tear up. "Thank you. Thank you Geraint."

"I couldn't leave him lying there." Geraint gets up off his knees. Job done.

Carole steps over and hugs him. "We're going to do the same thing with the Sea Captain's body."

Geraint breaks free. "Bury him here? You're kidding!"

"No, we're taking him to the lake. Burying him in the water."

Geraint races to object but thinks for a moment. "A burial and baptism? Absolving him of his sins?"

Carole nods. That makes perfect sense. "Making sure he has moved on. Gone forever."

Geraint and Peter pick up the canvas bag holding Ifan's remains. It's surprisingly light. Say half the weight of a bag of spuds. That's all that's left of this big man after all this time. Geraint had carried his father's coffin with five other bearers when he was fourteen. He felt as though his fingers would be severed. Felt as if he'd never reach the graveside from the cemetery gate. Not wanting to rock the body within. Desperate not to disturb his dad lest he wake him. Desperate. Just wanting everything over. Wanting to be alone so he could cry. Wanting everyone gone, despite their kind words and concern.

Yes, this is so much lighter. Bearable too now that the bag has been closed up. He couldn't look at that skull again.

It was disturbing. Seeing what was once angry vital life, stripped away by time, death and decay. He tried not to think about what these forces were doing to his Dad. And to Bethan, that gorgeous girl who died here in the forest. And would do to him when the time came. And that time almost came today, care of the man standing an arm's length behind him. Geraint thought he had faced death before. It stared him in the eye today.

That lime is getting everywhere. All over his hands and trousers and shoes. He leads the way out of the bedroom, through the living room and out of the front door, held open by Carole.

Out into the gloom of the thick mist. Mist so thick he still can't see the trees on the other side of the road. Walking into a netherworld where the living and dead are side by side. Maybe they always are in Cwm Celyn. Cwm Celyn has so many ghosts.

The mist is hiding them from sight. The mist is dampening their footsteps rendering them silent. The mist is also dampening Geraint's clothes and face. He coughs. The lime dust itching on his skin and irritating his lungs.

Carole has caught up and is walking alongside them now. Everyone moving silently through the mist on this blind-deaf journey to the lake to bury a man who died over a century ago.

Geraint spots something large at the side of the road. Peter's Porsche. He parked down here to avoid it being seen from the cottage. That's assuming that Carole was not out this way. But it isn't really hidden at all. Maybe he just didn't care. Didn't care if others spotted him here. That's far more frightening, someone who has no fear of consequences. And this man is so close Geraint can feel his breath on the back of his neck.

"Stop a minute. I'm losing my grip." Peter stops, almost wrenching the canvas bag from Geraint's hands. "Put it down."

Geraint and Peter place the bag down on the wet road. Sweat is pouring on Peter's face, dripping off his nose. "I need a minute." Peter's heavy breathing is the only sound now.

Geraint looks at Peter panting. Seriously? This isn't heavy. He could carry it himself, but that would be wrong. This bastard should at least share the load, if not carry it alone as penance for what he has done. But that would take all day. The sooner this is done, the sooner that bastard can go home. The sooner he can go home. "Put it on your shoulder. It'll be easier."

Peter and Geraint pick up the bag once more, resting it on their shoulders and head off down the road towards the glow in the mist; the sun descending in the sky ahead. Very red for the time of day. A trick of the light with this fog maybe.

Carole watches them go. She remembers her father telling her folk tales of the area. They look like a funeral procession headed by a *Canwyll Gorff*, The Corpse Candle her dad told her about all that time ago foretelling or marking a death. Red for a man. That light is unnaturally red. Is it really the sun?

Geraint and Peter are coughing now. The dust from the bag getting on their faces. "Don't let this stuff get in your eyes or mouth. It's alkaline. It burns."

"Acid?"

"No, the opposite." Geraint wonders how this guy became a city whiz kid with so little knowledge.

Suddenly the road descends beneath their feet. It gets rougher, the old tarmac making way for stone and gravel. They are entering the car park by the lake. As the surface levels out, Geraint can just make out the standing stone by the water's edge and heads for it. The end of the road, thank God. He leads the way and comes to a halt at the stone. "This is it."

Geraint and Peter lower the bag to the ground. Carole catches up to them, taken aback at what she sees. They are both covered in the lime dust, white, black and grey against the reddish mist. Looking like painted, prehistoric tribesmen carrying out a ritual.

"We should weight it down, we can't risk him floating up." Geraint being practical again beyond his years. "A few rocks will do it." He wanders around the edge of the car park and picks up four heavy stones. "Come on, give me a hand!"

Carole and Peter collect a few heavy stones and join Geraint. Geraint opens the canvas bag gingerly and lays the stones inside on Ifan's body. He places the rocks that Carole and Peter have brought too. He ties the bag tight.

"Should I say a few words? You know..."

Carole nods. "Yes, I think that's best. A Welsh boy with a chapel upbringing, you'll think of something."

Something, yes. From Bethan's funeral. A reading from a psalm. A handful of them from the school's sixth form were press ganged into it. He memorised that. How did it go? He looks at Peter standing idly by. "Come on. Let's get it done."

Geraint takes one end of the bag and starts dragging it into the water. Peter drags the other end. Peter was expecting to maybe roll the bag into the lake. Geraint wades in, the bag half submerged.

The lime in the bag and on their persons begins to smoke as it comes into contact with the water. As Geraint leads deeper into the lake, he, Peter and the bag are enveloped in smoke. They disappear, lost in a cloud moving across the lake surface in the mist. Carole can only hear the splashing as the two men take the bag further out from the shore.

Geraint begins to recite a Psalm in Welsh, from Bethan's funeral. Peter watches the white dust covered lad speak a language he hardly knew existed. "Na chofia bechodau fy ieuenctid, na'm camweddau: yn ôl dy drugaredd meddwl di amdanaf, er mwyn dy ddaioni."

The words are completely alien to him. But apt. Asking for forgiveness of sins and... Agh! Peter trips over a rock in the lake. He falls beneath the water, letting go of the bag. His eyes shutting as the water hits them. He is on his knees, under the water. The heat of the lime on his face. He rubs the lime off in panic.

Peter opens his eyes seeing the canvas bag sink in the water. Dropping beyond a ledge a little way ahead. Descending out of sight into the weeds of the bottom of the dark lake. Peter gets to his feet. Up to his shoulders in the water now. Fog all around. No sign of Geraint. No idea which way is back to dry land.

Silence. Then Geraint stands up. Around ten feet away, wiping the remainder of the lime from his face. Geraint turns around and walks away leaving Peter alone in the lake. He disappears in the mist.

Peter follows, back through the mist until he sees the standing stone and a figure. Carole. Geraint joining her, soaked from head to foot. Peter wades out of the water which gets shallower with every step.

"You boys better come back to the cottage to dry off."

Geraint shakes his head. "We should get back to our own lives. It's best if we don't see too much of each other again. Best not tempt fate. It's too easy to rekindle a fire on an old hearth."

Peter nods. "Yeah, old flames never die and all that... I have to get out of here Carole. Call me when you're back in town. We still have stuff to sort out."

Carole steps forward to hug him but he is gone. Heading off across the car park and up the road into the mist.

Carole watches Peter disappear out of her life.

Chapter 37: Wake

Peter walks briskly up the road, his wet clothes flapping against him. Looking down making sure he stays on the tarmac. He can only see a few feet in this mist. Out of nowhere the Porsche appears. Peter roots in his pockets for the keys. He taps the electronic fob. A thump as the car unlocks and the interior light comes on. Peter takes off his shirt and trousers and tosses them into the car.

He starts the engine and turns up the heating, shivering already. The car throws up mud as it gets back onto the road and roars off. The full headlights showing a wall of white ahead of Peter. Featureless, full of danger. A track not much wider than the car through a world of trees. He puts on the fog lights, killing the main beam. Better. The road lights up in front of him.

Passing the cottage on his left. A shiver runs through him again. He taps the sat nav and hits "Home". The windows misting up now from his wet clothes. An internal mist adding to the external one, but he hasn't felt as clear as this for days. The car follows the twists and turns of the road. If it hadn't been for the sat nav he would have missed the turn onto the mountain road.

The engine roaring as the car climbs steeply through the trees. Breaking out of the tree line, and out of the mist. A sunny summer evening on the mid Wales mountains. Sheep grazing on the open common.

Peter looks in the mirror at the wall of mist behind him, hiding Cwm Celyn as if it was a bad dream. But it wasn't a dream and when he gets back to London there will be hell to pay. Burnt bridges at work. A new place to find to live. And all he can say in his defence is that he wasn't himself this week. Fuck!

Peter puts his foot down sending the car roaring across

the open mountain road.

Carole and Geraint walk wordlessly, side by side through the mist. Carole instinctively glances around for Sammy. She lets out a sob.

"Are you OK Carole?"

She nods. "I was thinking about Sammy. I'll be alone in the cottage now."

Geraint smiles. "No ghosts though. And he's just outside the back door looking after you."

"He was a good dog."

"Lovely dog."

They are at the cottage. "Are you sure you don't want to dry your clothes in front of the fire?"

Geraint shakes his head. "No, I'll get home. If Mam asks, I'll tell her I fell off my bike. That will explain the bump on my head."

"But you're OK?"

"I get worse every week playing rugby." This is it. Goodbye. No point drawing it out. Geraint grabs his bike and rides off into the murk with no lights. In a few seconds he has gone.

Carole stands alone outside her cottage. Totally alone.

She walks into the cottage. Even in the gloom she can see the lime dust everywhere. She goes into the kitchen. She fills a bucket from the Belfast sink and picks up the mop and sets to work cleaning.

Into the bedroom. More mopping. Getting a hammer and nails and replacing the floorboards. Making it look like the whole thing never happened. All that redecoration and repair she hasn't done this week will have to restart in the morning.

Geraint rides the bike slowly through the mist. Wobbling a

little, losing his balance. Maybe he took more of a knock than he realised. He is shivering in his wet clothes in the cold air. Damn it's cold. He passes the pathway to Nant y Cadno and the Dark Grove. He could have ended up like that lad. It doesn't bear thinking about. He won't care if he never sees Carole again.

She's procrastinated enough. She picks up her phone, steps outside and dials 999. "Police please." She locks the door and walks down the road towards the village. "Hello. I'm out walking, and I've found a couple of bodies in the woods.... No, they are very old. Cwm Celyn..." Carole disappears in the mist.

Almost an hour of waiting at the track to Nant y Cadno. Headlights approaching through the mist. Blue flashing lights. Carole waves.

Up in the Dark Grove with two PCs, one seeming as young as Geraint, and the other a girl Carole's age. Looking down at Mari and Owain's bodies in the hollow. Carole telling the police a cock and bull story of how she found the bodies. It's plausible enough it seems. The important thing is that she is passing the wife and the boy on to the powers that be. They'll get a proper funeral. Her job is done. Her conscience clear. Time to move on.
Carole looks down at Mari staring back up at her from what has been her grave. Carole feels a strange sense of loss. Loss for what Mari gave her in that brief time. The fun part of Mari. The happiness. The sex. All of which she'll miss. Mari opened up a part of her she had forgotten existed.

Well over a couple of hours sitting in the back of the police car. In that time half a dozen vehicles have joined it, parking precariously at the edge of the narrow road. A Private Ambulance arrives. White suited Scenes of Crime Officers trampling down what was a secret pathway to the old forgotten Cwm Celyn. This is now a Crime Scene. Over a hundred years too late.

Carole sits alone in the back of the car, available for any further questions. Already an afterthought in this little drama that is unfolding in the thick June fog.

She could have been one of these bodies today. She and Geraint could have been murdered. With Peter hanging himself, that would have been the second murder suicide at the cottage. Geraint's words, 'It's easy to relight a fire on an old hearth' come back to her. History repeating itself.

Peter has been deeply affected by this, like Geraint. She has to admit, so has she. Maybe it's best she leaves too? Sell the cottage on.

No! It's her cottage. She bought it to remember her Dad. Tying another generation of her family to this little valley in the middle of Wales where most people have had to leave to make any kind of living. No! She's staying! It's not a haunted house anymore. History won't be repeating itself again. No!

The woman PC who was first at the scene taps on the car window. "It's OK love, don't cry. I'll take you home shortly, OK?"

Carole catches her reflection in the car window. She is in floods of tears.

Darkness has fallen. The police car pulls up outside Pantyfedwen. The female PC lets Carole out of the rear of the car. "There you go Miss Morris. Thank you again for all of your time and help this evening."

Carole smiles weakly and walks to the cottage door. The police car drives on up the road. Carole looks at her phone. Almost ten o'clock. They kept her for nearly four hours. Maybe in the scheme of things that's not too long to put this to bed. She fumbles for her keys and puts the key in the lock.

Carole unlocks the door. It jams. Carole pushes it. Stuck again. She barges the door open. Car headlights. The police car drives back up the road towards the village. Carole waves from the doorway.

The female PC does a double take at the two figures in the doorway. Carole closes the door, Phillips behind her, the sound of his electronic watch marking the hour. Beep beep.

THE END.